Travelling
Below the Surface

PJ Kropp

First published 2021

ISBN
Print: 978-0-6487292-2-8
Ebook: 978-0-6487292-3-5

Layout and typesetting: Busybird Publishing

Preface

It was in late-May 1990 when the overseas wanderlust venture began. After adopting an itinerant fruit-picking lifestyle throughout the three eastern states of Australia for nearly two and a half years, I decided it was time to commence travelling beyond the Australian shores.

This is the second book of a two-book series. The first book, *The Itinerant Way*, was published in October 2019.

During the early 1990s, I jot down handwritten notes as I constantly travelled within eastern Australia and abroad (European countries and New Zealand, in particular). Originally, I tackled both literary projects as autobiographical accounts. I soon realised, however, that a different approach was required: a fictional-based one.

Although, a sizeable content of this book is fictional, *everything* is based on actual events and real people. Yes, I've let the imagination run wild at times, enabling the scope of the literary experience (or journey) to be a more enjoyable one.

Thank you for reading this page! Now, sit back – relax – and hopefully, you'll enjoy my second attempt at achieving 'literary prowess'.

P.J. Kropp.

Contents

1

One Way Ticket to Wanderlust

After being actively involved in an itinerant fruit-picking lifestyle for two and a half years, Charlie decided it was time to travel outside Australia. By now, he had saved several thousand dollars and was looking forward to the commencement of a primitively-planned *wanderlust* adventure. Additionally, the relatively-quick sale of his motor vehicle would be an added financial bonus for him.

Two weeks before his departure, Charlie purchased an airline ticket from a travel agency in central Sydney: a one-way fare from Sydney to London (via the USA and Ireland). This would be the only time he would travel to Europe in an easterly direction. All future travel to Europe would be in a westerly direction, via stopovers in numerous Asian cities (Singapore, Kuala Lumpur, New Delhi, etc).

After being granted a two-year work permit for the United Kingdom and a multi-entry visa to travel throughout the United States, Charlie was now set for an *adventure of a lifetime.* He would not bother with pre-planned rigid travel plans. This included no pre-booked accommodation or travel insurance. This carefree approach was to be a major aspect of all of Charlie's future travel plans. He felt that a rigid approach to travelling would stifle his wanderlust spirit!

With minimal planning, Charlie just basically wanted to get from one destination to the next destination: fuss-free. Upon arriving at his final destination, he would immediately seek reasonably priced accommodation (typically for two or three days). During this short period, Charlie would decide upon his next course of action.

On a pleasant sunny afternoon in late May, Charlie waited in the lounge area of the Departures terminal at Sydney Airport. An hour or so later, passengers were called upon to board the aircraft. The Continental Airlines flight was going to Newark Liberty International Airport (New Jersey) via stopovers in Honolulu and Los Angeles. After the aircraft landed in Newark, he had to make his way to John F. Kennedy International Airport (New York). From JFK airport, Charlie would board an Aer Lingus Airlines flight destined for London (United Kingdom), via two stopovers in Ireland: Shannon Airport and Dublin Airport.

Before take-off, genial murmuring amongst the passengers dominated the overall vibe within the filled economic-class cabin. This peaceful vibe, however, was soon interrupted by the onboard safety demonstration which was delivered by several of the cabin crew. Charlie deemed the enthusiastic (and theatrical) demonstration as quite entertaining!

Half an hour into the flight, a boisterous group of Americans decided to violate the general vibe of peaceful civility amongst the other passengers by loudly discussing their recent Australian adventures. Unfortunately, their 'decibel-breaking' conversation triggered a similar action amongst an equally irritating group of Australians. They decided to discuss their past travel adventures in a tone what could be best described as being 'a nasally-driven and ockerish-like whine'.

Eventually, these two groups of passengers started conversing with each other. A plethora of combative and competitive dribble soon followed! Fortunately, sets of earplugs were being handed out to the passengers. After receiving a set of earplugs, Charlie immediately tuned into an in-flight music channel. Now blissfully relaxed, he could no longer hear the competitive bouts of boisterous drivel!

During his twenty years of travelling, Charlie flew with many different airlines: twenty-eight to be precise. This Continental Airlines flight was his first. Throughout the journey, Charlie was quite intrigued by the appearance of the cabin crew who he deemed as being decidedly plastic: hairstyles contained copious amounts of hairspray or hair gel; suntans seemed to be solarium-influenced; constantly smiling, displaying sets of perfect-white teeth (perhaps they were recruited from toothpaste commercials); and, 'iron-smoothed' skin which lacked wrinkles and facial lines.

After more than ten hours in the air, the aircraft touched down at Honolulu International Airport. A small percentage of passengers made their way to the luggage carousel but for others, it was a two-hour stopover. By now, the novelty of first-time flying for Charlie had largely eroded and he was still a long way from London. The next stage of the journey was a flight to Los Angeles. The aircraft touched down at Los Angeles International Airport at 4.10 pm (local time). The flight from Sydney to Los Angeles had taken nearly sixteen hours. The Continental Airlines flight had left Sydney at 4.30 pm (eastern Australian time) – his life had gone back by twenty minutes.

Inside the terminal at Los Angeles International Airport, Charlie had to collect his luggage from the carousel and, thus, check-in for a domestic flight from Los Angeles to New York. However, with seven hours to spare, he decided to store his luggage inside a locker. Charlie then ventured outside the airport and casually strolled along several nearby roads for the next several hours.

After rechecking his luggage at the check-in counter, Charlie waited in the lounge area for the boarding call. By now, he was feeling quite haggard. Several hours later, the aircraft descended towards Newark Liberty International Airport (New Jersey) just as the sunrise was beginning to dominate the morning sky. After passing through the Customs area and exiting from the Arrivals terminal, Charlie walked to a nearby bus stop. A short time later, he was aboard a bus, heading towards Grand Central Terminal train station (New York City).

The bus journey turned out to be quite an interesting one. The affable bus driver, delightfully, delivered a running commentary on the city of New York, highlighting and describing many of its key landmarks. The informative and light-hearted commentary style eased Charlie's 'jetlag woes' – to a point. As the bus approached central New York City, however, the overwhelming sight of continual blocks of high-rise buildings somewhat dampened his enthusiasm for the city. A high-rise metropolis lifestyle held little appeal for Charlie as he had become quite accustomed to a 'rustic-dwelling' existence for the past several years.

At Grand Central Terminal (also known as Grand Central Station), Charlie alighted from the bus and graciously thanked the driver for his light-hearted commentary on New York. Sitting on his backpack, he waited for over forty-five minutes for a connecting bus to JFK International Airport: located in the New York borough of Queens. When the bus arrived at JFK airport, it dropped passengers off at numerous bus stops. Charlie got off at the last bus stop. He thought to himself, 'This airport is way too large.'

Charlie, by now, was severely sleep-deprived. He was keen to obtain several hours of quality 'shut-eye' time before the departure of his next flight, still ten hours away. His attempt to gain any amount of quality sleep time, unfortunately, was largely thwarted by the continual buzz of activity within the terminal. There was no partitioned area to minimise or eliminate unwelcomed noise. Even worse, the rock-hard plastic seats didn't provide any level of physical comfort to anyone who tried to sleep or even just to nap!

Two hours before the departure of the flight from New York to London (via Shannon and Dublin airports), Charlie checked-in at the lone Aer Lingus service desk. As he was waiting in the small queue, a group of five females (who appeared to be related to each other) became embroiled in a heated argument with a waif-like, middle-aged Irish woman who was seated behind the check-in desk.

The hostile group hadn't made a pre-booking for this particular flight but they steadfastly insisted that a group of seats should be made immediately available to them. The Aer Lingus representative casually repeated (numerous times) that there were no 'group' seats available and insisted that they need to book a later flight. The absurd confrontation continued for a further twenty minutes. The two youngest females, in particular, would not take no for an answer. The Aer Lingus check-in clerk, however, remained steely calm and repeatedly stated to them that they needed to book a later flight. The group of females eventually conceded defeat and left the check-in area: cursing, hissing and uttering vulgar expletives amongst themselves. Feeling quite pleased with the outcome, the Irish woman happily snapped, 'Next!'

After dragging his luggage to the check-in desk, Charlie casually quipped, 'Hi there… you deserve a medal for the way you handled that situation.'

With a wry smile, she politely replied, 'Oh, I've had plenty of practice with these types of people over the years!'

A short time later, Charlie's luggage was checked-in and he made his way to the waiting lounge. Whilst waiting to board the plane, Charlie managed to have a one-hour nap. The Aer Lingus flight departed JFK International Airport and six and a half hours later, the aeroplane touched down at Shannon Airport (Ireland). During the flight, he was fortunate to have two seats to himself. Charlie managed to have several bouts of quality sleep. In stark contrast to the Continental flight crew, the Aer Lingus stewardesses (all Irish) were quite friendly and chatty. Throughout the flight, they walked up and down the aisles and talked to all of the passengers, even it was just for a few minutes.

At Shannon Airport, a quarter of the passengers disembarked. The remaining passengers stayed onboard and forty-five minutes later, the flight continued onto Dublin (Ireland). At Dublin Airport, Charlie was issued with a transit visa to London (UK). Two hours later, he was on a domestic flight to London's Heathrow Airport: the last leg of the gruelling fifty-two-hour journey. Onboard the aircraft, casually-dressed Charlie was surrounded by passengers – all dressed in business attire. He sensed that these types of passengers commuted between the two capital cities regularly.

One week later, Charlie was inside the Home Office (Westminster, London) waiting to have his two-year work permit validated. He was in and out of the Home Office just under four hours. Charlie was one of the 'lucky ones'; he later learnt that many foreign nationals would be inside the Home Office building for six to eight hours, frantically dealing with (Home Office) personnel!

During his three-month stay in London, Charlie learnt that deportees (South Africans, in particular) were able to re-enter the United Kingdom via domestic flights from Dublin airport – often dressed in business attire. Identical to Charlie's experience, Irish customs officials would issue them with transit visas to the UK and, subsequently, their passports would not be checked by British customs officials. Another common method for deportees to enter the United Kingdom was via ferry services operating between Ireland and Wales: either from Rosslare (Ireland) to Fishguard (Wales) or from Cork (Ireland) to Swansea (Wales).

The fifty-two-hour journey from Sydney to London had certainly taken its toll on Charlie; he had well and truly succumbed to severe and chronic jetlag. At Heathrow Airport, Charlie boarded a train. Travelling along the Piccadilly Line, he alighted at Earl's Court tube station forty-five minutes later. Earl's Court, popularly known as 'Kangaroo Court' or 'Kangaroo Valley' at the time, was an area well known for its large transient population of Australian and New Zealand travellers.

Charlie made his way up the escalator and walked towards the roadway. [Note: the first escalators on the Underground network were installed at Earl's Court in 1911].

After a brief stroll along Earls Court Road, he came upon a backpacker's hostel: one of many in this area. Charlie stayed in the hostel for the next seven days. Still feeling the effects of long-haul jetlag, he was unable to adjust to a normal sleeping pattern for the first three days. On the fourth day, Charlie forced himself to stay awake during the daytime by engaging in many hours of sightseeing and walking. He slept for eight hours straight that night – despite sharing the room with five other people.

During his last three days in Earl's Court, Charlie regularly patronised the 'Aussie' hotels. The *Australian-themed* hotels made him feel a little bit homesick: the majority of the beers (both on tap and bottled) were Australian brands; one's footwear would be partially stuck with each step taken on the 'sticky' carpet (due to multiple beer spillages); and, the vast majority of the staff could be best described as *bogans* (the wearing of flannelette shirts and mullet haircuts were prevalent). Additionally, the majority of the patrons were either Aussies (Australians) or Kiwis (New Zealanders).

[Note: the word *bogan* is an Australian/New Zealand slang term used to describe a person whose behaviour may be regarded as 'unrefined' or 'unsophisticated'].

Originally, Charlie intended to use London, primarily, as a base for employment purposes. His travel itinerary was to include well-known backpacker pastimes: attending the Munich Beer Festival; the *Running of the Bulls* in Pamplona; and, short stays on the Greek 'party' islands (e.g. Ios and Santorini). Within the first few weeks, however, he was unable to gain full-time employment. Through several employment agencies, Charlie only managed to obtain single-day jobs. At one stage, he was registered with more than thirty employment agencies and Charlie quickly became quite disillusioned with the way they operated.

Eventually, he did manage to obtain full-time employment at a C&A retail store (near Marble Arch tube station), courtesy of an Australian-staffed employment agency: Centacom. Charlie worked in the C&A store for the next two months.

As time went by, the novelty of living and working in London for Charlie had largely eroded. Fortunately, though, he did enjoy his period of employment at the C&A retail outlet, largely due to the multiracial camaraderie amongst the majority of its employees. The nationalities of employees included: British, Irish, Australians, New Zealanders, South Africans, Zimbabweans, West Indians, French, Moroccans, Algerians and a crew of Portuguese cleaners.

During his two-month period of employment, Charlie was mostly employed in the 'Maintenance' section. Occasionally, he would work in the 'Merchandising' section of the department store. Both sections were located below the main store area. In the Maintenance section, the personnel consisted of numerous nationalities. In stark contrast, however, the personnel in the Merchandising section were mostly British, female and over the age of thirty.

Charlie soon learnt that several of the women in the Merchandising section had been employed in this store for more than a decade. Each day, the women complained, whined and moaned in regards to their employment situation. Most of their disdain or contempt, however, was largely directed at managerial personnel. Charlie, though, didn't particularly like most of the managers either. He regarded them as an *exclusive group of elitists* as they rarely engaged in any form of conversation with the 'peasants' (the general employees). Inside the staff canteen area and during every meal break, they would congregate around a large table – well away from all the other tables.

During the latter half of his employment period at the C&A department store, the desire for Charlie to return to an itinerant fruit-picking lifestyle had continually gained momentum. He felt that he had inadvertently become *trapped* within London's Australian/New Zealand community. Charlie regarded this environment as detrimental to his overall purpose of travelling, preferring to 'meet and mix' with a wider array of nationalities. After residing in London for three months, Charlie boarded a train which took him to Maidstone (51 kilometres south-east of London). The large town was located in 'The Garden of England' (county of Kent). Little did he realise at the time, Charlie's true *wanderlust spirit* was just about to begin.

2

The North Pole, Poles and New Age Travellers

The one-hour rail trip from London Victoria to Maidstone East was a pleasant and scenic one. For the duration of the train journey, Charlie spent most of the time just gazing through the window and marvelled at the picturesque fields intertwined with the numerous idyllic villages that passed by. At Maidstone East railway station, he alighted from the train and headed straight to the nearby Maidstone Tourist Information Centre. His main purpose was to seek reasonably-priced and comfortable accommodation for the next three days. Half an hour later, Charlie was unpacking his backpack in a spacious room within a B&B (Bed and Breakfast) establishment. As he rested on the bed, Charlie began to devise a viable strategy in his endeavour to obtain apple-picking employment.

Early the next morning, Charlie ventured on foot through the outskirts of Maidstone in a westerly direction. Initially, he strolled along Tonbridge Road but over the next few hours, Charlie wandered from orchard to orchard: many of them located on seldom-used laneways. He soon discovered that the commencement of the apple-picking season was still a few days away. Several orchards, though, did offer Charlie employment. Unfortunately, they didn't have any accommodation facilities.

One of the orchards, however, did offer Charlie both employment and accommodation. The accommodation involved sharing a caravan with several Eastern European students. He was fine with that arrangement. A major problem, though, the orchard had no showering/bathing facilities but did have several taps located on the side of the packing shed. The expectation was that one had to wash themselves using these low-to-the-ground taps! Charlie declined the offer. An essential accommodation condition for him *must* include a warm shower at the end of any working day.

A few minutes after midday, Charlie espied a licenced premise: the North Pole Hotel. Close to a road junction, the hotel was located in-between villages but it was part of the village of Wateringbury. Feeling partially-despondent, due to his futile attempt to obtain a suitable combination of employment and accommodation, he ventured inside. By 1.30 pm, Charlie was the only person in the hotel; except for Diana (the bartender). He soon struck up a conversation with her, largely focusing on his morning 'adventure': namely his unsuccessful quest for the combination of apple-picking employment *and* suitable accommodation arrangements.

Just after Charlie ordered another pint of ale, Diana casually informed him that several local orchardists, along with numerous orchard managers were frequent patrons at this hotel. After several phone calls, she informed Charlie that one of the local orchardists was immediately seeking pear-pickers. The orchard also had several large caravans and a large amenities block: male/female bathrooms and a laundry facility. At 3.00 pm, Diana closed the hotel (it was a common practice for many village hotels to be closed for several hours in the afternoon). She drove Charlie to a nearby orchard and introduced him to the orchardist: Angus.

After Charlie discussed with Angus the employment and accommodation arrangements, Diana drove him to a bus stop. Twenty minutes later, he boarded the bus and went back to Maidstone. Charlie spent another night at the Bed & Breakfast lodging. The next morning, he packed his backpack and walked to the bus stop. Half an hour later, Charlie was at Angus's orchard.

Angus led Charlie to the tract of land where the caravans were located; they were mostly occupied by Eastern European students. The caravans were also near a hayshed. Not overly keen to dwell in one of the caravans with several other people, Charlie casually asked Angus if he could pitch his tent on the loose bundles of hay. 'No problem' was the response. Ten minutes later, Charlie had pitched his tent on top of a bundle of hay, practically providing him with a comfortable bed to sleep on.

In the evening, Charlie walked to the North Pole Hotel. After thanking Diana for her assistance, he consumed a sit-down meal. Just after 10.00 pm (and after quite a few pints), Charlie gingerly strolled back to the orchard. By now, all activity within the accommodation area had ceased as the interiors of all eight caravans were in darkness. He opened a bottle of brandy inside his tent and after several swigs, Charlie was asleep.

Early the next morning, Charlie met his co-workers (twenty in total). The group consisted of thirteen Polish nationals, three Czechoslovakians (Czechoslovakia would soon split into two separate countries as a result of the *Velvet Revolution*), a Bulgarian and a Russian family of three (parents and daughter). Charlie was the only person from an English-speaking country.

Most of the group was transported to the block of pears on a large dray towed by a tractor. Throughout the trip to the orchard block, one of the Polish ladies conversed with Charlie in English. Helena, who was from a village near the southern Polish city of Krakow, was a student studying English Literature (at one of the universities in Krakow). For the next few weeks, Helena would be one of Charlie's two translators whenever he attempted to converse with the other Eastern European nationals.

Upon arriving at the block of pear trees, Charlie was formally introduced to the Polish tractor driver: Tadeusz. He would be Charlie's other translator. Besides English, Taddy was fluent (or near-fluent) in several other languages: Russian, German, French and Greek. Waiting at the pear block was the orchard manager (John). The rows of pear trees in the orchard block were no more than three metres high. This meant that minimal ladder work would be required. The entire group soon broke up into smaller groups of either two or three people – except for Charlie. John casually asked him if he wanted to work with anyone. 'No!' was the emphatic response.

Whilst fruit-picking in Australia, Charlie had rarely worked with anyone else. Each team of pear pickers were soon allotted a double row of pears. Before the commencement of any pear-picking, there was quite an amount of excitable chatter, especially amongst the young Polish students. Although Charlie had no understanding of the Polish language at the time, he sensed that the sniggering amongst them may involve him; their continual sly glances towards him certainly aroused suspicion!

Charlie suspected that the Poles thought that he was English. At that stage, only John knew that he was an Australian. Charlie sensed that they had already stereotyped him as not being a *useful orchard worker*. The group was oblivious to the fact that he was an experienced fruit picker. A determined Charlie, there and then, decided he would 'push hard' that day. He'll show them! The pear picking was being paid at piece-rate instead of an hourly or daily rate. To the left of Charlie, a young Polish couple (both students) were working together. On the other side of Charlie, two young male Polish students were working together.

Throughout the first two hours of pear picking, the two young Polish lads were constantly chatting with each other – regularly glancing in Charlie's direction. After three hours, Charlie was still level with them as he moved along the double row of pear trees. The young Polish couple was now well behind. By now, the jovial manner of the two young males working together had transformed into one of 'baffling bemusement'.

By the end of the eight-hour working day, Charlie had forged ahead of the two Polish lads and well ahead of the young Polish couple. At the far end of the pear-tree block, the entire group congregated in readiness to be transported back to the accommodation facilities. Whilst waiting for the tractor and dray, most of the weary group was engaged in a form of clamorous and excitable chatter. Charlie stood a few metres away from the group.

Helena shuffled wearily towards Charlie and asked him how his day went.

'Not too bad.'

He then asked Helena how her day went.

'We three Polish ladies picked eight bins today.'

After a brief silence, the inevitable question was asked, 'So… how many bins did you pick today?'

'I picked a few.'

Helena continued. 'Umm… three, four bins… five bins perhaps?'

Charlie cheekily grinned. 'Nine bins for me today!'

A shell-shocked Helena immediately informed the group of Charlie's *super-human* pear-picking effort. She was immediately met with looks of scepticism by the students. However, the two young Polish males (Arak and Piotr) working beside him, confirmed Helena's statement. They had managed to pick a total of eight bins between them whilst the young couple, who worked on the other side of Charlie, had only picked six bins.

As the group was transported back to the accommodation facilities, Charlie casually discussed with Helena that he had been a seasonal fruit-picker in Australia for the past few years. At that point, she excitedly informed the others that Charlie was an Australian – not an Englishman. In an instant, excitable chatter broke out amongst the group. The words koala, kangaroo and the mysterious 'Ko-shoo-shko' were uttered numerous times! Helena cheekily asked, 'How do you pronounce that famous mountain in Australia?'

Australia's highest mainland peak is Mount Kosciusko (later corrected to Kosciuszko). Charlie responded, "Koz-see-us-ko!"

Fits of laughter immediately broke out. Helena informed Charlie that the correct spelling is K-O-S-C-I-U-S-Z-K-O and the mountain should be pronounced 'Ko-shoo-shko!'

For the next five days, Charlie's daily total of bins would be either eight or nine. After the short pear-picking season had ceased, there was no employment for the next three days. During these three days, Tadeusz informed him that the apple-picking was only going to be paid at an hourly rate. Charlie sensed that he would be soon seeking another orchard. Tadeusz firmly suggested to the Eastern Europeans and Charlie that they should only pick three bins of apples each day.

Tadeusz, who preferred to be called Taddy, had quite an interesting background. A former civil engineer specialising in bridge construction, he had been employed throughout Poland and Germany over several years: mostly on short-term contracts. Taddy was always paid in Deutschmarks (the then-German currency) instead of being paid in Polish currency (the złoty).

In between bridge construction projects and especially during the colder months, Taddy would relocate to northern Greece (on several occasions) and seek employment on farms/orchards. A multi-linguist, he had learnt Russian,

French, German and English at school. Taddy claimed that his periods of employment in Greece enabled him to become fairly fluent in the Greek language. He further stated that his level of spoken English, largely due to being employed on Angus' orchard the past five seasons, had improved significantly.

Charlie tried to negotiate with Angus a piece-rate for the upcoming apple-picking season but to no avail. The orchardist wanted the apples to be *handled like eggs*. During the first two days of the apple-picking season, the orchard manager (John) attempted to use 'standover tactics' in an endeavour to persuade each apple-picker to pick at least four bins of apples each day. Every apple-picker (including Charlie), however, would only fill three bins on each of these two days!

On the first day, Taddy told Charlie that the piece-rate for a bin of apples was between £6 and £7. The hourly rate was a meagre £2.50. An eight-hour day, therefore, netted £20 for each individual apple-picker. This equated to about three bins per day on piece-rate. During the second day, Taddy informed Charlie that Broadacre Wood Orchard (located between the village of East Malling and the town of West Malling) was seeking apple-pickers.

The next morning (Saturday), Charlie walked a distance of just over three miles (or nearly five kilometres) and entered Broadacre Wood Orchard. Fortunately, the orchard manager

(Colin) was in the office. After a brief cordial discussion, Colin showed him the camping ground. The next day, Charlie pitched his tent and commenced apple-picking the following morning.

As Charlie pitched his tent, he was quite amused by the odd array of 'motorhomes' which dominated the landscape of the camping ground. The vehicles were either well-used Bedford vans or antiquated ice-cream vans. Most of the converted vehicles, however, had a 'special' feature that immediately caught Charlie's eye – a chimney. Over the next few weeks and especially around dinner-time in the evenings, large puffs of smoke would flow effortlessly out of these chimneys and often merged to create one large haze throughout the camping area. Within this prominent haze, however, one's olfactory organ would also be subjected to a substantial whiff of a well-known substance – marijuana.

Charlie estimated that about forty people were dwelling on the campsite. During the six-week apple picking season, he conversed with only a few of the campsite residents. Most of these 'alternative' lifestylers regarded themselves as *New Age Travellers* (also known as NATs). Their chosen lifestyles were, in some ways, an attempt to mirror the stereotyped lives of nomadic gipsies. Coincidentally, there were several actual gipsy communes within the local area. The Romanichal (a Romani sub-group) gipsies were easily recognisable: largely by their quite colourful and extravagant forms of caravan accommodation. Most groups tended to occupy authorised tracts of land and, thus, pay local council taxes.

On the camping ground, meanwhile, Charlie deemed the NATs as mostly being quite *snobbish*. The majority of them tended to only communicate amongst themselves: an elitist type of behaviour. He felt that he was being treated as an outsider and, subsequently, Charlie was ignored by most of the group. Their behaviour, however, didn't faze him too much; he soon took a dislike to most of them anyway!

Whilst Charlie regarded himself as a 'true' traveller (as opposed to a working tourist), his lifestyle was largely incompatible with the NATs. He was on the orchard to work hard and save a substantial amount of money. The NATs, on the other hand, were fortnightly social welfare recipients. The majority of them appeared to be more interested in the free accommodation that the orchard provided. Charlie would regularly fill 8-10 bins of apples within eight hours. Many of the NATs, however, would only fill 2-4 bins per day and within a 4-6 hour timeframe.

This particular season would be the first of four apple-picking seasons for Charlie on Broadacre Wood Orchard. Before the commencement of the apple-picking season the following year, another campsite had been set up. It was located about 500 metres from the main camping ground. Colin (the orchard manager) created this second campsite specifically for the New Age Travellers who owned dogs. The site was just cleared land and the only access to water was from several taps. There were no amenities on this campsite.

On the campsite, during the first apple-picking season, Charlie had to endure nightly sing-alongs, along with the continuous (but gentle) strumming of acoustic guitars. These nightly sessions took place near the warmth of a communal campfire and they continue right through to the early hours of the next morning. A combination of a hard day's toil and a copious amount of brandy, though, enabled Charlie to sleep reasonably well inside his tent. If woken up, he would just gulp a few more swigs from the bottle of brandy and occasionally turn on his transistor radio (at a low audible level) and place it near his head.

There was a small amenities block on the campsite which only had two showers. Out of the forty or so camping residents, Charlie suspected that only a few people used them on a regular or semi-regular basis. The vast majority of the NATs never showered or washed at any stage during the six-week apple picking season and quite a few of them never changed their clothes either!

Charlie would walk to the town of West Malling (and occasionally to the village of East Malling) every late afternoon and patronise one of the hotels for at least a couple of hours. He'd never cross paths with any of the campsite residents inside any of the licenced premises. During the third week of the apple-picking season, Charlie briefly conversed with several dishevelled NATs. When he mentioned one of West Malling's hotels in the conversation, they immediately complained to him that they had been barred from every hotel in the area. In unison, they ranted on how they were largely 'discriminated' by the local (supposedly upper-middle class) community and how the NATs were generally treated as *downtrodden lower-classed citizens*. Charlie then casually informed them he had never encountered any problems with hotel staff (or patrons) at any of the local hotels. This admission was not well received by them and, subsequently, they never spoke to him again!

Throughout several evenings, Charlie discussed with hotel staff and patrons (many of them wearing business attire) the issue of 'discrimination' towards the NATs. All the responses related to one common factor: the NATs general disregard for personal hygiene. In previous years, patrons had complained to hotel management the ever-present whiff of unpleasant body odour inside the premises. Eventually, all the local hotels enforced a policy where the NATs were sternly told that they would only be welcomed if they abided by two key rules: they needed to shower/wash before entering; and, they needed to wear clean and mostly odourless clothing.

On the campsite, there was a room attached to the main packing shed which was meant to be used as a kitchen. The kitchen contained tables and chairs, a microwave oven and two very old refrigerators. Several hours after pitching his tent (first apple picking season), Charlie opened the kitchen door and was immediately met with several unsavoury sights: the aftermath of recent food fights; food scraps and empty/half-empty food cans were strewn over tables and on the floor; numerous empty beer cans/plastic cider bottles had not been binned; a large number of cigarette butts laid on the ground; and, several dogs were eating leftover scraps of food. He decided not to use the kitchen for the entire apple-picking season!

The kitchen was initially closed the following apple-picking season, but several of the campsite residents (including Charlie) successfully *lobbied* Chris to have the kitchen reopened. In turn, he sternly informed the majority of the campsite dwellers (the NATs) that the kitchen was strictly out of bounds for them. Chris added if the kitchen ever looked like what had happened the previous year, it would be padlocked.

For the first several weeks of the second apple-picking season, Charlie mostly distanced himself from most of the campsite dwellers. Towards the end of the season, though, he began to converse regularly with several individuals. Unfortunately, his next-door neighbour (Clifford) wasn't one of those amicable individuals! From the first day, Charlie deemed Clifford as *a bit strange* and automatically decided to limit any verbal contact with him. As it turned out, he was quite a reclusive character anyway, rarely talking to anyone.

Clifford lived in an old refurbished Bedford van which also had a chimney protruding from the top of the vehicle. Charlie suspected that he might have underlying mental issues: he frequently talked to himself and largely distanced himself from the other campers. Charlie only discovered that his name was Clifford – courtesy of a conversation with himself.

A large number of the NATs owned dogs: mainly whippets or greyhounds. Clifford, however, had two goats as travelling companions! Every afternoon, he would sit in a rocking-chair near his Bedford van, calming smoking a 'ganja' joint (a rolled cigarette paper containing marijuana) and would occasionally sip on a large plastic bottle of apple cider. As the darkness of the evening began to slowly creep in, Clifford would alight from his rocking chair and take his pet goats for a walk. He would lead them through the orchard or along a public bridle path for at least an hour.

The goats were chained to individual steel stakes that had been hammered well into the ground. Each chain was about five metres in length. They spent a good part of the day just eating grass or food scraps, provided by Clifford and other campsite residents. During the apple-picking season, he relocated the steel stakes on several occasions. By the end of the season, there was quite a large bare (and brown) patch surrounding Clifford's van!

During the first two weeks of the second apple-picking season, Charlie arrived back to his tent after a hard day's toil, only to discover that it had been broken into on three separate occasions. He knew it wasn't the goats as they were secured to steel stakes. Charlie presumed that the free-running whippets were the culprits. They had broken into his tent, purely to steal food. Bread and processed ham were the desired items. These misbehaved pooches, however, put several holes in the tent. He managed to repair the holes, haphazardly, with shoelaces. After the third break-in, Charlie confronted several of the whippet owners. In unison, they denied that their 'well-trained' pooch was responsible!

Charlie, however, came up with a solution. After informing Colin of his predicament, he was provided with thick sheets of clear plastic – and lots of bricks. Charlie's tent was soon *fortified*. There were no more break-ins from that moment. Additionally, the thick sheets of plastic provided extra warmth for the inside of his tent and importantly, it was also an effective way to prevent any rain seeping into the tent. On the first day of the subsequent apple-picking seasons, he covered his tent with large sheets of plastic, all firmly held down with numerous bricks. Charlie never had a problem with opportunistic pooches again.

During Charlie's third apple-picking season on Broadacre Wood Orchard, a large percentage of the NATs decided to dwell on the newly-established second campsite. The less 'feral' ones decided to remain on the main campsite. In general, they were friendlier than their counterparts and

Charlie regularly conversed with them throughout the apple-picking season.

Charlie's next-door neighbour (Roger) was from the city of Oxford. Roger's well-maintained Bedford van was in an immaculate condition. Although he regarded himself as a NAT, Charlie viewed him more as a 'proper' traveller. Roger had travelled and worked extensively throughout Europe for more than a decade. He had been involved in numerous *vendange* seasons in France, fruit picking in Denmark (mainly on the island of Funen/Fyn), undertook various forms of employment throughout Greece and had been employed on several fishing trawlers within the Scandinavian region. His main goal on Broadacre Woods Farm was to work hard and save plenty of English sterling pounds.

Regarding the overall itinerant fruit-picking scene within Europe, Roger was an excellent source of useful information. Charlie reciprocated by providing him with a substantial amount of information concerning the itinerant fruit-picking lifestyle throughout Australia and New Zealand. During several conversations, he learnt that Roger embraced a 'minimalist existence': a simple lifestyle where one would try to minimise their weekly or overall living costs. He mainly ate vegetables and fruit, purchased from small markets (instead of supermarkets). Every Sunday afternoon, Roger would 'raid' the supermarket skip bins after they were closed. He would return to the orchard campsite with a wide array of discarded foodstuff: mainly partially-damaged cans of food (that were still properly sealed with little to no risk of being contaminated) and loaves of bread.

Roger's chosen lifestyle would partially influence Charlie to adopt similar *frugal tactics* when attempting to save a substantial amount of money within a relatively small timeframe. A disciplined mixture of 'hard toil' and 'hard saving' for several weeks (or even for several months) enabled him to be placed in a comfortable financial position and, thus, allowed him to then travel for the next few weeks or even longer.

Another campsite resident, who Charlie conversed with regularly, was London-born Angelique. Originally from the west end of London, she had been a practising lawyer (as were both of her parents) but after a failed relationship, Angelique decided to undertake a dramatic lifestyle change. Although she had adopted the NAT sub-culture as a lifestyle choice, Angelique had also been an active participant in the *European wanderlust* for more than ten years. Now aged in her late thirties, she was quite comfortable in discussing her lifestyle choices with Charlie. Similar to Roger, Angelique had also travelled and worked in numerous European countries: Portugal, The Netherlands, France, Spain, etc.

Charlie felt that Angelique's physical appearance was largely one of rebellion and to possibly blend in with the NAT community as well. She only wore hessian-fabric dresses and a pair of black boots laced up to just below her knees. Along with numerous facial piercings (eyebrows, nose, ears and lips), Angelique also had a unique Mohawk hairstyle – dyed in a distinct pattern of rainbow colours. However, behind the façade of an intertwining *Medieval Period meets Punk-Era* dress sense, she was quite an attractive woman. Along with sparkling blue eyes, Angelique had a smooth and wrinkle-free face, stating that she hadn't worn any makeup for years.

Charlie, meanwhile, wondered why the orchard manager was so tolerant towards the NATs. During the third apple-picking season on Broadacre Wood Orchard, Colin revealed to Charlie that he had a 'soft spot' towards them and firmly believed in looking after the *locals* first. Colin also regarded 'colonials' (such as Charlie) as being part of the local population! He was quite bewildered by what was happening on a lot of the other orchards: namely, the Eastern European 'invasion'.

A sizeable number of Polish nationals (both students and non-students), by now, had travelled to the United Kingdom for the fruit-picking seasons for more than a decade. During this particular apple-picking season, however, students from other eastern European countries (Romania, Bulgaria, Latvia, Belarus, etc) had arrived in large numbers. Colin felt that *all* the orchards (plus other industries) in the United Kingdom would soon be 'overrun' by the Eastern Europeans, causing a massive reduction in employment opportunities for the local population or the itinerant traveller.

After Charlie had completed his third apple-picking season at Broadacre Wood Orchard, Colin remained as the orchard manager for a further ten years. He ensured that the NATs occupied both campsites and were employed for the duration of each apple-picking season. When Colin departed, the new orchard manager (Neil) immediately signed contracts with several employment agencies and, thus, mostly hired Eastern European students. He closed the second campsite and arranged for portable accommodation to be brought onto the first campsite. The NATs were no longer welcomed on the orchard.

Charlie eventually returned to Broadacre Wood Orchard – eleven years later. Neil offered him three weeks of cherry-picking employment but the accommodation was not offered. During these three weeks, he camped in a small tent at the Gate House Wood Touring Park: 5 miles (8 kilometres) from the orchard. On each working day, Charlie would walk to a nearby bus stop and board a bus which took him to West Malling. He would then walk two and a half miles to the orchard!

During the first apple-picking season, Charlie never forgot his Polish friends. Every Sunday morning, he would walk from Broadacre Wood Orchard to Angus's orchard: a distance of about 3 miles. Charlie enjoyed the *therapeutic* journey, breathing in and appreciating the morning crispness of the idyllic countryside. The walk, lasting just over an hour, consisted of a mixture of walking along bridle paths through paddocks (and a tract of woodlands), footpaths in sleepy villages and on narrow roads or laneways where he would occasionally having to 'skilfully' dodge the odd car or tractor at times!

Every Saturday morning, Charlie boarded a train at West Malling railway station, taking him to the town of Maidstone. Then he would walk to the Maidstone Market and a short time later, ordered a large sumptuous breakfast. For the cost of three pounds, Charlie would always select the *Big Breakfast*: beef and pork sausages; rashers of bacon; two scrambled eggs; a serving of baked beans; several slices of roasted potato; a sliced roasted tomato; two pieces of toast; and, a large mug of coffee.

After downing his breakfast, Charlie would casually amble throughout the outdoor market place. He would often cross paths with several of the Polish students employed on Angus's orchard. Helena also explored the Maidstone Market every Saturday morning for several hours. In the afternoon, Charlie and she (along with several other students) would stroll along several walkways beside the River Medway; the river sliced the town into a western section and an eastern section. Most of the students on Angus's orchard used bus services to and from Maidstone. Helena, however, preferred to hitchhike – instead of paying bus fares. When Charlie queried her on the preference for hitchhiking, she casually explained that this method of transport was common practice within Poland. Helena, further added, that she regularly hitchhiked from her home village to and from the city of Krakow.

By the end of the apple-picking season, Helena and Charlie had struck up a close friendship. The diminutive little lady, standing at a mere four feet and ten inches (1.47 metres) tall would have quite an alluring effect on him! She only came to the United Kingdom on this sole occasion but the pair would keep in contact for several years. Two years later, Charlie travelled around Poland for two months. He would catch up with Helena during his nine-day stay in Krakow.

Charlie enjoyed conversing with the talkative lady but it was her ever-present twinkling and 'mischievous' eyes that soon captured his attention. The apple-picking season on Angus's orchard finished two weeks before the one on Broadacre Wood Orchard. Nearly all the students left the orchard within three days. Helena, however, decided to stay for a further two weeks; she was now living in a caravan on her own. Charlie stayed with her on the weekends. The romance between the two blossomed (but only kissing and cuddling). He attempted to take things *a little further* but was always met with the same response, 'No sex before marriage... I'm a good Catholic girl!'

Amongst Helena's student peers, she was well-known for being quite cunning and *ridiculously* frugal at times. Her ultimate moment of frugality occurred a week before the end of the apple-picking season. When Helena first arrived in Maidstone, she purchased a camera in one of the town's stores. Over the next few weeks, Helena took a large number of photographs. Then one day her camera was mysteriously damaged. The following Saturday morning, Helena stormed into the store. With the receipt in her tiny hand, she demanded a refund for the 'faulty' camera. Two of her fellow countrymen accompanied her to the store and later recounted the incident to Charlie.

After initial hesitation, the store manager decided that he would replace the 'broken' camera. The diminutive Helena, however, was adamant and persistent that she should receive a full refund for this 'poor quality' camera! A heated discussion then took place for the next few minutes. The store manager eventually conceded defeat – primarily as a means in persuading Helena to leave the store. She received a full refund!

Helena returned to Poland and stayed in contact with Charlie via the postal service. Two years later, he met up with her in Krakow. Helena, three years later, decided to relocate to the USA to reunite with her father. She hadn't seen him for nearly fifteen years. Helena stated to Charlie that her father had escaped to the USA for 'political' reasons. She further added that her father would most likely have faced criminal charges if he ever returned to Poland and, subsequently, would be imprisoned. After relocating to the USA, Helena ceased contact with Charlie.

As the end of October approached, Charlie relocated to the city of Peterborough (county of Cambridgeshire): 75 miles/120 kilometres north of London. He would stay in the area for the next four weeks. At the end of November, Charlie returned to London and several days later, returned to the C&A retail store (near Marble Arch tube station) where he had been employed the previous summer. Two months later, Charlie left London and decided to move to a warmer location: the Greek island of Crete.

3

The Cockney Rebel

Charlie first encountered Dave inside a hotel in the village of Yalding (county of Kent). After entering the hotel, he sat on a stool at one end of the bar and ordered a pint of John Smith Bitter. At the other end of the bar, several patrons were engaging in quite a lively discussion. The eldest patron in the group, however, dominated the conversation. Clutching a pint of Guinness, Charlie deemed his manner as being boisterous and aggressively animated.

Five minutes later, the elderly gentleman walked towards Charlie. In a gruff and a very distinct Cockney accent, he introduced himself as Dave. Upon hearing Charlie's *colonial* accent, he loudly and excitedly introduced the 'Antipodean' to the other hotel patrons and the publican.

'He's an obnoxious old prick,' thought Charlie.

A few days later, the pair crossed paths again, inside the Wateringbury Hotel (Wateringbury, Kent). At the time, Charlie was working on an orchard located between the villages of Yalding and Wateringbury. He, firstly, had walked to the village carrying a fully laden backpack with clothing that required the services of a launderette (also known as a laundromat in other English-speaking countries). Charlie trundled cautiously down a steep, narrow and windy lane – trying to avoid any contact with a vehicle or tractor.

As Charlie approached the main street in Wateringbury, he walked across the railway crossing and then onto the train platform. Large manually-operated wooden gates were still being used to close the road just before the arrival of a train! Charlie checked the timetable for the next train going to the small town of Paddock Wood (two train-stops away from Wateringbury). He was only going to the town to use the launderette but the next train was nearly two hours away. The Wateringbury Hotel was less than a hundred metres away.

Charlie entered the hotel and was only planning to have two pints. Just after he had walked through the opened double-oaked-door entrance, Charlie noticed a familiar face! Dave noticed his arrival and immediately greeted him. Putting his bear-like arm over Charlie's shoulders, he *loudly* introduced him to the hotel patrons and staff. In an overbearing and paternalistic manner, he enthusiastically declared that Charlie was one of his 'kids'.

'Dave, I'm 26 years old.'

One of the bemused local patrons then sarcastically quipped, 'Geez Dave… how many bleedin' kids have you got!'

Several hours (and pints) later, Charlie realised that Dave had *a heart of gold* and several patrons explained to him that he was a decent and honest character, despite his boisterous nature. They further explained, however, that Dave did possess a fiery temperament from time to time: one that had seen him barred (on numerous occasions) for short periods from many hotels within the Maidstone district!

Charlie never made it to the laundromat that Saturday afternoon. Feeling the effects of several pints, he eventually left the hotel and doggedly made his way back up the hill, returning to the orchard. The next morning, he walked back to Wateringbury railway station and caught the train to Paddock Wood. Charlie soon found the launderette and a vital chore was accomplished.

In the ensuing years, Charlie returned to the Maidstone region for several more fruit-picking seasons. Throughout each season, he would visit Dave (who lived in Yalding) on several occasions. Charlie, however, would mostly cross paths with him inside the same Yalding hotel where he had first met him. Before the commencement of each fruit-picking season, Charlie would arrive in the area virtually near-penniless: a result of a recent bout of extensive travelling. A perceptive Dave sensed that his financial situation was in a perilous state and, subsequently, supplied him with food, coffee, tea and bottles of beer – all acquired courtesy of a 'back-of-the-truck' deal with one of his lorry-driving friends.

Due to long-term connections with several lorry drivers, Dave was regularly supplied with heavily discounted food and beverage items. The drivers, who were returning from continental Europe (France, Spain or Eastern European countries), would have their vehicles laden with cheap grocery items and alcohol. In return, Charlie would supply Dave with a constant supply of fruit (strawberries, cherries, pears and apples) throughout the weeks of the fruit-picking season.

Whenever Charlie was not in the Maidstone region, due to travelling or employment commitments elsewhere, he still kept in contact with Dave – solely with postcards. At the end of the first fruit-picking season, Dave informed Charlie that he liked to receive numerous postcards from all of his *travelling kids*, regardless of where they were travelling or working. Inside Dave's house, the large double-door and the sides of the refrigerator (along with a section of the lounge room wall) were covered with postcards.

In his younger days, Dave had been quite an adventurous traveller himself and openly bragged of his bygone escapades. One day, to escape from his period of *juvenile delinquency* (whilst living in an eastern borough of London), he decided to board a train to northern England. Within a few days, Dave managed to obtain employment in a coal mine. He was seventeen years old at the time.

After working in the coal mines for two years, Dave decided to join the army. This career change enabled him to travel to numerous countries in both Europe and in the northern regions of Africa. After serving in the army for over a decade, he was 'honourably' discharged. Now newly-unemployed, Dave recounted to Charlie how the next few years of his life could be best described as the *turbulent years*. He described this period as a 'rebirth' of his juvenile delinquency days. As a result, Dave spent several stretches in Her Majesty's prisons.

Outside of paying 'patronage' to the British prison system, Dave mostly drove lorries/trucks throughout the United Kingdom and across the European mainland. Several years later, he became involved in the hotel/nightclub industry, as a part-owner or a manager (or both). Through a mixture of Dave's employment history and his extroverted persona, he managed to establish a flourishing network of contacts throughout the United Kingdom and other European countries as well. In Dave's 'retirement' years, his long-established network of contacts would enable him to indulge in a fair bit of *wheeling and dealing*: primarily as a means of eking out a living.

On the occasional Saturday afternoon, Charlie would be in the passenger seat of Dave's large Ford Transit van, along with his beloved Jack Russell terrier: Princess. She would mostly rest herself on top of the wide single-benched seat.

Occasionally, though, Princess would rest her front paws on Charlie's shoulder but with her hind legs still on top of the seat. The vehicle was laden with a vast array of plants and shrubs. They had been brought into the United Kingdom from continental Europe. Dave had purchased them from lorry drivers at *mates' rates.*

Seeking potential customers, Dave would drive along the streets in new (or relatively new) housing estates throughout the Maidstone area. His sales technique was purely a door-to-door approach. Beaming with self-confidence, Dave's favourite sales technique was to try and convince the householder(s) how certain types of plants and shrubs would look *just divinely and lovely* in their front yard. Additionally, he would offer potential customers a 'special deal' if they decided to purchase a certain quantity of plants/shrubs. These special deals included: young family rates; cockney-born rates; new-to-the-area rates; and, elderly/pensioner rates. Charlie's lone role in Dave's money-making venture was purely physical: unloading and carrying the plants/shrubs from the van to the front yard or garage.

Dave regarded his Saturday afternoon making-money venture mainly as a social pastime. Charlie, on the other hand, regarded the whole exercise as a priceless piece of entertainment! Several times during the afternoon, the pair would patronise a hotel establishment for a 'quick' half-pint of Guinness. As the sun was descending over the horizon in the late afternoon, the day's plant/shrub selling venture would eventually come to a halt at a hotel, owned by one of Dave's longtime friends: a fellow cockney named Ross. Charlie would take all the unsold plants and shrubs out of the van and carry them to a small room inside the hotel. Ross would then purchase the unsold items at a reduced rate.

When Charlie returned to Australia, he continued to send postcards to Dave. However, after Charlie got married (a marriage that only lasted for several years), he ceased sending postcards to him. On the last postcard sent to Dave, Charlie wrote that he had recently married and would be settling in Australia. Charlie, though, further added that he hoped to return to the United Kingdom one day.

Charlie did return to the United Kingdom – eleven years later. After staying in London for two nights, he boarded a Maidstone-bound train. For the next several days, Charlie stayed in a Bed and Breakfast in the village of Coxheath (2.5 miles/4 km south of Maidstone). On the first evening, he entered the village's lone hotel. As Charlie drank a pint of Guinness, sitting on a stool at the bar, an elderly couple approached him. They had recognised him! The couple had been former next-door neighbours of Dave and his wife. They informed Charlie that he had passed away five years ago at the age of seventy-eight.

Charlie had only intended to stay in the hotel for two pints of Guinness but ended up having dinner (and several more pints) with the elderly couple. Over several hours, he conversed earnestly with them. They had known him for several decades and, thus, the evening was primarily an anecdotal history of Dave: the *Cockney Rebel.*

4

The Land of the Crows

When the apple-picking season in county Kent had ended in late-October, Charlie decided to relocate to the East Midlands region of the United Kingdom in an endeavour to seek further employment. After staying in London for two days, he boarded a train which took him to the northern environs of London. Charlie alighted from the train and walked towards the motorway (M1). At a road junction, he attempted to hitch a ride. Within fifteen minutes, Charlie was on his way to the city of Peterborough: 75 miles (120 kilometres) north of London.

From Peterborough, Charlie hitchhiked along the A47 to the market town of Kings Lynn, located in the county of Norfolk. He would stay at the youth hostel for a week. For the first three days, Charlie actively explored local employment opportunities. His quest to seek employment during this time, however, was unsuccessful. For the next two days, he resorted to a mixture of sightseeing and walking, just to pass the time away.

On the sixth day, Charlie boarded a local bus to the nearby market town of Wisbech (county of Cambridgeshire). After alighting from the bus, he proceeded to walk away from the town centre, wandering in a mostly southerly direction. Eventually, Charlie came upon a hotel, located amongst picturesque fields and orchards.

As Charlie sipped on a pint of beer, he was informed by several of the patrons that outdoor employment within the 'Fens' (also known as the Fenlands) was relatively scarce at this time of the year. Plus, employment in local factories and packing sheds was mostly filled by the local population. One of the hotel patrons, however, provided him with the phone number of a *gangmaster* who resided in the city of Peterborough. Charlie was further informed that gangmasters within Cambridgeshire were often a good source of employment – especially for non-locals.

Charlie rang the gangmaster the next day and was immediately met with an assurance that there was plenty of employment available within the Peterborough region. The gangmaster further informed him that share accommodation in a large house was also available. Charlie boarded a bus in the centre of Kings Lynn and arrived in Peterborough one and a half hours later. A short time later, he was inside a spacious office room. 'Gangmaster' Robert outlined the employment and accommodation options for him. For the next two weeks, Charlie would reside in the nearby village of

Eye and share a five-bedroom house with nine people. The other occupants were either Eastern Europeans or from northern African countries.

The employment options for Charlie involved day, afternoon or night shifts. He chose the night shifts (8-10 hours) as it was the best-paid option. Charlie would work five nights a week. All shifts were cleaning jobs. During his second week of employment, Charlie began to consider other employment options. Most of the employment vacancies in newspapers and on communal notice boards, however, were low-paid factory jobs – and, there was a high demand for onion-peelers. An employment position for celery-cutters (listed in the local newspaper), however, caught his eye. The four-week season, in the nearby town of Crowland, was to commence in 3-4 days. The advertisement further stated that caravan accommodation on the vegetable farm was also provided.

During the recent apple-picking season in the county of Kent, one of the New Age travellers had warned Charlie about working for gangmasters. Standing in the office that afternoon, he soon understood their concern. Robert (aged in his early-fifties) had the general appearance of a slick car salesman. Besides being well-groomed, he seemed to have a penchant for anything gold: a gold watch; numerous gold tooth-fillings; and, a prominent (and expensive-looking) gold chain around his neck. Robert's four 'office' employees were uncannily alike: they all had heavily-built physiques; shaved heads; and, spoke with Cockney accents. Charlie wondered if they were all retired henchmen!

Charlie's two-week stay in the large house would be quite an enjoyable experience as he managed to achieve a high level of amicableness with the other nine occupants. All of them had secured many hours of employment: typically 50-70 hours per week. Charlie soon learnt that all the occupants had one goal: to save several thousand pounds sterling and return to their homeland. With their hard-earned savings, each individual intended to purchase a house or start a business venture (or both). Charlie, who had a two-year work permit at the time, suspected that he was probably the only legal worker in the household!

After leaving the large household, Charlie boarded a bus in Eye which took him to the small town of Crowland, Lincolnshire: 9 miles north of Peterborough. Besides his large backpack and a small-sized carrier bag, he was also carrying two large plastic bags of *communal goodies*. Located in the hallway of the large household, these 'communal goodies' were contained in several large boxes and contained the following items: large tins of coffee; loose onions and potatoes; canned vegetables/spam; packets of soup; bottles of discount-priced wine; discarded clothing; and, several items of footwear.

When the bus arrived in Crowland, Charlie walked to the vegetable farm: a distance of about 200 metres from the bus stop. He was met by the vegetable farm's owner (Nigel) on the front lawn of his house, situated near the farm's main entrance. The front lawn contained numerous ornamental wheelbarrows and perky garden gnomes. Charlie felt that Nigel was still living as if he was still stuck in a bygone era: the *hippy-flippy* times of the Sixties. Besides his long, thick and dishevelled hair (along with a lengthy and straggly greying beard), Nigel was wearing a green and purple paisley shirt; easily visible underneath an open and tattered duffel jacket.

After a discussion which barely lasted five minutes, Nigel introduced Charlie to the vegetable-farm foreman (Basil). Moments later, Basil (who spoke with a distinct 'west-country' accent) directed him to the accommodation area which contained eight large caravans. He would be sharing a caravan with two other people. Charlie left his luggage inside the caravan and strolled to the village hotel. Several hours later, he returned and was soon conversing with the other two occupants of the caravan: Mick and Dan (both New Zealand nationals).

Both Mick and Dan were originally from the south island of New Zealand. They had been residing in England for nearly two years and had solely been employed in rural industries. A large amount of their employment evolved around driving harvesting machinery. Dan, whose parents were Swedish-born, had also lived and worked on farms in Sweden before deciding to relocate to the United Kingdom.

Whilst the interior of the caravan was in good condition, the same could not be said for the amenities block. It was in an appalling condition. Built into a section of an unused packing shed, several windows were broken and numerous fragments of glass were scattered on the cement floor near the doorway. Charlie suspected that the windows had been deliberately damaged; most likely by former disgruntled employees. The lone shower only had a single-handle hot/cold control of the water. This meant that if you wanted hot water, the water would just trickle out. If you wanted more water (along with an increase in water pressure) it would be quite cold. Combined with the chilly evening draught, effortlessly seeping through the damaged windows, one would shiver helplessly whilst showering!

The employment conditions for the next four weeks could be best described as *character building*. The inclement weather, persistent throughout these weeks, generally made working conditions quite unpleasant. Although the celery-cutters were provided with wet-weather gear, the muddy conditions ensured that inner clothing would also be mud-stained. At the end of the celery-cutting season, Charlie promptly put all of his mud-stained clothing into a garbage bin.

Another major hazardous work condition involved the use of a large knife. The large regularly-sharpened knife was used to cut the celery at the base of the plant. The muddy conditions ensured that the knife handle was quite difficult to grasp properly at times. By the end of the celery-cutting season, Charlie's hands had numerous minor cuts and they were well and truly *weather-beaten*. Away from the celery fields, drying clothes for the next day's work was also a constant problem. Inside the caravan, Mick constructed an indoor clothes-line. Using the heat from the gas stove-plates, the three of them managed to dry their clothes.

Outside the work environment, the social atmosphere within the accommodation area was harmoniously amicable. All the celery-cutters were male and many nationalities were represented. Charlie was the lone Australian. The rest of the group comprised of four Kiwis (New Zealanders), a Scotsman, a South African, a Dutchman, a Nigerian, two Turks, five Czechs, five Poles and 'Scouser' Roy (a Liverpudlian).

Within the first several days of the celery-cutting season, the *entire* group quickly took a dislike to both Nigel and Basil. Noel (a New Zealander) soon had nicknames for both of them. Nigel was regularly referred to as 'Nigel No Mates' and Basil as 'Faulty' (adopted from the television show *Fawlty Towers*). The group, however, rarely saw Nigel who turned out to be quite an elusive character; his wife mostly controlled the everyday activities of the packing shed. 'Faulty' Basil, on the other hand, seemed to be *always* nearby. During work hours, he would regularly park his vehicle close to where the celery-cutters were working and walk up and down the rows. Any drops of rain, though, saw Basil hastily retreat to the inside of his vehicle.

The celery-cutters soon learnt to limit any communication with Basil. A boring conversationalist, he would constantly moan and groan about his 'past misadventures' which included: numerous failed marriages and relationships; several failed business ventures and failed employment opportunities; three bankruptcies; and, his declining 'societal statuses'. Noel suggested to his peers that Basil should have included *failed personality* to his list of many woes and regrets!

The celery-cutters had moved to this vegetable farm, solely for employment purposes, except for 'Scouser' Roy. He had left his home city of Liverpool for an entirely different reason: one that saw him trying to reconcile with his ex-wife who resided in nearby Peterborough. Smooth-talking Roy was the first person to arrive on the vegetable farm. He managed to persuade Basil to allow him to solely occupy one of the medium-sized caravans (all the other caravans would contain shared occupancy). This caravan was the only one that had a television. Roy's caravan, on most evenings, would transform into a *television room* as he was regularly visited by the other caravan dwellers.

Thirty-something Roy managed to 'sweet-talk' his way into obtaining the coveted job of transporting bunches of celery from the field (via a tractor and a dray) to the packing shed. He was paid a daily rate. In between deliveries, Roy would occasionally cut some bunches of celery – especially when Basil was inside his vehicle power-napping or sheltering from unfavourable weather conditions. On the way to the packing shed, he would park the tractor and dray near his caravan – stockpiling bunches of celery into a wardrobe. On the weekend, he would then sell the celery at various places in Peterborough: hotels, food markets and small convenience stores!

The working week on the vegetable farm was from Monday to Friday only. On the weekends, Nigel and Basil were nowhere to be seen: a fact that Roy was well aware of! On two consecutive Sundays, he decided to 'borrow' one of the registered farm tractors and drove it to Peterborough to sell bunches of celery – and to visit his ex-wife. He mostly drove the tractor along the lesser-used roads, purposely keeping away from the A-roads as much as possible. The two-way trip was a distance of around 20 miles (32 kilometres).

On Monday morning (after the second Sunday), however, Nigel was driving this particular tractor on the vegetable farm when the engine suddenly 'died'. It had run out of diesel fuel! A short time later, he came to the field where the celery-cutters were working and, in a quite an exasperated manner, demanded to know who had been using the tractor for *recreational purposes.* All the celery-cutters knew that Roy was the culprit but they just stood there 'innocently' and denied any knowledge of his tractor-driving escapades over the previous two Sundays. Nigel, however, repeatedly looked at Roy. Several minutes later, he blurted out bewilderedly, 'Roy... it wouldn't be you by any chance?'

'It was certainly not me... sir!'

Most of the celery-cutters were now struggling to maintain a calm composure and desperately tried to muffle obvious sounds of sniggering. From that moment on, Nigel instructed Basil to do regular fuel checks on all of the tractors. The following weekend, Roy boarded a bus to visit his ex-wife in Peterborough. He was also carrying two large plastic bags of celery!

Whilst life in the celery fields could often be deemed as *character-building,* the humorous camaraderie within the group provided light-hearted relief. After work, the celery-cutting crew would regularly discuss the day's events in jest. Basil (in particular) was a key element of these jovial conversations!

During work hours, (Faulty) Basil would regularly repeat his tales of woe. But even more annoying, he often looked over people's shoulders as they worked. Charlie *hated* anyone looking over his shoulder as he worked. Whenever Barry was behind him, he (Charlie) would stop working and confront him face-to-face. Charlie regarded this type of behaviour as a form of intimidation. Basil, however, continued to ramble about his life's *moments of bleakness.*

Charlie would then typically respond along the following lines.

'Well, Basil… that's life.'

'Get over it… time you moved on.'

Basil, despondently, would walk away and Charlie recommenced celery-cutting.

The four-week celery-cutting season came to a halt just after midday on a Tuesday. An hour later, most of the crew went to the packing shed to collect their final cheques. Nigel's wife, however, insisted that the final cheques were usually mailed to a nominated forwarding address. She further added that all caravans needed to be vacated by 4.00 pm today.

A now-bewildered group then declared to her that they wouldn't be leaving the property until they got paid. Charlie sarcastically responded, 'Guess I'll just have to pitch my tent on your front lawn… until I receive my cheque!'

All cheques were available one hour later! Nigel, though, insisted that the caravans still had to be vacated by 4.00 pm. By 3.30 pm, however, most of the celery-cutting crew had already had their cheques cashed in one of Crowland's hotels and were now enjoying an alcoholic beverage. After consuming two pints of John Smith Bitter, Charlie left the hotel and boarded a bus for Peterborough. After staying in

Peterborough for two nights, he decided to hitchhike to London. It was the first week of December.

Charlie stayed in London for the next two months and returned to the C&A store where he had worked several months previously. As a means to boost his financial position within a short time, Charlie undertook a second job: industrial cleaning (on weekends and the occasional evening shift during the week).

On the last day of January, Charlie boarded a Dan-Air aircraft (a now-defunct airline which was merged into British Airways in 1992). The flight took him to the Greek capital city of Athens. He would live and work on the Greek island of Crete for the next four months. Charlie returned to London aboard a Malév Hungarian Airlines flight. He soon discovered that the start of the strawberry-picking was still a few weeks away. Charlie, therefore, decided to venture back to the small town of Crowland (Lincolnshire) for the upcoming leek-cutting season.

After discussing the upcoming leek-cutting season with Nigel's wife (via a telephone call from a public phone booth in Crowland), Charlie casually ambled towards the vegetable farm. As he approached the packing shed, he crossed paths with 'Faulty' who, quite startlingly, greeted him with the *encouraging* words, 'Surprised to see you here again… no-one ever comes back.'

A semi-bemused Charlie responded, 'Well… I do!'

A few minutes later, Charlie was unpacking his backpack in the same caravan that he had stayed in during the celery-cutting season. Charlie would be sharing the caravan with two other males: an Australian (Dave) and a South African national (Scott).

Unlike the celery-cutting season, the weather conditions this time were far more favourable. Financially, however, the leek-cutting season would be even less lucrative. Charlie stayed for only two weeks. On the second day of the leek-cutting season, he was already planning his next travelling venture: hitchhiking throughout France and Germany, with the possibility of obtaining fruit-picking employment.

On the third day, Charlie deemed the leek-cutting season, primarily, as a scam. The ever-annoying Basil rigidly enforced the rule that each bunch of leeks had to be *washed, trimmed and manicured* before they could be placed in the crates. Just like the previous celery-cutting crew, the entire leek-cutting group quickly took an immense dislike to Faulty. On the fourth day, there was a 'workers revolt' which prompted Basil to nastily suggest, 'If you don't like it... leave!'

The result: over half of the leek-cutting crew (mainly the Polish nationals and those from northern African countries) left the vegetable farm the next day. The majority of them returned to Peterborough to be employed by gangmasters – the 'lesser of the two evils'.

The remaining leek-cutters, meanwhile, worked 10-11 hours per day and earning a paltry amount each day. Charlie viewed the dire situation as just a notch above *slave labour*. Nevertheless, he persevered for the next two weeks and managed to save just over 200 pounds sterling. On Charlie's last day of employment, his level of motivation was at rock bottom. South African Scott's level of enthusiasm was even worse. During the morning leek-cutting session, he regularly threw a leek (or several) over a high bricked-wall. The wall divided this field of leeks and a seldom-used laneway. Basil, meanwhile, had spent most of the morning *power napping* inside his vehicle.

Just after 11.00 am, an irate Nigel speedily drove to the field on one of his tractors. Sheepishly, Basil alighted from his vehicle. The duo then stormed towards the leek-cutters and a flustered Nigel demanded, 'Who has been throwing leeks onto the laneway… one of them just landed on a passing motorist's windscreen!'

The leek-cutting crew, however, ignored Nigel's rant and continued working, with their backs facing towards him and Basil. The group were mainly trying to hide their sniggering and smirking facial expressions. Charlie then decided to provoke Nigel even further and quizzically asked him, 'Hey, Nigel… sure it was one of us?'

Charlie then categorically stated to Nigel and Basil that he was unaware of any 'juvenile behaviour' – despite working only a few metres away from Scott. Charlie, quite theatrically, then threw his arms in the air and forthrightly declared that it was unfair that management was making 'unsubstantiated accusations'. He cheekily added that the leek-cutting group were *genuinely concerned* about the 'welfare' of the washed, trimmed and manicured bunches of leeks!

A now-flabbergasted Nigel was quite taken back by Charlie's antics! Speechless, he simply turned around and walked away from the group. Basil, meanwhile, was practically choking himself on stifled laughter and was unable to verbally respond to Charlie's 'flamboyant' rhetoric. Once Nigel had left the vicinity, he attempted to employ a tactic of reverse psychology with the leek-cutting crew. Basil tried to be 'friendly' with the group. '*Please...* don't throw any more leeks over the brick wall and onto the laneway!'

Just after midday, Charlie (along with Scott and Dave) decided to have a lengthy lunch-break in the communal area of a nearby packing shed (not the main one near the accommodation facilities) where bunches of leeks were being sorted and packed. During the luncheon interval, the trio conversed with a group of elderly packing-shed workers who were also on their luncheon break.

Twenty-five minutes into the luncheon interval, 'Faulty' Basil entered the complex and demanded that the trio should return to work immediately. An unperturbed Charlie reminded him that the leek-cutters were being paid piece-rate and that there was no set time limit for meal breaks. Perplexed, Basil then babbled on how the 'piece-rate' was the method of payment and management *decides* on the length of any meals breaks. In unison, the trio strongly chastised him for uttering such nonsense.

A bewildered Charlie rose from his chair and stood in front of Basil, practically standing on his toes and eyeballing him.

'Hey, Faulty… that's absolute bullshit.'

Before Basil could even respond, one of the elderly gentlemen gave him quite an earful.

'Basil, your behaviour is disgraceful… you should be far more hospitable to our colonial friends!'

Another elderly chap then wanted to take Basil outside for a *friendly discussion* – flexing his knuckles on his weathered spade-like hands as he spoke. Faulty quickly retreated, turned around and hastily left the complex. After the lengthy luncheon break, the three 'colonials' returned to the field for the afternoon session of leek-cutting. Basil, however, had other ideas.

He intercepted them and ordered them to leave the field immediately! Basil then ordered the trio to pack their belongings and vacate the caravans by the end of the day. An angry Charlie demanded that they needed to be paid in cash within the hour. Basil's face was now a glowing red but the trio stood their ground and glared at him. Charlie clenched both of his fists – he wanted to drop him. Basil went to his vehicle and drove to the main packing shed. Forty-five minutes later, he returned with three envelopes of cash. After opening the envelope and counting the money, Charlie cheekily quipped, 'Hey, Faulty… can you put my name down for the celery-cutting season!'

Two hours later, the trio was on a London-bound train. Scott and Dave remained in London for the next several months. Charlie, on the other hand, only stayed in London for two nights. For the next four weeks, he hitchhiked throughout France and Germany. Charlie soon lost contact with Scott but he kept in contact with fellow-Australian, Dave, for several years. Several months later (in November), he received a letter from him. Dave was cutting celery on Nigel's farm. Charlie thought to himself, 'Yep… only stupid Aussies return to Nigel's vegetable farm!'

5

The Ellaniki Experience

Charlie boarded the Dan-Air aircraft from London's Gatwick Airport in the late evening. Amidst typical cold wintry-like conditions, the flight was bound for the capital of Greece. He was hoping the weather conditions in Athens would be far more favourable. Just after take-off, however, the pilot announced the weather forecast (for Athens): fine, but with a current temperature of -2 degrees. Passenger Charlie Ash was not amused!

[Note: Dan-Air is a now-defunct British airline which was sold to British Airways in 1992].

After disembarking from the aircraft and passing through the customs area, Charlie and a group of his fellow passengers were soon engaged in earnest conversation, discussing an array of upcoming ventures. The group huddled together on the cold marble floor in the lounge area of the arrival terminal inside the small airport. The then-international airport, Ellinikon International Airport, was located quite a distance away. There was no heating within this terminal.

The vast majority of the group would only be staying in Athens for one or two days. Eventually, everyone would be venturing to one of Greece's well-known islands: either by air travel or a ferry trip from the port of Piraeus (12 kilometres from central Athens). Two blonde-haired English ladies travelling together planned to go to the island of Rhodes via a ferry service later that day. Charlie was also planning to be aboard a ferry later in the day but the island of Crete was his intended destination. After chatting together for half an hour, the trio decided to share a taxi ride to the port of Piraeus.

Just after 6.00 am, the three casually strolled through the exit door of the airport terminal. Outside, there was a fleet of idle but 'eager-waiting' taxis. In front of the first taxi stood several seemingly-bored taxi drivers, barely engaged in any form of discussion with each other. Suddenly, all eyes were focused on Charlie's new-found blonde-haired companions!

One of the taxi drivers asked, 'Where do you want to go?'

The idle chit-chat amongst the drivers was soon replaced by audible childlike sniggering.

Charlie replied, 'We're going to the port of Piraeus. How much will the taxi fare cost?'

Another taxi driver slyly quipped, 'The cost will be 3,500 drachmas.'

Before Charlie could even respond, one of his blonde-haired companions blurted out,

'That's quite excessive!'

Before departing from London, Charlie had read in a travel brochure that the taxi fare from the domestic airport to Piraeus should be about 600 drachmas. Without hesitation, he coolly relayed this piece of information to the drivers – only to be met with icy stares.

As a form of compromise, Charlie suggested, 'We're quite happy to pay 900 drachmas… 300 drachmas from each passenger.' He further informed the taxi drivers that the bus fare to the port of Piraeus was 150 drachmas. The first taxi driver then snarled, 'But there are no buses for at least an hour.'

Charlie was content to continue 'negotiations' but the English ladies had already made up their minds; they were already heading back to the inside of the terminal. Just over an hour later, the two English ladies and Charlie (along with several other passengers on the Dan-Air flight) were aboard a Piraeus-bound bus. As the bus drove past the group of taxi drivers, who were still waiting for their first fare for the day, many of the bus passengers smiled and waved at them. Needless to say, there was no reciprocated response from the taxi drivers!

Once inside the port of Piraeus, the two English ladies and Charlie immediately tried to book ferry trips to the islands of Rhodes and Crete, respectively. All ferry services to the Greek islands, however, had been cancelled for the entire day. Due to the atrocious weather conditions, port authorities had deemed that any ferry crossing across the Mediterranean Sea would be too dangerous to undertake.

Charlie attempted to extract information from ferry terminal staff, concerning the recommencement of ferry services. Alas, he was frequently met with the response, 'I don't know'.

Eventually, a female customs officer icily declared:

'There will be no ferry services for at least the next two days!'

'Flying to the islands via Ellinikon International Airport is the only option for the next two days'.

She further stated that afternoon flights were available to both the islands of Rhodes and Crete later in the day. The trio left the port and boarded a bus which took them to the international airport.

The two English ladies booked a 2.00 pm flight to Rhodes whilst Charlie booked a 4.00 pm flight to Crete. A few hours later, he was aboard a small but 'antiquated' aircraft bound for Chania Souda Airport (Crete). The flight took just over 45 minutes. In stark contrast, the ferry crossing would have taken at least eleven hours!

The aircraft flew at a relatively low altitude for the entire journey. For the duration of the flight, Charlie spent most of the time just gazing through the small window, viewing the rippling waves of the *nearby* ocean. He sensed that the aircraft was probably passed its 'use-by-date': the occasional cough and splutter of the plane's engine was hardly reassuring in one's overall confidence in airline safety!

Charlie firmly believed that there was a clear logic to why the pilot had chosen a relatively low flight path for this aircraft: less distance for *free-falling* or the need to *glide* along the water in an attempt to reduce the impact of any impending crash. Continuing to gaze at the nearby ocean, he began to visualize himself in an inflatable floatie – desperately clinging to the partly submerged plane – and waiting anxiously for the delayed ferry from Piraeus to rescue him as it passed by.

The aircraft safely arrived at Chania-Souda airport. As no bus services were operating at that time of day, Charlie began to walk towards the city of Chania (sometimes spelt Khania or Xania). Initially, he thought the distance to the city from the airport was only several kilometres. After walking a few hundred metres, a kind-hearted motorist stopped and gave him a lift to the city. Charlie soon learnt that the distance to Chania was *fourteen* kilometres.

In central Chania, Charlie boarded a bus. He showed the elderly bus driver a piece of paper which had an address for a YHA hostel. The driver just shook his head and verbally responded. Charlie, unfortunately, didn't understand a word of the Greek language at the time and thus, had no idea what the gentleman was trying to tell him. He, however, insisted on wanting to go to the hostel and ten minutes later, the bus stopped in front of the YHA hostel.

Charlie immediately sensed that the youth hostel was probably closed. It was! A nearby resident explained to him (in English) that the youth hostel was only opened during the tourist season: May to October. With a laden backpack and a small carrier bag, he started walking back to central Chania. As Charlie casually ambled down the street, he noticed numerous spent cartridges strewn along the roadway. With an instant sense of uneasiness, Charlie thought he may have unwillingly entered a recent gangland war zone. He later learnt, however, that the strewn spent cartridges were most likely linked to recent overzealous wedding celebrations! As Charlie walked nervously along the street, he half-expected the sound of gunfire to erupt at any given moment. The eerie silence further enhanced his cautious fears. There was no-one outside and no vehicles were being driven along this particular road.

After walking for just over half an hour, Charlie was once again in central Chania. He immediately sought accommodation and located a *pension* (a type of guest house or boarding house which typically provided comfortable and affordable accommodation). Charlie was shown to a room where he would be sharing with two other people.

The next morning, Charlie boarded a bus which took him to the village of Gerani: 14 kilometres west of Chania. After alighting from the bus, he entered a nearby *kafenio* (a café/coffee shop). The kafenio was mostly occupied by

'Westerners': a mixture of French, German, English, Irish, Canadians, etc. The itinerant travellers patronised this venue, primarily as a means to obtain employment during the orange-harvesting season.

For half an hour, Charlie sat at a table and sipped on a cup of coffee as he read an English newspaper. The general atmosphere within the kafenio could be best described as quite 'frosty'. But there was a reason for this. The financial situation for most of the itinerant workers was perilous. Even worse, current employment opportunities were scarce. Charlie, however, did manage to converse with two French nationals (Alain and Francois).

Whilst Alain did not speak English fluently, his level was still proficient enough for Charlie to understand the current dire situation in the area. The availability of employment was severely limited at the time. Francois would occasionally express his views (in French) and Alain, subsequently, translated these views to Charlie in English. At one point during the discussion, Charlie decided to purchase three bottles (500ml) of the Dutch-brewed Amstel beer. Alain and Francois were grateful as neither of them had consumed any alcohol for the past two weeks. Alain further admitted that both of them had only been eating oranges (taken directly from orchards) for the past four days!

Opposite the kafenio, Charlie noticed a small *taverna* (a tavern, bar or inn). He managed to persuade the reluctant pair to continue the conversation over there. Inside the taverna, Charlie purchased six mini-souvlakis. Three days later, Alain and Francois did manage to secure semi-regular orange-picking employment. When Charlie entered the kafenio that afternoon, they immediately bought a bottle of Amstel beer for him. In the evening, the three of them went to the nearby taverna. Alain and Francois purchased two mini-souvlakis for Charlie, thanking him for his previous generosity.

During his four-month stay in Crete, Charlie became 'addicted' to mini-souvlakis and consumed at least four of the *savoury delights* every day! At the time, a mini-souvlaki cost between 90-100 drachmas: equivalent to about 30p (UK).

Charlie slept in a partly-constructed building during his first night in Gerani. Partly-constructed buildings were commonplace (at the time) throughout Greece, largely due to the financial collapse of the economy. Before deciding to sleep in the building, he had already sought accommodation in Gerani and the nearby village of Platanias (and in between the two locations as well). Due to the lateness of the evening, though, and his advanced level of *social inebriation* (intoxication), Charlie had little hope in securing accommodation that night.

The next morning, Charlie consumed a hearty breakfast in the village of Platanias. Afterwards, he attempted to seek accommodation once more. Several minutes later, Charlie knocked on the door of a modest-looking homestead. It had a sign 'Accommodation' above the doorway. Whilst waiting for a response, he sensed that this place looked kind of familiar! After waiting for a couple of minutes, Charlie rapped on the door again. A short time later, a woman yelled from the balcony, located directly above the doorway. He asked her if she had any accommodation available. The woman gazed at Charlie for a few seconds and then blurted out, 'Wasn't you here last night?'

Sheepishly, Charlie replied, 'Yes…I think so.'

She then threw her arms in the air and exasperatingly responded, 'Same as last night… all full!'

Charlie then calmly requested, 'Do you know where I may find some accommodation?'

On hearing Charlie's accent, her demeanour suddenly changed as if she was having a 'light-bulb' moment.

'Where are you from?'

'Australia!'

Now with a sudden realisation that Charlie wasn't English, she responded excitedly.

'Why didn't you say you were from Australia?'
'I lived in Melbourne for over twenty years… working mostly at the Ford Motor Company in the northern suburbs of Melbourne. By the way, my name is Soula.'

For the next half an hour, Soula and Charlie discussed all things *Australian*:

1. Her extensive life in Melbourne;

2. His itinerant fruit-picking lifestyle throughout the eastern states of Australia; and,

3. Australian politics.

Soula came downstairs and led Charlie to a small self-contained villa: one of eight similar-sized buildings. She stated to him that she rarely allows English males to stay in any of the units anymore – especially the 'lager louts'. Soula further explained that she had encountered major problems with several English drunkards within the last few years and added, other local accommodation providers were also wary of them.

Charlie stayed in the fully-furnished complex for the next two weeks. The daily rental cost was reasonably priced. During the main tourist season, however, he learnt that the rental costs of these self-contained villas increased three-fold! The other residents were of several different nationalities: Scottish, Irish, Canadian and American. All the occupants of the villas were either couples or lone females, except for a Mexican-born American named Frank.

Charlie would have happily stayed in the self-contained villa for the next several months but the availability of employment within the local region was quite scarce. During his two-week stay, he only obtained four days of employment, solely by working with Frank.

Employment for Frank suddenly came to an abrupt halt one day and this also meant that further employment opportunities for Charlie were now even less. Frank left the area the next day. He relocated to Israel and commenced employment on a *moshav* (a co-operative agricultural community of individual farms). Later in the day (in Gerani), Charlie learnt that there were better employment opportunities in another nearby village: Alikianos. The next morning, he walked five kilometres (to Alikianos) to make 'further enquiries'.

6

The Road to Alikianos

After walking along the main thoroughfare in the village of Alikianos, Charlie came upon a cafe: *Καφενείο Ευφτίσια* (Kafenio Eftesia). A group of 'westerners' were seated around a large table in the courtyard of the kafenio. They conversed with each other in English. He went inside the kafenio and was immediately greeted by the owner (Eftesia). Aged in his mid-sixties, Eftesia spoke little English. Charlie, however, had already learnt a few Greek words and phrases and promptly requested: *Μία býra parakaló* (one beer please). He went to the outdoor area and sat at an empty table. As Charlie sipped on a bottle of Amstel beer, he read an English newspaper. Several minutes later and upon seeing the English newspaper, one of the English lads asked inquisitively, 'Hi… where are you from?'

Joining the rest of the group, Charlie soon learnt that the availability of orange-picking employment within the region of Alikianos was far more plentiful than the Gerani/Platanias area. One major problem, however, the availability of accommodation was relatively scarce. Nearly all the kafenio patrons were residing in the city of Chania: 12 kilometres away. Every day, they would travel back and forth via a bus service.

Two of the Englishmen, Gerry and Mick, were residing in Chania and they shared a large room inside a pension. The room contained four single beds, two wardrobes and a hand basin. As a means to reduce their daily accommodation costs, the pair was looking for two more people to share the room costs. The cost of the room was the same regardless of the number of occupants. Charlie and Gunther (a German national) quickly took up their offer.

Charlie and Gerry would get along quite well with each other. Unfortunately, they would soon have issues with both Mick and Gunther. The 'happy household' would only last for a couple of weeks. Ten days earlier, Gerry and Mick had crossed paths in the Italian port city of Brindisi whilst staying in a hostel. Before they arrived in Crete, there had already been *personality clashes* between the two.

Gerry had gradually been making his way through Europe after residing in Amsterdam for several weeks, eking a living as a 'professional' beggar. To boost his finances even further, he decided to sell his passport. Claiming that his passport was *stolen*, Gerry soon obtained a new one and left the Dutch capital the following day. As he slowly made his way through the European continent in a south-easterly direction, Gerry resorted to begging in three major cities: Frankfurt, Munich and Venice. He would occasionally hitchhike between destinations but mainly chose to 'play' the rail system. Gerry would board a train without a valid ticket and proceeded to *train hop*: alighting from one train — only to board the next one that came along. He would be caught by ticket inspectors on the odd occasion and, thus, forced to get off the train at the next stop. Gerry boasted: 'France and Italy were the best countries to play the rail system!'

According to Gerry, Mick had largely 'over-funded' his journey from London. As an example of (Mick's) financial recklessness, he gleefully recounted to Charlie of an incident that occurred whilst they were staying at the hostel in Brindisi. Mick was constantly complaining of having sore ankles and heels. Gerry, jokingly, suggested to him that he should seek *urgent medical attention*. Amazingly, Mick did indeed visit a doctor to complain about his sore ankles and heels, only to be told that his boots were *too tight*.

'The visit to the doctor cost the clown about 40 quid (British pounds)!'

Gerry would not be the only person that was unhappy with Mick. A compulsive moaner and groaner, he was soon disliked by most of the itinerant group and soon became known as *Miserable Mick*. Even worse, Mick regularly attempted to spin his moments of wastrel spending (paying too much for accommodation, buying meals in upmarket restaurants, short-distance taxi fares instead of walking the distance, etc) as 'hard-luck' stories. The itinerants condemned his spending habits as being naively stupid. One of the young Irish lads summed it up best. 'Mick… you can't travel as a tourist on a traveller's budget!'

For the next three months, Charlie's employment situation was generally quite good. He lived comfortably and even managed to save a reasonable amount of money each week. The availability of employment, however, could be limited from time to time: mainly due to the competition from a sizeable influx of Albanian males.

Despite the Albanians being prepared to be employed on a much lesser hourly rate, many employers at the time still preferred to hire 'westerners'. In Alikianos, Eftesia (with regular assistance from local police and the majority of citrus growers) ensured that the Albanians were kept a reasonable distance away from his kafenio – especially large groups of them. Most of the local citrus growers in the local area would either approach Eftesia directly or telephone him when they were trying to fulfil labour requirements for the day or several days. Charlie's work ethic did not go unnoticed and he soon emerged as one of Eftesia's *favourites*. His daily effort in obtaining employment, subsequently, was largely successful.

Large groups of Albanians throughout the Chania region were often a problem for local authorities. They regularly gathered in large numbers in Chania's square of *Eleftherios Venizelos* (Old Town) and even in some of the nearby towns and villages (e.g. Platanias). A common tactic used by the Albanians was to firstly surround an employer's vehicle. Next, they would try to persuade him that he should hire them – and, at a lesser hourly pay rate than what westerners would work for.

Citrus and olive growers, in particular, disliked this *mob* tactic. They preferred to approach kafenio/taverna owners either in person or by telephone. Occasionally, teams of police officers would pose as potential employers. A group of Albanians, for example, would board a vehicle and instead of being taken to an orchard, they were taken to the police station! After being 'processed', they would then be deported back to Albania. Within weeks, however, many of the deported Albanians would simply *walk* back into Greece. They would, firstly, cross the mountains on the Albania-Greece border and over the next several weeks, continued to walk onwards to various regions in Greece. Some of them would board a ferry service, taking them to one of the Greek islands (e.g. Crete).

In Alikianos, meanwhile, employment opportunities for the itinerant travellers could be best described as 'tight' on some days. A simple rule within the group, however, was to allow the *needier* to have the first preference regarding employment availability; especially with the eight-hour orange picking jobs (typically commencing between 8.00 am and 9.00 am). Charlie (along with several others) regularly shunned orange-picking employment and opted instead to take the 'later jobs': loading and unloading trucks of full orange crates or packaging materials. This type of employment was mostly one to three hours in duration and the hourly rate was much higher than orange picking. Charlie, with assistance from Eftesia, would regularly secure two or three of these types of jobs within a single day. He also worked with Gerry on many occasions.

Gerry was also another one of Eftesia's favourites, having quickly gained a reputation as a reliable and hard worker. On several occasions, both he and Charlie would be quietly relaxing at the kafenio (after completing a job), casually drinking half-litre bottles of Amstel beer when suddenly, Eftesia would excitedly inform them that another job was immediately available for them. The pair would attempt to finish their bottles whilst still inside the kafenio but soon found themselves in a vehicle – still drinking their beers. Even whilst they loaded/unloaded trucks of full crates or packaging material, they were sometimes given a bottle (or two) of beer to consume!

The itinerant collective, meanwhile, had developed a serious disdain for Miserable Mick – especially at the kafenio. Having already earned a reputation as a habitual winger, several acts of blatant meanness had irked people even further, even annoying Eftesia to a certain degree. The itinerant travellers had created a policy of *caring and sharing* where the following items were shared: food (packets of biscuits, bags of crisps, plates of hot fries, etc); carafes of wine; and, even English newspapers purchased in Chania. Mick, on the other hand, would read his newspaper and eat a packet of biscuits. After he finished reading the newspaper, Mick never asked anyone if they would like to read it and would drop it in a garbage bin instead – and, he never offered anyone a biscuit.

Most of the itinerant workers, in general, would spend any earnings within 24 hours – especially on alcohol and cigarettes. Eftesia, however, made sure that everyone in his kafenio would be fed daily. He regularly put certain individuals on *me pístosi* (credit) list. When these individuals were paid at the end of the day (typically 5000 drachmas) they would pay Eftesia any outstanding credit. Several 'needy' itinerant travellers deliberately took advantage of this system, purely as a means to secure daily employment. Supposedly *poverty-stricken*, these veteran itinerant workers made sure their 'reserve fund' was untouched. The saved or unspent money was kept aside solely for their departure from Crete: mainly via the ferry trip to Piraeus. Then, they'd either catch a flight from Athens to another European city or they would be aboard the infamous (but now defunct) *Magic Bus* which travelled from Athens to London, via several former-Yugoslavian countries.

Throughout the orange-picking season, Charlie's level of spoken-Greek steadily increased. Eftesia, meanwhile, was constantly learning and remembering new English words and phrases. As his son (Thaddeus) and daughter (Eleni) were relatively fluent speakers of English, they would regularly translate for their father. Most of the local orange growers could not speak English or very little, therefore a basic knowledge of Greek words and phrases could be quite useful at times. Many of the veteran itinerant travellers, however, were relatively fluent with the Greek language – and, they were useful people to work with.

During the third week of the orange-picking season, Miserable Mick decided to depart from the Chania area, opting to relocate to the 'party' island of Ios. The itinerant community were quite thrilled with his decision! Charlie and Gerry, however, had another problematic roommate to deal with: Gunther.

Muscularly-built Gunther had physical features that possibly indicated a past usage of anabolic steroids. Along with an 'English bulldog-like' head, he also possessed a large and distinct square-shaped jaw and, thus, displayed quite a menacing persona. Despite Gunther's sizeable physique, it soon emerged that he had a relatively 'soft' personality, one that would see him being largely deemed as a *baby elephant.*

Two days before Mick's departure, there was a near-physical altercation between him and Gunther. Before the commencement of his wanderlust venture, Mick had been employed at a well-known toy company. He regularly annoyed the itinerant travellers with his high appraisal of the company. Charlie and Gerry soon learnt, however, that this particular company had been Mick's *only* place of previous employment.

One afternoon, Mick and Gunther (along with several others) were engaged in a conversation, primarily concerned with the topic of 'past employment'. At one point, Mick casually asked an inebriated Gunther, 'Are there any Toys "R" Us in Germany?'

What followed next was quite comical! Aghast, Gunther's square-shaped jaw virtually dropped. Enraged, he stood up, raised his fist and glaring menacingly at Mick. For the next few seconds, there was an eerie silence. Then Gunther angrily blurted out, 'Not now we do… but in the past we had torturers!'

What saved Mick from a beating was the instant howls of laughter from the rest of the group at the table. A red-faced Mick was physically trembling. Gunther (originally from East Berlin) had never heard of the company.

For the first several weeks, Gerry and Charlie had been quite amicable with Gunther. Despite the menacing physique, his simplistic and harmless nature still made him an affable character. A particular event, however, was about to alter the 'harmonious relationship' – Gunther's birthday. The day before his birthday, Gunther's bank account had been significantly boosted by his parents (living in Germany). Instead of just celebrating his birthday for a day or two, he decided to indulge in a drinking 'bender' for the next eight days! Even worse, Gunther mixed his heavy intake of alcohol with an array of pills. The mind-altering concoction transformed his simple-natured persona into one which resembled a blubbering mess. During these eight days, he didn't seek any form of employment and instead, opted for daily shopping sprees and extensive patronage of bars/night clubs in Chania.

On three occasions (during these eight days), Gunther travelled to Eftesia's kafenio. He proudly displayed his brand-new and colourful shirts, along with an expensive pair of designer sunglasses, and numerous gold chains around his neck. Gunther may have been trying to *impress* his fellow itinerants but his spoilt teenager-like antics were largely met with an air of disapproval.

Every night, Gunther partied in Chania. In the early-morning hours, he would noisily enter the pension room. After *bouncing* off wardrobes and walls, Gunther would eventually fall onto one of the two empty beds – face-first and fully clothed. On two occasions, the badly-disoriented 'baby elephant' accidentally wandered into the wrong room, immediately sparking a barrage of Serbian swear-words!

Light-sleeper Charlie would be awoken each morning as Gunther came crashing into the room. Gerry was seemingly undisturbed by the noisy encounter although Charlie suspected he was attempting to ignore the drunken antics. One morning, just before 6.00 am, Gunther staggered into the room and sat at the end of Gerry's bed. Then he tried to wake him by grabbing and shaking his foot!

Charlie whispered angrily.

'Gunther, fuck off. Gerry is asleep.'

'But, I need a cigarette.'

Then, Gerry did wake up. 'Gunther, fuck off.'

'I have no cigarette. I want a cigarette.'

'No… fuck off.'

A now-irate Gerry placed his feet into Gunther's back and with considerable force, practically catapulted him from the end of his bed and into the opposite wall! He (Gunther) started crying and left the room. Charlie burst out laughing but Gerry buried himself beneath his blanket. Two minutes later, the sound of screeching car tyres could be heard and barrages of Greek swear words quickly followed: *malaka* and *pousti malaka* featured prominently. In amongst the verbal onslaught, Gunther's voice could be heard.

'Do you have a cigarette, cigarette… *parakalo?*'

By now, both Charlie and Gerry were laughing heartily. But upon hearing Gunther's heavy footsteps trundling up the staircase (their room was on the first floor), the mood suddenly changed. Gerry declared, 'It's time for Gunther to go!'

Charlie readily agreed.

Instead of entering Charlie and Gerry's room, Gunther was knocking on several other doors.

'Cigarette, cigarette… *please.*'

Eventually, Gunther returned to the room. With a broad cheesy grin, he proudly announced to Gerry and Charlie, 'Look… I have six cigarettes!'

'Good for you. Now leave or Gerry and I are going to pick you up and throw you headfirst over the balcony onto the street below… no more Gunther!'

With a smug cheesy grin, Gunther slyly replied, 'Okay, I will leave… you sleep now!'

Later that day, Gunther boarded a bus in central Chania, one that took him to the port of Souda. He then boarded the overnight ferry, destined for the port of Piraeus on the Greek mainland. Gunther was never heard of again. Charlie and Gerry stayed in the pension for a further six weeks. Every morning, they continued to travel by bus to the village of Alikianos.

The daily 7.30 am bus service from central Chania to Alikianos was largely occupied by the itinerant collective. If the quest for daily employment in the morning was fruitless, most individuals would consider returning to Chania at noon or shortly afterwards. Some itinerants, however, opted to walk back to the city: a distance of eleven kilometres (or just under seven miles). The metropolis of Chania offered far more than the sedated village of Alikianos: beach-side walks, tourist bars, cafes/restaurants, etc.

Late one Saturday morning, Charlie and Gerry decided to walk back to Chania as there was a scarce amount of employment available that day at Eftesia's kafenio. As they walked along the side of the road, a car suddenly pulled up in front of them (less than two kilometres from Alikianos). The driver alighted from his vehicle and walked towards them. In an excitable state, he instantly babbled to them in what could be best described as incomprehensible Greek. Charlie and Gerry's level of spoken Greek was still quite minimal at that stage. They soon sensed, however, that the excitable gentleman wanted them to do some work for him as he frequently used the word *douleiá* (work).

Charlie and Gerry were unable to ascertain the nature of the type of employment involved but assumed it had nothing to do with orange-picking as the word *portokália* (oranges) was never mentioned. The driver (who had already introduced himself as Yani) gestured for them to get in his vehicle. Yani drove for three kilometres and stopped at the entrance of a large paddock. Charlie and Gerry soon realised what the nature of employment was going to be: fencing – and plenty of it.

Yani had already hammered numerous fence posts into the ground and had already measured the perimeter of the area to be fenced. Four sizeable rolls of fencing were laid on the ground. He wanted Charlie and Gerry to assist him to extend each roll from one large post to the next one. Smaller posts had also been hammered into the ground, in between the larger posts. It soon emerged, however, that Yani appeared to have minimal knowledge of fencing. After an hour had passed, Charlie exclaimed, 'Hey, Gerry… I'm no expert in fencing but I'm sure he's doing this the wrong way though!'

Just after 1.00 pm, Yani took Charlie and Gerry back to his house where they would enjoy a wholesome and scrumptious meal prepared by his wife. A bottle of red wine accompanied the meal. He did not dine with them and instead drove off to an unknown destination. An hour later, Yani returned and the trio returned to the paddock.

A now-upbeat Yani adopted a more jovial approach to the task that he wished to have completed. As a result, most pre-luncheon fencing efforts were about to be redone. It was quite clear that he had used the luncheon break as a means to discuss with someone who knew how to do the fencing properly! The afternoon, therefore, was much more productive than the pre-luncheon efforts. Each roll of wire was stretched out, a metre at a time, then tied and nailed to each post. Several hours later, the fencing of the perimeter was completed. Yani paid Charlie and Gerry 5000 drachmas each and then drove them back to the same spot where he had first met them. They recommenced walking back to Chania but as it was late in the afternoon, they attempted to hitch a ride. There were no local bus services at that time of day. After walking several kilometres, however, a bus did stop for them. The driver was returning the empty bus to Chania.

Charlie and Gerry, eventually, decided to swap the 'bright metropolis lights' of Chania for the quaint and idyllic village of Alikianos. An opportunity to relocate to the village arose when Gareth (a veteran Welsh itinerant) moved into a room of a two-room house in Alikianos. For the past two months, he had been living in a small tent near the *Rema Keritis* (river Keritis). The second room was being occupied by an English couple. Gareth was looking for two more people to share the monthly rent of the first room.

The monthly rental cost of each room was 15,000 drachmas (equivalent to about 50 English pounds sterling) at the time. This would equate to Gerry, Charlie and Gareth each paying 5000 drachmas for a month's accommodation: equivalent to one eight-hour day of orange picking. In comparison, Gerry and Charlie had each been paying 5000 drachmas for their pension room each week. Before moving into the room, Charlie casually asked Gareth for more information about the room and was met with the response, 'It's just a room.'

And the room was exactly that – one ceiling, one floor, four walls, two windows and one door. There was no furniture. Numerous empty beer and retsina (white wine) bottles, lined up against one of the walls. On the floor, however, there were several 'mattresses': flattened cardboard boxes lay side by side.

Charlie stayed in the room for just one month. Besides being cheap to rent, the room was conveniently located – forty metres from Eftesia's kafenio. His daily alcohol consumption increased significantly. Charlie's daily routine would commence around 7.00 am with several shot glasses of *tsikoudia* (also known as *raki* or *rakomelo*) and two cups of coffee: primarily used as 'chasers' after consuming an amount of spirit. The locally-made spirit drink was flavoured with honey and cinnamon. If he hadn't commenced employment by 9.00 am, Charlie would be drinking his first 500ml bottle of Amstel beer for the day!

On some days (mainly in the evenings though), Charlie would consume a copious amount of wine. As there were plenty of wine drinkers within the itinerant community, carafes of wine were often shared inside the kafenio. Home-made red wine was also in plentiful supply in and around the village of Alikianos. Inside the room of the house, Charlie regularly kept several plastic bottles of home-made red wine. When he first moved into the room, Charlie purchased bottles of mineral water at the nearby supermarket. He would then empty the water from several of the bottles. The reason for doing this was that the cost of the wine was charged by the litre and home-made winemakers did not provide any containers for their customers.

Life in the village could be best described as mostly mundane and uneventful. Life inside the kafenio, however, could regularly be deemed as *entertaining* – and there were plenty of 'entertainers' within the travelling itinerant community.

Firstly, there was Toby. Aged in his thirties, the English itinerant was a proud 'leftover' of the 1970s punk rock era. He wore a Sex Pistols singlet/vest or a t-shirt – every day. An ardent fan of Johnny Rotten (the lead singer of the Sex Pistols), Toby had bleached his hair a cherry-blonde colour which blended in well with his pale white skin. He also had safety pins pierced into his ear lobes and nose. Toby's comical attempt to be a *fearsome* punk rocker was quickly dissipated by the wearing of thick-rimmed spectacles and a pair of oversized-boots, loosely attached to his 'pencil-like' legs. The boots also affected the way he walked. Unable to lift his feet at times and especially when intoxicated, Toby tended to 'shuffle along' when moving from one place to another.

Toby largely survived on a *retsina* diet, drinking litres of the potent liquid. His daily food intake was quite minimal and regularly consisted of the following: a large bowl of soup; two bread rolls; two fried eggs; and, a basket of fries. The poor diet and large intake of retsina severely affected Toby's capacity to engage in physical activity (e.g. orange picking). On any working day, the 'retsina blues' would take control over his physical well-being – even by midday on some days. Occasionally, he would manage to pick oranges for eight hours, although his co-workers would often have to 'carry' him for the last two or three hours!

Toby's name would regularly be at the top of Eftesia's *me pístosi* list. This meant that Eftesia would ensure that he obtained enough employment to pay off his 'retsina' debt. Toby, surprisingly, was still one of Eftesia's favourites but he had returned to the Alikianos area each year (for the past eight years) and for 5-6 months, would be a regular at Eftesia's kafenio. Toby, however, would irk the itinerant workers from time to time, particularly when in a state of 'social inebriation' (drunkenness). He could be quite boisterous and over-opinionated – and aggressive. On several occasions, Toby clashed with one of the veteran itinerants (Zico) over Greek-Macedonian politics. Zico was a diehard Yugoslavian-Macedonian and the fiery political debate would often climax with some sort of physical altercation.

Toby, quite foolishly, tried to evoke some involvement from the other itinerants. They, in turn, refused to take part in any of the political discussion. Making sure that they had a firm grip on their alcoholic beverages, the itinerant collective would just simply create extra space for the upcoming 'physical disagreement'. The fracas, though, would be short-lived and usually ended when Zico threw Toby over one of the vacant tables. He (Toby) would be quite upset that his 'fellow westerners' did not offer any support but the group would constantly remind him that he was the *actual* instigator. To add further insult, Toby soon realised that they were more concerned about spilling or losing their drinks!

Zico wasn't the only person that Toby clashed physically with. One afternoon, he was involved in a scuffle with Benji: a Jamaican-born Londoner. Jockey-sized Benji wasn't overly popular amongst the itinerant collective either as he would regularly boast about his 'connections' with *Yardie* gangs in Brixton (a London suburb), in a delusional attempt to assert his toughness within the group. Several of the itinerants, however, constantly reminded Benji of his lack of stature and that 'Yardie culture' was irrelevant in this part of the world.

A heated discussion over the 'Yardie culture' in London eventually evolved into a scuffle between Toby and Benji. For the next ten minutes or so, the would-be pugilists provided what could best be described as a *spectacle of entertainment.* Both of them were heavily intoxicated and the physical altercation mainly involved the pair trying to remove each other's eyeglasses! It was more like a wrestling match: the pair grappled *ferociously* with each other, desperately trying not to fall over. No punches were thrown and due to physical exhaustion, both of them relented. Toby resumed drinking his bottle of retsina, whilst Benji resumed drinking his bottle of Amstel beer. They sat on separate tables. Gerry sarcastically (and loudly) announced, 'The bout between Mr Retsina and Mr Amstel has officially ended in a draw!'

Over the past few fruit-picking seasons, Toby had developed a reputation amongst many of the local orange-growers as being mostly *unemployable.* He would, therefore, struggle to obtain employment at times (even with assistance from Eftesia). On some days, Toby would shun any thought of food and instead opted to drink several bottles of retsina throughout the morning. At some point, he would fall asleep and slump his head on the table in front of him.

Twice a week, Eftesia would require assistance in bringing crates of alcoholic beverages into his kafenio. He would carry the crates of bottled beer; Toby would carry the crates of retsina bottles. A bemused Eftesia was quite confident that he (Toby) wouldn't drop the *precious* crates of retsina. He was right! Toby struggled to carry the crates and sweated profusely – but he never dropped one. As a reward, Eftesia's wife (Maria) would cook his favourite meal: two fried eggs, a basket of fries and a bread roll.

Despite Toby's irksome behaviour at times, the itinerant community and Eftesia's family did develop a 'soft spot' towards him when they learnt that he was in regular contact with his ailing mother. Toby would ring her each week at the telephone exchange in Chania and was noticeably sad after each phone call. He wanted to return to England but had violated his latest parole conditions (and had previously been incarcerated within the British prison system). This meant that Toby would face jail time if he returned.

On the day that Charlie departed from Eftesia's kafenio, Toby was fast asleep on a table. When he (Charlie) returned to Alikianos nearly three years later, Charlie learnt that Toby had changed his life around considerably. Firstly, he stopped drinking alcohol. Then Toby relocated to Athens and taught English for several months to newly-arrived migrants. Then one day, he decided to board a flight to Gatwick Airport (United Kingdom). Toby was immediately arrested on arrival. After spending nine months in jail, he was released. Toby then stayed with his mother; her health had steadily declined.

Another English itinerant worker of notoriety was Alastair. He was born and brought up in the *Black Country* area, located west of the city of Birmingham (West Midlands region of the United Kingdom). Similar to Toby, he rarely ate any food and largely survived on a liquid diet: beer and red wine. On an almost daily basis, Alistair would rant incessantly about his beloved Black Country, sparking an atmosphere of bemused ire amongst several of the other British itinerants. Gerry, a proud Cockney Londoner, would sarcastically (and with an element of malice) suggest to him, 'If it's such a great place, why don't you go back there. Why are you still here?'

The pair soon developed an intense dislike towards each other. For several weeks, the only conflicts between them were ones of a verbal nature. Then one afternoon, a highly intoxicated Alastair tried to hit Gerry in the head with an empty wine bottle. In retaliation, he (Gerry) punched him flush on the jaw. A startled Alastair fell to the ground. From that particular moment, the pair never spoke to each other again.

Alistair had arrived in Chania with two former schoolmates (Robert and Timothy) via a ferry service from Piraeus. Robert and Timothy only drank alcohol at a moderate level (unlike Alistair) and they also possessed a very good work ethic. Eftesia, in turn, ensured that the pair would secure a reasonable amount of employment throughout the orange-picking season. The pair's long-term friendship with Alistair, however, meant that they felt somewhat obligated to constantly 'look after' him which prompted the itinerant collective to regard them as Alistair's *babysitters*.

The trio shared a pension room in Chania, located above a restaurant colloquially known as 'Testicules de Porcs' (Pig's Balls). *Testicules de Porcs* was also listed as the main 'delicacy' on the restaurant menu! They travelled to and from Alikianos nearly every day via the local bus service. Outside the work environment, the trio would be regularly involved in Chania's thriving nightclub scene and frequently attempted to 'pick-up' a female companion. Whilst Robert and Timothy were unsuccessful, Alastair did manage to hook-up with a holidaying French woman (Marie) for a couple of weeks.

According to Robert and Timothy, Marie was at least ten years older than Alastair and she adopted him as her *toy boy*. She regularly purchased food, alcoholic beverages and even new clothes for Alistair. The pair partied nearly every night and would return to the pension room in the early-morning or even as daybreak was emerging. Robert and Timothy would be regularly woken up by the sound of an intense and vigorous sexual romp – taking place in or on top of Alastair's bed.

On some nights, Alastair returned to the pension room with Robert and Timothy, whilst Marie would continue nightclubbing. Several hours later, however, the socially inebriated French woman would enter their room and proceeded to wake Alistair up by grabbing and shaking his arms. Once he was awake or partially awake, Marie would then attempt to sexually arouse him – using the 'hand relief' method. A few minutes later, she would place herself on top of Alastair and proceeded to *give his bones a good rattle* – using the 'bounce and ride' method.

During the morning bus trip to Alikianos, Robert and Timothy would describe in detail the early morning escapades in their pension room. Any doubt to the authenticity of the story was soon quashed by several of the other bus passengers; they were either staying in adjacent or nearby rooms and further stated that the walls of the pension rooms were *paper-thin.*

Besides the large contingent of English itinerant workers in the Chania/Alikianos area there was also a group of middle-aged French gentlemen: commonly referred to as the 'French Connection'. Marko, Christo, Jean and Alain were either aged in their late-forties or early-fifties. These veteran travellers had a lot in common: they were multi-lingual; heavy smokers; chronic alcoholics; and, all had craggy weather-beaten and scarred faces largely due to past drunken pugilistic bouts. But they were affable characters and were generally well-liked by the local population and the itinerant workers.

Marko and Christo, in particular, would regularly assist other itinerant workers in translating Greek words and phrases into English. As each day passed, Charlie became more proficient in speaking 'pidgin' Greek and steadily increased his vocabulary as well. He would also gain a wealth of information regarding the numerous fruit-picking seasons throughout the European continent. By the completion of the orange-picking season, Charlie's work diary contained the addresses of numerous future-potential employers (along with the starting dates of the fruit-picking seasons).

The French Connection was mostly a well-behaved bunch. Occasionally, however, they would engage in a boisterous and animated discussion and, thus, provide a source of priceless entertainment for other people – especially the more-reserved contingent of English-speaking itinerants. These frantic discussions usually involved the following: wild animated hand gesticulation; a lot of arm-waving and shoulder-shrugging; and, reddening of the face (and neck as well). To the casual observer, one expected that the noisy discussion/debate/argument could erupt at any time into some form of physical altercation. Instead, the vociferous spectacle would just simply come to an abrupt halt – especially if there were empty beer bottles or empty wine glasses/carafes on the table.

One Saturday afternoon, inside Alikianos' lone taverna, the French Connection became embroiled in a scuffle with a group of young local males. The heavily-intoxicated quartet was involved in a heated political discussion with several other patrons. Eventually, the fiery discussion evolved into a minor physical fracas, although no punches were thrown. What happened next could be best described as a typical scene from an old Western movie!

The four of them were flung through the saloon-style doors and onto the outside road. Marko tried to re-enter the premises several times but was repeatedly pushed back outside. On his *last* attempt, he was picked up by several of the patrons and hurled through the air, landing heavily on the tarred surface. Heavily intoxicated Marko then decided to just lie on the road and sleep.

His compatriots, however, lifted him off the ground and managed to get him to stand up. Even though it was a sleepy Saturday afternoon, motor vehicles still used this road – even the occasional donkey with an elderly gentleman aboard. The quartet slowly then staggered down the middle of the road towards Eftesia's kafenio. Eftesia, however, received a phone call from the owner of the taverna, alerting him of four heavily intoxicated Frenchmen! When they did finally reach the kafenio, he refused to serve them alcohol and instead, managed to persuade them to rest their heads on the tables. For the next couple of hours, patrons had to endure what may be best described as *thunderous synchronized snoring*.

The French Connection tended to only seek employment when they had either run out of money or had a sizeable tab to pay at Eftesia's kafenio. When their desire to seek any form of physical labour had seriously subsided, all four would resort to begging near the Chania markets – especially Christo. He had been a regular visitor to the Chania area for many years and was well-known locally: particularly by the market stall-holders. Christo's regular appearances at the markets earned him *near-celebrity* status and he was often provided (by food stalls) with food. During the official tourist season (June to October), however, the local police would either ask or forcibly remove all the beggars to leave Chania altogether and ordered them not to return to the area until at least November.

Another itinerant of notoriety was 'Popeye' Shane. The Englishman was a typical exponent of the 'lager lout' culture. When he was sober, Shane was a hard-working individual and quite a likeable chap. After a substantial amount of alcohol, however, he could be quite an unpleasant character: a *Dr Jekyll and Mr Hyde* persona. At the time, Shane was thirty years old and he had been travelling throughout the European continent since the age of sixteen. Shane preferred to avoid the orange-picking jobs and opted instead for the better-paid heavier types of employment: loading and unloading trucks containing crates of oranges or packaging material. Similar to Charlie, he would regularly obtain two or three of these jobs during a single day.

The solidly-built Shane regularly attempted to intimidate his fellow itinerant travellers, especially when intoxicated. He would stretch out his arms and utter slurringly, 'Feel this… these muscular forearms!' Shane soon earned the nickname 'Popeye'. He further irked the itinerant community with another oft-used catchphrase, 'I am going to hit you so hard… you think you are surrounded!'

Gerry and Charlie would regularly try to provoke an intoxicated Shane. But they were also wary of him. He would occasionally respond to their taunts by swinging his arms at their heads! Laughably, though, Shane would occasionally swing at the air *too hard* which saw him lose his balance and, thus, fall to the ground.

Charlie enjoyed his four-month stay in Crete, largely regarding the experience as *character building*. By the end of the orange-picking season, however, he was quite happy to leave. Charlie left the Chania area in the last week of May as the availability of agriculture employment had diminished considerably. A large number of the itinerant workers had either saved no money or very little. Some of them couldn't even afford the ferry trip back to the port of Piraeus. A combination of excessive alcoholism and scarce availability of employment resulted in numerous physical altercations within the itinerant group during the last few days of the orange-picking season. Charlie left the kafenio without saying goodbye to anyone except for Eftesia and his wife Maria.

In the late-afternoon, Charlie boarded a bus in central Chania, one that took him to the port of Souda. Several hours later, he was aboard the overnight ferry to Piraeus. Twelve hours later, Charlie disembarked from the ferry. Next, he boarded a bus, taking him to the centre of Athens. Charlie was hoping to be aboard a London-bound flight later that day but the earliest one available was a Malév Hungarian Airlines flight departing the following day. He filled in the rest of the day by exploring the sights of Athens and just after 6.00 pm, Charlie was inside the departure lounge of Ellinikon International Airport. Eighteen hours later, he was aboard a London-bound flight. After a one-hour stopover at Budapest Ferihegy International Airport (now known as Budapest

Ferenc Liszt International Airport), the aircraft landed at London's Heathrow Airport in the late afternoon.

7

Life on the Road

Charlie's experience of *life on the road* (hitchhiking), over many years, was mostly a positive one: a venture that enabled him to travel extensively throughout various European countries (France, United Kingdom, Germany, Spain, The Netherlands, etc) and in New Zealand. Eventually, the novelty of hitchhiking for Charlie was replaced by more conventional means of land travel: namely cars, buses and trains. During his 'life on the road' travel phase, he obtained between 1200-1500 lifts from (mostly) kind-hearted motorists

Charlie's hitchhiking experience was a relatively safe one, albeit for the occasional uncomfortable situation from time to time: middle-aged/elderly homosexuals trying to 'hit' on him; inebriated or partially-inebriated motorists who were somewhat hazy with their driving abilities; and, the 'would-be Grand Prix' drivers who drove well above the speed limit and regularly overtook slower-driving motorists. The type of motorist that stopped to offer him a ride was quite diverse at times: company representatives (who had previously been involved in the *wanderlust spirit* themselves); lorry/truck drivers; modern-day 'hippies' (e.g. new-age travellers); and, of course, local inhabitants who only drove a short distance from one place to the next.

The most enjoyable aspect of hitchhiking for Charlie was the numerous amicable discussions that took place between the motorist and himself. He acquired, in turn, a vast amount of knowledge from them concerning local history and politics within various European countries. Charlie was also quite fortunate to view numerous key landmarks firsthand: centuries-old castles; historical churches and homesteads; and, numerous waterways (e.g. lakes, rivers, canals, etc).

Charlie's hitchhiking venture began at the Port of Le Havre (near the city of Le Havre) in northern France. After an overnight ferry trip from Portsmouth (England) and across the English Channel (or La Manche), he arrived at the port early in the morning. After disembarking from the ferry, Charlie walked towards the start of the autoroute (A131): five kilometres away. After waiting for over an hour, he obtained his first lift. Charlie's intended destination was the town of Saumur (located near the Loire River), where he intended to seek cherry-picking employment within that region. Saumur was only 349 kilometres away from La Havre, but it would take Charlie three days to reach the town.

On the first day of hitchhiking, Charlie's efforts in obtaining lifts were largely fruitless. By the end of the day, he had only travelled a distance of about fifty kilometres and twenty kilometres covered was by walking! He was also carrying a large backpack (with a small tent attached to the base of it) and a medium-sized bag as hand luggage. Charlie sensed that his main mistake was leaving the autoroute system and attempting to thumb lifts along lesser-used roads. As he walked through a village, in the early evening, the clouds opened and in torrential-pouring rain, Charlie desperately sought some form of shelter.

As Charlie walked towards a bus shelter on the outskirts of the village, a car suddenly pulled up beside him. The motorist wound down the passenger-side window and began speaking in French but was quickly interrupted by Charlie, politely stating (in basic French) that his spoken level of the French language was quite minimal. The young male then spoke in English and asked him where he was going. Pointing at the nearby bus stop, Charlie calmly replied, 'Right there!'

The driver (Michel) then promptly informed Charlie that he could stay at his parent's place that night if he wished. Inside the vehicle, Michel stated that he was a student and was staying in the house on his own as his parents were on holidays at the time. Charlie was quite grateful for Michel's hospitality. He, also, managed to get his clothes and luggage dried by the next morning. After a good night's rest, Charlie hitchhiked towards the town of Saumur.

For the first few hours, Charlie made little progress, having only managed to obtain two short-distance lifts: both lifts were from village to village. Just before midday, he obtained a lift with two middle-aged males; they were going to a tavern in the nearby commune (a level of an administrative division in France) of Orbec. Both of them had 'battle-scarred' faces and the driver had a black eye, along with minor bruising on one side of his face. They, excitedly, chatted to each other in French but the language barrier soon thwarted any form of effective communication between them and Charlie.

Fifteen minutes later, the trio was inside the tavern, each enjoying a large glass of refreshing lager. Fortunately for Charlie, the bartender spoke a reasonable amount of English and for the next hour or so, he took on the role of translator. Charlie, however, attempted to input a few French words and phrases into the conversation. The bartender stated that the two gentlemen (Rene and Louis) were mainly good fellows – and heavy drinkers. He further added that Rene's black eye was a result of a scuffle (in another tavern) two nights ago.

After consuming a hearty lunch (along with several more lagers), Charlie left the tavern and walked towards the outskirts of the commune. Displaying a thin white cardboard sign with 'Saumur' written on it, he patiently waited for his next lift. Two and a half hours later, a vehicle finally stopped next to him. The attractive driver, who Charlie regarded as having an uncanny resemblance to that of a young Nana Mouskouri (a well-known Greek singer), would take him to the outskirts of the city of Le Mans, 130 kilometres away. Amelie spoke English fluently but with a distinct American-influenced accent. The pair chatted amicably throughout the journey.

For the past several years, Amelie had been residing in the USA. She was also a devout member of the Unification Church. In recent weeks, Amelie had been dwelling in a *commune* (as in a religious or cultural commune). It was owned by the Unification Church and was located near Le Mans. She added that her everyday existence was greatly inspired by the teachings of 'her' church. At one point during the conversation, Amelie invited Charlie to come with her to the commune for a 'spiritual retreat'. He politely declined. Initially, Charlie had never heard of the Unification Church – or so he thought. When Amelie began to discuss mass weddings and the South Korean origins of the church, however, Charlie then realised he knew them better as the *Moonies.*

Amelie dropped Charlie off at the northern outskirts of Le Mans. He then walked several kilometres until he came upon an entrance to the A11 autoroute. By now it was late in the afternoon. An hour later, Charlie obtained his next lift when a sporty-like hatchback vehicle stopped beside him. The occupants were three cheerful females who were aged in their mid-twenties. Through a mixture of English and French, he was able to communicate effectively with the young woman who sat beside him on the backseat. Ten minutes into the journey, she asked him where he was staying for the night. Pointing to a nearby field, Charlie responded, 'On a comfortable bed of luscious green grass!'

When she translated Charlie's response, her two companions reacted with instant laughter. Then the driver told her friend that he could stay at her place that night. She was residing in a village (40 kilometres south-west of Le Mans) and was renting a house with one of her brothers. Charlie politely accepted her offer.

Throughout the evening, Charlie managed to communicate with Satine and her brother (Henri) via the use of a French-English dictionary and a French-English phrasebook. Both of them were students and they also had part-time employment. Their parents lived in suburban Paris. The next morning, Henri took Charlie (on his motorbike) to an autoroute entrance. He obtained a lift within half an hour and, several hours later, arrived in central Saumur just after midday. Ten minutes later, he located a campsite situated near the Loire River (the longest river in France). Charlie camped there for the next four nights. During the daytime, he sought information concerning the upcoming strawberry and cherry-picking seasons.

Every day, Charlie walked for many kilometres throughout the countryside that surrounded Saumur. He came upon several large vineyards but Charlie soon realised that the orchards were far more difficult to locate. By the third day, he had realised that most of the orchards were a considerable distance away from Saumur which meant that having a motor vehicle would be essential. Charlie further learnt that the start of the fruit-picking season was at least a week away.

With ever-diminishing finances, Charlie decided to telephone a German woman who he had befriended in Australia (in the town of Bowen, North Queensland) during a previous fruit-picking season there. Heidi, who lived in the city of Reutlingen (located 40 kilometres from Stuttgart), was studying at the local university. She invited him to stay with her for a few days. Charlie regarded this opportunity as a means of seeking fruit-picking employment in a region 80 kilometres south of Reutlingen: specifically between the town of Ravensburg and the city of Friedrichshafen, located near Lake Constance (which separated southern Germany from northern Switzerland).

On the fifth day, Charlie was 'on the road' again. He eventually obtained a lift and was in the city of Tours forty minutes later. After consuming a meal and several lagers, Charlie walked to the outskirts of the city. Several hours would pass by before he obtained his second lift for the day. The elderly motorist was only going to a nearby town (30 kilometres away) but Charlie was happy to be on the move again.

Throughout the trip, the elderly gentleman chatted incessantly – in French. Charlie, on several occasions, reminded him that his knowledge of the French language was still fairly limited. Ten minutes into the journey, the elderly male suddenly put his hand on one of Charlie's thighs! A startled Charlie turned his head and just glared at him. He immediately removed his hand but was silent for the rest of the journey. Although Charlie was annoyed by the incident, he was also quite bemused and thought to himself, 'I'd have no problem in overpowering this short, pudgy, elderly guy.'

Charlie also carried a small fishing-knife in one of his trouser pockets. He could easily conceal the knife in his hand and then quite *masterly* use it as a flick-knife in a fraction of a second. Ten minutes later, Charlie was dropped off.

Whilst waiting for his next lift, Charlie wrote a new hitchhiking sign: Orléans. Twenty minutes later, a late-model Volvo sedan with dark-tinted windows pulled up beside him. The rear right-hand side door was automatically opened for him. Peering inside the vehicle, he saw that the driver was dressed similarly to the literary character *Sherlock Holmes*, wearing an old-style suit and a deerstalker hat – and he had a tobacco pipe in his mouth. Charlie immediately thought to himself, 'This isn't my day!'

The driver then opened the vehicle's boot/trunk by pressing a button on the vehicle's dashboard. There was already a backpack and other luggage items in the spacious boot. Charlie placed his luggage in there and then sat down on the vehicle's rear bench seat. A young male was sitting in the front passenger seat: another hitchhiker. A few minutes into the journey, the driver explained to Charlie that he was employed as a chauffeur for VIP's (very important people). Hence, the attire he was wearing. When the driver wasn't talking he would casually puff away on his pipe. The smell of the tobacco was quite pleasant and Charlie thought, 'Top-notch stuff!'

As the driver was returning to Paris, he decided to drop Charlie off just outside the city of Orléans. After walking for barely a kilometre, Charlie came upon a café. He went inside and ordered a meal and a coffee, using a memorised phrase: '*Je voudrais un sandwich jambon-fromage avec un grand café* (I would like a ham and cheese sandwich with a big coffee). Half an hour later, Charlie left the café and walked towards the A19. When he reached the entrance to the autoroute, Charlie created a new sign (Strasbourg) and casually waited for his next lift.

Charlie waited for several hours. As the late evening was approaching, he began to plan his 'sleeping arrangements' for that night. The weather was quite pleasant and there were plenty of *comfortable-looking* paddocks nearby. Charlie was about to give up trying to hitch another ride for the day but amidst diminishing daylight, a large lorry stopped beside him. The driver introduced himself as Francois and stated that his final destination would be the city of Dijon, (ESE of Orléans). As the vehicle trundled along the autoroute, Francois contacted several other lorry drivers to determine whether any of them were driving in an ENE direction, towards the city of Strasbourg. Francois's efforts, unfortunately, were unsuccessful and he dropped Charlie off at a *péage* (toll booth): near the junction of autoroutes A5 and A31. It was now 1.30 am!

In near-pitch darkness and a reasonable distance away from the péage, Charlie came upon a comfortable grassy knoll. One problem though: it was on a forty-five-degree decline. A now-tired Charlie laid his sleeping bag out, placed it inside the rolled-out tent and covered everything with the tent's sizeable fly. Lying down in a diagonal position, he soon fell asleep. On several occasions, however, Charlie woke up – as he started to roll down the steep decline.

Just after 4.30 am, daylight began to seep through the darkened sky. A now-awakened Charlie folded his sleeping bag and tent. Then he walked sheepishly towards the péage. The sole operator at the péage (who probably saw Charlie when he first arrived several hours earlier) gave him quite a stern look as he walked towards the toll booth! An undeterred Charlie simply ignored the operator's prolonged gaze and commenced an attempt to hitch his next ride, holding a sign in his left hand and a protruding right thumb. Five minutes later, a dark blue van with the word *Gendarmerie* written on the side of it suddenly emerged. It came to a screeching halt and stopped less than two metres from where Charlie was standing.

The three military officers immediately requested to see Charlie's passport. He duly handed over his Australian passport to the senior-most officer. Realising that Charlie was unlikely to be any type of a 'national threat' (such as someone who indulges in terrorist activities), they soon handed back his passport. The youngest military officer then spoke to Charlie in English and casually asked him where he had stayed the previous night (although the péage operator had probably already informed them). Charlie responded, 'Nearby!'

With a nonchalant shrug of the shoulders, the young gendarmerie officer then informed Charlie that hitchhiking was only allowed *in front* of the péage. After bidding farewell, the gendarmerie officers left and Charlie casually ambled to the other side of the péage. Twenty minutes later, the first vehicle that passed through the péage stopped and gave Charlie a lift. For the next half an hour or so, he desperately tried to stay awake; the previous night's *embankment-rolling* moments had largely thwarted any quality sleep.

An hour later, the driver arrived at his workplace and tapped Charlie on the shoulder. He (Charlie) woke up, thanked the driver and alighted from the vehicle. A lethargic Charlie gingerly walked away from the centre of the commune. Followed the signs that directed him towards the city of Nancy, he soon found himself walking up a very steep hill. Half an hour later, Charlie made it to the top of the steep incline and immediately espied a nearby café.

Inside the café, a hungry and thirsty Charlie ordered breakfast. '*Je voudrais un sandwich jambon-fromage avec un grand café – s'il vous plaît*' (I would like a ham and cheese sandwich with a big coffee – please). Fifteen minutes later, he was happily gorging on a large ham and cheese-filled baguette roll. The coffee came in a 'soup bowl': the large mug had no handles and required *two* hands to lift it to one's mouth. Charlie's bodily mechanisms were now recharged!

For the rest of the day, Charlie mainly obtained numerous short-distance lifts. He arrived at a tiny village, near the western outskirts of Strasbourg, in the early evening. Just outside the village, Charlie came across a partially-built house (with no roof) on a sizeable tract of vacant land. He walked to the rear side of the house and out of view from any motorists driving along the nearby road.

Not far from the partially-built homestead, stood a now-closed supermarket. At the side of the building, there were two skip bins/dumpsters. A short time later, Charlie was 'fossicking' through the two bins and was amazed at the quality of the food that had been disregarded. He returned to his makeshift camp with a collection of edible food and a short time later, managed to start a small campfire. Charlie would later enjoy a meal of fairly fresh vegetables which he had boiled in washed aluminium cans (half-filled with water) and placed on a makeshift grill hovering just above the campfire. Charlie removed the cans by using two small tree branches as makeshift prongs.

Early the next morning, Charlie packed his gear and walked towards Strasbourg. An hour later, just as he was entering the outskirts of the city, a police vehicle and two police officers on motorcycles pulled up beside him. One of the motorcycle riders, in quite an exasperated manner, spoke in French to Charlie who barely understood a word he said. When the police officer paused, Charlie said to him, '*Je suis australien et veux-tu voir mon passeport?* (I am Australian and do you want to see my passport).

Charlie handed the passport over to the police officer. The details of his passport were checked by one of the officers inside the motor vehicle on a dashboard computer. Several minutes later, the passport was handed back to him and he continued walking towards Strasbourg. The police officers appeared to be looking for someone in the area: the same vehicles drove pass Charlie several times.

After walking through the city of Strasbourg, Charlie arrived at the France-German border. On the French side of the border, his passport was checked but there was no border control on the German side of the border. He walked a further kilometre before coming upon a rest area: an ideal spot for hitchhiking. Using his black pen-marker, Charlie wrote a new sign: Reutlingen. The city was located 40 kilometres south of Stuttgart. After waiting for nearly an hour, a motorist finally stopped beside him. The driver was going to the university town of Tübingen: ten kilometres from Reutlingen.

For the next hour or so, the vehicle passed through the breathtaking scenery of the Black Forest via a series of windy roads and with varying elevations. After being dropped off in the centre of Tubingen, Charlie then walked to the eastern outskirts of the town. After waiting for just over five minutes, he obtained his next ride which took him directly to the nearby city of Reutlingen. Charlie soon met up with Heidi and ten minutes later, they were conversing and consuming large mugs of beer inside a bustling tavern. He recalled his recent hitchhiking adventures which Heidi found quite amusing!

After staying with Heidi for two nights, Charlie decided to seek fruit-picking employment in the Upper Swabia region of southern Germany: especially in the region between the town of Ravensburg and the city of Friedrichshafen. Heidi, meanwhile, was going to stay in the city of Stuttgart for the next several days.

Charlie hitchhiked from Reutlingen to Ravensburg: a distance of 115 kilometres. For the next several days, he camped in woodlands southwest of Ravensburg. With limited finances, Charlie decided to 'raid' the skip bins of one of the supermarkets. He returned to his makeshift campsite with an assortment of edible vegetables. After starting a campfire, Charlie boiled some of the vegetables in washed label-less cans; he had also collected a few potatoes and onions. Instead of boiling them, Charlie peeled the skins off with his fishing-knife. Next, he wrapped them in pieces of aluminium foil and then placed the food items in the embers of the campfire. Using small thick branches as tongs, Charlie later retrieved the cooked potatoes and onions from the embers.

For the next three days, Charlie searched for potential fruit-picking employment opportunities. He soon realised, though, that the majority of orchards were either 'pick-your-own' or small-scaled family ones. Feeling quite dejected, Charlie decided to hitchhike back to Reutlingen and arrived there in the early (Saturday) evening. Heidi would not be returning home until the following day. Charlie, initially, was quite content to just sleep out 'under the stars' that night but a sudden weather change prompted him to seek a more viable option.

At the front of Heidi's house, there was a thick hedge. Charlie managed to squeeze himself (and his luggage) through the hedge and onto the front sheltered porch. A short time later, heavy torrential rain pelted down. During the night, he woke up several times due to thunder and lightning. Charlie, though, still managed to sleep fairly well. Just after 7.00 am, he squeezed through the dampened hedge and walked towards the centre of Reutlingen.

Despite the atrocious weather conditions during the night, some kind of festival had taken place. Large canvas shelters (used as food stalls) were still erected. The area was eerily quiet, albeit for a few inebriated individuals trying to walk back home and the sounds of snoring seeping out from the inside of several of the canvas shelters. A hungry Charlie searched for food and soon discovered a lot of untouched food in cardboard containers. After deciding which food looked the most edible, he carried several cardboard containers back to Heidi's place. Squeezing back through the hedge and onto the front porch, Charlie quickly quelled his hunger pangs. For the rest of the day, he wandered throughout the city and indulged in a bit of sightseeing.

Heidi returned that night and soon sensed that Charlie's current financial situation was in a dire state. She offered him an amount of money and he gratefully accepted it. Charlie, however, explained to Heidi that a money order had been sent to him from Australia but it would take several more days for it to arrive. As Heidi's exam week was about to commence, she subtly suggested to Charlie that a week of *peacefulness* was required for her. The next morning, he was 'on the road again' and, thus, enabling Heidi to study for her exams in a more relaxed environment.

Charlie walked to the northern outskirts of Reutlingen and after a ten-minute wait, obtained a ride that took him to central Stuttgart. He then walked for the next two hours and eventually reached an entrance road to the autobahn (Bundesautobahn 8 or A8). After obtaining several rides on the A8 and the A5, he arrived in central Heidelberg (Bergheim-Ost) in the late afternoon. Charlie then decided to walk in an easterly direction, basically following the nearby Neckar River. An hour later, he came upon a steep set of steps. Charlie walked down them and came across a grassy area which contained remnants of previous makeshift campsites. This area was fifteen metres below the surface of the road and just slightly above the banks of the river. He pitched his tent and stayed there for the next several days. Charlie would occasionally have a small campfire in operation, but only if the weather conditions were relatively mild. He discovered on the second day that any gust of wind resulted in the smoke (of the campfire) drifting upwards and, thus, onto the thoroughfare above!

Each day, Charlie casually strolled throughout the city of Heidelberg for several hours, viewing key historical landmarks. The rest of the time, however, he was content to just stay at the makeshift campsite and engage in the following: reading a book; slowly sipping on cheap cask wine; and, watching the numerous marine vessels (barges, cruise ships, etc) gliding elegantly and quietly along the Neckar River.

After departing from Heidelberg, Charlie hitchhiked to Munich, via Bundesautobahns 6 and 9 (A6 and A9). In the late evening, he was comfortably resting at a railway station complex near the Glockenspiel. Charlie intended to sleep the night there, along with several other 'homeless' individuals. He eventually drifted off into a peaceful slumber but two hours later, was woken up by a gentle boot to his ribs. Several police officers were hovering above him. They demanded that everyone should leave the vicinity immediately as the railway station would be closed for the next several hours. After leaving the railway station, Charlie soon discovered a large doorway area of a nearby building. For the next few hours, he sat upright and occasionally drifted off into a temporary sleep mode – with his fishing-knife firmly clutched in his right hand, in case of a physical attack.

Charlie, initially, had planned to stay in Munich for two days. The *overnight experience*, however, dissolved any desire for him to explore the city. As soon as daylight began to emerge, he started walking in a westerly direction. Two hours later, Charlie was at an entrance point of Bundesautobahn 96. He held a cardboard sign (Landsberg) with his left hand and stuck out his right thumb. The town of Landsberg-am-Lech was his next destination.

Charlie arrived in the town of Landsberg-am-Lech just after 10.00 am, not far from the historical Landsberg Prison. The prison's most famous inmate was Adolph Hitler and this was also the place that *Mein Kampf* was dictated by him to Rudolf

Hess in 1924. He walked around part of the prison perimeter before venturing away from the residential area. Heading southwards, Charlie soon came upon a woodlands park reserve where free camping was permitted. He decided to walk past the main camping area and, thus, delve deeper into the tranquil and picturesque woodlands. Consisting of different varieties of trees and shrubs, the park reserve also possessed numerous streams of clear-running water. Twenty minutes later, Charlie came upon a small piece of land, consisting of an inhabited hut and several other campers.

After Charlie had pitched his tent up, he decided to explore the nearby surroundings. Charlie came upon a stream where the water flowed over a large rock and, thus, into a lower level (of the stream). Catching the cool, crisp and clean water as it bounced off the rock, he filled two half-litre plastic bottles. Charlie stayed in the park reserve for the next three days and indulged in the following: read two books; sipped on cask wine throughout the day; walked for two to three hours at a time; and, implemented his culinary skills (using a small campfire) twice a day.

After departing from Landsberg-am-Lech, Charlie hitchhiked back towards the city of Reutlingen. Hoping to reach the city that night, all was going quite well, until he arrived in Stuttgart. Charlie was dropped off in the centre of the large city and then spent the next several hours walking towards the southern outskirts. At an entrance point to Bundesautobahn 27, he attempted to thumb a ride but the sky was fading quickly. Even worse, raindrops started to fall and eyeing a nearby partly-constructed bridge, Charlie decided to seek shelter in the concreted tunnel beneath it. There was a torrential downpour a few minutes later.

An hour later, the heavy downpour had finally subsided. Leaving his luggage in the concreted tunnel, Charlie decided to walk to a nearby village to purchase food. During the day, a kind-hearted middle-aged woman had given him a lift – and twenty Deutschmarks. As he entered the village, Charlie came upon a small street festival which included several under-covered food stalls. He had originally planned to go to a supermarket but instead decided to purchase a cheap meal at one of the food stalls. Later, Charlie bought a bottle of beer and conversed with several of the local villagers. He returned to his temporary accommodation two hours later.

Early the next morning, Charlie walked to the entrance point of Bundesautobahn 27 and only had to wait about five minutes for a lift: one which took him directly to Reutlingen. Inside Heidi's residence, he was given an envelope. It contained a letter and an American Express cheque. Two hours later, Charlie cashed the cheque and promptly paid back what he owed Heidi.

In the mid-afternoon, Heidi took Charlie on a guided tour of Reutlingen. She had completed her exams. Later, the pair met up with several of Heidi's student friends in a local *Bierhalle* (Beer Hall). In the evening, the group went to a popular picnic area (located halfway between the city and the town of Tubingen) for a barbeque. After creating a campfire, all cuttings of meat (mainly beef and lamb) and vegetables (potatoes, carrots and onions) were wrapped in aluminium foil and cooked within the embers of the fire. Using several large steel-pronged forks, the wrapped food items were turned over on several occasions. An hour later, all food items were removed from the embers. The sumptuous meal that followed was accompanied by bottles of German-brewed lagers.

Later in the evening, the group decided to go for a stroll in the night darkness via the use of several small torches. They came upon a ditch, partially covered with large branches. A slightly inebriated Charlie, quite foolishly, moved to the edge of the ditch to see what was in it. Suddenly, the dirt beneath his feet gave way. Fortunately, the ditch was only two metres deep. Unfortunately, he was lying on his back and his right leg was trapped between several branches. Charlie was dragged out of the ditch by Heidi's friends but, alas, he now had a badly sprained knee.

The next morning, Heidi massaged a lotion into Charlie's injured knee. She then applied a thick bandage. Despite experiencing a fair amount of discomfort and pain, he was still determined to hitchhike back to the United Kingdom (via Germany and France) the next day. Charlie was keen to return to the English county of Kent for the upcoming strawberry harvest. The next morning he hobbled to the outskirts of Reutlingen and attempted to thumb his first ride for the day. It would take a *hobbling* Charlie three days to hitchhike to the northern French port of Calais.

On the first day, a wounded Charlie eventually made it to a service station (on the Bundesautobahn 8) in the late afternoon. The service station was twenty kilometres east of the city of Saarbrücken (near the German-French border). Before he entered the service station café, Charlie was quizzed by a man standing just outside the entrance, wondering why his knee was heavily bandaged. He informed him of the previous night's hapless sequence of events. The gentleman then introduced himself (Carl) and stated that he was waiting for his girlfriend to pick him up. As they continued to converse, Carl offered Charlie the option of staying at his place for the night. A few minutes later, a BMW sedan pulled up beside them. The driver alighted from the vehicle and Carl introduced her as Inga. He then explained to Charlie that she could treat his injured knee. Inga was a nurse.

Inside Carl's large house, Inga applied an ice pack to Charlie's knee. She later re-bandaged it with a new bandage. During the evening, Charlie learnt several things about Carl: he was a relatively-successful author, scriptwriter and screenwriter; he came from a very wealthy family; and, he had been in a relationship with Inga for over ten years (both were aged in their mid-thirties).

In the late morning of the next day, Inga drove Charlie to the southern outskirts of Saarbrücken. Although his leg was feeling better than the previous day, he was still limping as he walked through the German-French border and into France. The French border officials stopped Charlie but only to stamp his French visa. After walking for half a kilometre, he attempted to thumb his next lift. In his left hand, Charlie held a new sign: 'Reims'.

After waiting for several hours, Charlie eventually obtained a lift from a lorry driver. An hour and a half later, he was dropped off at an Autoroute 4 peage: a few kilometres west of the city of Metz. As nightfall began to creep in, Charlie decided to walk away from the toll booth, searching for a nearby 'comfortable-looking' paddock. Finding shelter under a large tree, he slept well that night. When Charlie woke the next morning, dark and menacing clouds were already dominating the daybreak sky. A hundred metres away, he noticed what he thought might be an abandoned farm hut. Charlie walked towards it, went inside and took refuge. A few minutes later, the 'heavens' opened up and for the next several hours, there was a torrential downpour.

After the substantial downpour had ceased, Charlie walked back to the péage. As he attempted to hitchhike *in front* of the péage, a familiar-looking dark blue vehicle drove up and stopped beside him. Even before any of the Gendarmerie officers uttered a word, Charlie held out his passport for them! Two minutes later, they handed the passport back to him and drove away. Nearly five hours later, a 1960s-model Citroen DS finally stopped beside Charlie. For the next two hours, the elderly driver drove along the inside lane of the A4 and at quite a leisurely pace. Speaking in fluent English, Jacques eloquently chatted throughout the entire journey, whilst a mostly-silent Charlie spent most of the time just nodding his head!

Jacques was quite an interesting character to listen to as he gleefully reminisced his *wonder years*. At one time, Jacques had been a chef to American servicemen, stationed in France during World War II. He first learned to speak English courtesy of regular conversations with these servicemen. Jacques relocated to the USA in 1951 and several years later, married an American woman. From the late-1950s to the early-1970s, the couple travelled extensively worldwide and eventually settled in the French city of Reims in 1972.

Charlie was dropped off in central Reims near a McDonald's restaurant. Somewhat surprisingly, this was the first McDonald's restaurant he had encountered in France. It would also be the only time that he would eat a McDonald's meal in France. After leaving the restaurant, Charlie walked towards the northern outskirts of the city. After obtaining numerous short-distance lifts throughout the afternoon and early evening, Charlie arrived in a village: less than 100 kilometres from the port city of Calais. On the outskirts of the village, there was a football (soccer) ground. After climbing the fence, Charlie entered a small undercover grandstand; the sheltered area was to be his accommodation that night.

At 5.30 am the next morning, Charlie stood on the side of the road and attempted to thumb his first lift for the day. In his left hand, he held a new sign (Calais). Nearly two hours later, a motorist finally stopped. After obtaining several lifts along Autoroute 26, Charlie arrived at the port of Calais just after 4.00 pm. A ferry crossing to Dover (United Kingdom) was scheduled to depart at 6.30 pm. As the ferry calmly made its way across the Strait of Dover, he rested his weary body, happily sipping on a pint of ale.

8

Strawberry Fields Forever

After hitchhiking throughout France and Germany for six weeks, Charlie returned to the United Kingdom. His financial situation was now in a parlous state of uncertainty and he needed to obtain employment – quickly. After the ferry had docked in at the Port of Dover, Charlie walked to the outskirts of the town of Dover and proceeded to hitchhike along the A20 (which later merged with the M20) towards the large Kent town of Maidstone.

Upon being dropped off in the centre of Maidstone, Charlie walked for about two miles (3.2 kilometres) before coming across a small area of woodlands. He pitched his tent between several bushes, in an attempt to be hidden from public view. Charlie's finances had now dwindled to less than ten pounds sterling! As the strawberry-picking season was about to commence, he went searching for strawberry farms. On the first day, Charlie's job-seeking venture was fruitless but on the second day, he managed to obtain employment on a large orchard located between the villages of Yalding and Wateringbury. The orchard contained a large strawberry farm; it also harvested cherry, pear and large apple crops. Charlie, however, would have to sleep out for another night. He would meet the orchard manager (Rupert) the following day.

The next morning, Charlie met Rupert and was immediately directed to the living quarters: two converted horse stables. The accommodation blocks consisted of a total of sixteen small bedrooms, each containing a bed and a large set of drawers. The larger accommodation block contained a spacious kitchen area and was connected to a large communal (or lounge) room via an open doorway. The communal room contained the following: a large television; several well-used lounges; and, a medium-sized table surrounded by six cane-woven chairs. The amenities (part of the smaller accommodation block) was in an excellent condition, compared to normal orchard amenity 'standards'. It was divided into three sections: a male restroom; a female restroom; and, a decent-sized laundry facility.

In the late afternoon, Charlie met some of the other *stable-dwellers*. Other than Jack, who was from the city of Birmingham, all other residents were Polish nationals. After consuming his dinner in the evening, Charlie conversed with three of them: Agnieszka (a student from Warsaw) and a couple (Ivana and Matthias) from the western Polish city of Poznan. The couple were aged in their late-twenties whilst Agnieska was twenty years of age.

Agnieszka spoke relatively fluent English, albeit in a partially-influenced (and monotonic) American accent. She translated for both Ivana and Matthias as they only spoke a small amount of English. Charlie, at that stage, did not speak any Polish. By the end of the fruit-picking season, however, Ivana's level of spoken English had improved dramatically. Charlie had even built-up a reasonable vocabulary of Polish words.

Later in the evening, several of the other residents and Charlie were in the spacious communal room. In the corner of this room, an excitable and tempestuous card game was in progress. Seated around the table were four young Polish males: Alek, Bartosz, Tomasz and Marcin. Three of them were students from Warsaw but non-student Marcin was from the town of Piaceszno: 20 kilometres south of Warsaw.

Of this group of four, Charlie would mostly converse with Marcin throughout the strawberry-picking season. He (Marcin) had been living in London for the past several months and had been employed as a chef – without an employment permit. Just six days earlier, Marcin revealed that Home Office (Immigration Department) officials and police officers had raided his place of employment. He managed to escape, however, by climbing onto the roof of a nearby building!

Charlie was to learn his first Polish swear words from watching this card game. Alek and Bartosz, in particular, were quite animated (a lot of arm-waving and hand gesticulation) throughout the evening. They were frequently losing games – along with a sizeable amount of Polish złoty notes and coins. On numerous occasions, Charlie heard the words *kurwa mać, kurwa jego mać, kurwa twoja mać, cholera jasna* and *gówno prawda.* Marcin, with an ever-increasing pile of notes and coins in front of him, gleefully translated to Charlie the English equivalent of these words!

Early the next morning, the 'stable-dwellers' congregated in readiness, in front of a block of strawberries ready for select-picking. Between each row of strawberry plants, there was plenty of thick straw; it was easier to pick strawberries when working on your knees. The strawberry plants were close-planted on long strips of black-coloured plastic sheets. Thin trickle hose ran underneath the plastic sheets. Two other large groups of strawberry pickers (the *East-Enders* and the *Travellers*) had also gathered nearby. The 'East-Enders' was from London's eastern suburbs whilst the 'Travellers', on the other hand, mostly lived an itinerant lifestyle. They were actually 'Romanichal Travellers' (or Rumneys) but commonly referred to as *Romani.*

[Note: Romanichals or Rumneys are a sub-group of the Romani people].

After the third day of strawberry picking, Charlie realised that this financial venture will be barely profitable. Life in the strawberry fields, however, was generally harmonious – and, entertaining. Charlie deemed the Travellers as quite an interesting group of people to work with. The large group collectively resided on a block of land (which they owned) located less than a mile from the main orchard. From the roadside, one could see an array of unique-styled gipsy caravans and wagons. A few of the latter were still horse-driven!

On the strawberry field, the young female Travellers would leave their babies in prams at the top of a row. Children, typically from the age of four or five, would assist their mothers or grandmothers with strawberry picking. Throughout the working day, the 'extended' family tended to the babies regularly. The young mothers tended to be aged from their mid-teens to their early twenties. The grandmothers were mostly aged in their thirties or forties and the great-grandmothers were aged over fifty.

Several local women were employed to weigh and record each tray of strawberries brought to them by the individual strawberry picker. Additionally, they often found themselves in the position of having to 'tend' to the small children who had *escaped* from the tedium of strawberry picking.

The weighing station was at a designated location where full punnets of strawberries, on a tray, would be taken to be weighed. Each tray had to be of minimum weight. The strawberry picker would then have their tally cards hole-punched for each tray collected. At the end of the day, the individual strawberry picker (or family group) would present their tally card at the cash office, located inside the packing shed. Each individual or group was paid in cash. One's daily earnings were calculated by the set price of a tray of strawberries and multiplied by the number of trays picked.

The East-Enders made the 'annual pilgrimage' to the county of Kent for the entire fruit-picking season: typically from June to October. The older members of this group had been engaged in seasonal fruit-picking employment for several decades. During the fruit-picking season, they resided in caravans permanently stationed on a block of land owned by the orchardist. By early-November, most of them had returned to their homes in London's East End.

Away from the strawberry fields, Charlie's social life largely centred on his daily verbal interaction with the Polish contingent within the living quarters. They soon 'adopted' him as their main English teacher. Each day, he fervently assisted them in their endeavour to steadily improve their level of spoken English, their reading ability and writing skills. Charlie was also keen to extend his Polish vocabulary – beyond popular swear words.

After purchasing an English-Polish book from a bookstore in Maidstone, he attempted to learn and memorise basic Polish words and phrases – much to the amusement of the Polish students. Initially, his pronunciation of many Polish words was quite awful but once Charlie understood the basic pronunciation rules, his spoken Polish improved rapidly. Nevertheless, he soon realised that some words were near-impossible for native English-speakers to pronounce correctly. Two years later, Charlie travelled throughout Poland for six weeks; his basic knowledge of spoken and written Polish would prove to be quite useful.

Throughout the strawberry picking season, there were *meal-sharing* evenings; especially on the weekends. Close to the converted stables stood a large two-storey house. The house contained a family of five: John, Lucinda and their three teenage sons (Teddy, Rob and Billy). The couple worked on the orchard throughout the year. As there was a constant problem with rabbits and hares on the orchard, John and his sons would often go into the orchard with rifles. Returning with several or numerous furry pests, the 'stable-dwellers' would occasionally feast on a rabbit stew or slowly-baked rabbit meat!

Besides rabbit being on the 'communal' menu at times, eels from nearby waterways would be occasionally captured and, thus, would also be consumed. Several Polish male students would, firstly, cut them into smaller pieces. Then, they would wash the bits and cover them in breadcrumbs. The next stage of the cooking process involved the eel pieces being pan-fried on the stove's hotplates. Chef Marcin would usually cook the rabbits or hares. After they were skinned, the remaining meat would then be either slowly boiled or slowly roasted in the oven for four to six hours. Charlie and several others would prepare side dishes: stir-fried or boiled vegetables; pasta-based dishes; and, *barszcz* (a Polish beetroot soup).

Occasionally, Charlie would venture to one of the local village hotels, either in Yalding or in Wateringbury. Inside these licenced premises, there was a mixture of Travellers, East-Enders and local patrons. Over several pints of ale (and the occasional game of pool), Charlie would be involved in quite a lot of interesting discussions – especially with the Travellers.

An inquisitive Charlie enjoyed discussing with the Travellers their cultural and nomadic lifestyle. The group, in turn, were quite bemused with his enthusiastic interest in their itinerant lifestyle as they were often scorned by local communities. Throughout the United Kingdom, the Travellers (along with other itinerant groups) were often referred to as *pikies* or *pikeys*: a derogatory term used for gipsies/travellers in a pejorative manner. The group, however, was equally fascinated with Charlie's adopted nomadic/itinerant fruit-picking lifestyle within Australia over the past few years. The parallels between the two lifestyles contained many similarities!

Charlie returned to the same orchard two years later. Little had changed. The East-Enders and the Travellers were there (and still in large numbers). However, a new group of Polish people (except for Marcin) were now in the converted stables.

In the communal room that evening, he conversed (via a mixture of Polish and English) with three Polish women: Danuta, Margorzata and Renata. Aged in their late-twenties, the three non-students had travelled from Poland in Danuta's German-registered automobile.

Danuta had been working in Germany for the past few years. She also had German citizenship and a German passport. Danuta later explained to Charlie that the trio encountered a few minor hassles when they tried to enter the United Kingdom via the port town of Dover. But after producing wads of British pound notes and German Deutschmarks (and several credit cards) to justify their 'self-funded holiday', customs officials allowed them to enter into the country.

The three women were from the city of Konin (located in the central-western region of Poland) and had known each other from their schooling days. Charlie soon had a nickname for them: the *Konin Sisters*. Over the next two days, he would meet the other stable-dwellers. All were Polish students. Charlie, however, soon took a dislike to most of them – especially the fluent English-speaking students. This particular group possessed annoying traits of childish and snobbish disdain towards the non-students (the 'Konin Sisters' and Marcin). Throughout the strawberry-picking season, the students would regularly converse with each other but largely ignore the non-students. Appalled by the group's *blatant* snobbery towards their countrymen and countrywomen, Charlie would mostly converse with Marcin and the three Konin ladies.

On the first day of the strawberry-picking season, all field employees were subjected to a 'meet and greet' session with the new orchard field boss: Richard. A rotund character, he had a distinct Cockney-accent and wore an ill-fitting beret, seemingly just perched on top of his head. Perhaps even more amusing, Richard wanted everyone to call him 'Guvna'! Even before a strawberry was picked, Charlie felt that the *rotund prat* was going to be a major problem for the strawberry pickers.

Over the next two weeks, Richard's behaviour was largely one of bullying and intimidation. Although he succeeded in harassing and intimidating the Polish contingent (especially the naive students), it was largely a different story with the East-Enders and the Travellers. Individuals from both groups argued with him frequently.

Richard attempted to intimidate and bully Charlie on several occasions. He (Charlie), however, had previously encountered similar types of individuals on the itinerant fruit-picking circuit in Australia. And Charlie knew how to deal with them: mainly through the use of sharp-witted humour and sarcasm, but also with *strong physical posturing* (toe to toe, eyeball to eyeball). Several of the Travellers would often intervene and assist Charlie, as he attempted to irk and undermine Richard's abuse of authority.

Although Richard easily bullied and intimidated the Polish contingent, Danuta was a notable exception! A strongly-built woman and 1.80 metres tall, she could be quite *fiery* at times – as the Polish students would discover throughout the fruit-picking season. Richard would occasionally attempt to converse 'amicably' with the Polish students but was often met with the *not understand English* routine. Danuta, however, was never afraid to converse with Richard, albeit in broken English and numerous Polish swear words.

One morning, Richard stood behind Danuta and asked her, 'What's the picking like today?'

Danuta snapped back, 'Gówno!' (Polish slang word for shit)

Richard than raised his shoulders, puffed out his chest and pointed to himself.

'No… I'm the *Guvna.*'

The Polish contingent burst out laughing and Richard, quite stupidly, joined in with the laughter, despite not understanding what they were laughing about. Moments later, a straight-faced Danuta explained to Richard what the Polish word translated to in English. His demeanour suddenly changed!

After two treacherous 'character-building' weeks, the large group of strawberry pickers was split into two separate groups. Richard remained in charge of the first group: the Travellers and the East-Enders. The second group consisted of the 'stable dwellers' and a contingent of the local population (within the Maidstone district). The majority of the locals had avoided the first two weeks of the strawberry-picking season. A Yalding villager (Jim) was the foreman of this group.

In stark contrast to Richard, Jim was a pleasant chap to deal with and his people's skills were excellent. As a result, the general atmosphere within this group was largely one of harmonious bliss. Even the Polish students relished the positive behaviour being displayed towards them and in response, they suddenly understood (and spoke) the English language so much better!

Jim was an ardent follower of English cricket. At the time, there was an Ashes Test match series in progress (in England) between England and Australia. Charlie was also a keen cricket follower and, therefore, regularly discussed with him the history of the Ashes series between the two nations. Unfortunately for Jim, the English cricket team were being *hammered* by the Australian cricket team in this particular Ashes series. Australia would eventually win the six-match test series 4-1 (with one drawn result). After the last test match of the series, a down-hearted Jim declared to Charlie, 'We'll bounce back… one of these days!'

Inside Yalding's Two Brewers Inn, Charlie would regularly be engaged in friendly banter with other patrons.

The performance of England's test cricket side was well below par during that particular Ashes series. Wallace, one of the Travellers, cheekily suggested that the Australian cricketers' performance was a *successful revenge plot* against England for shipping convicts to Australia in the past.

The strawberry-picking season, again, was not an overly profitable one for Charlie. But what he lost from a financial perspective, Charlie would gain in the form of a thriving social life. He enjoyed the company of the Konin Sisters and Marcin. Besides sharing cooked meals, the group also shared alcohol. The three women had brought two boxes of bottled home-made spirits (twenty-four bottles in total) with them from Konin and often shared a drink with the two males. Charlie, in turn, bought numerous bottles of French-made brandy and bottles of Scotch whisky, regularly sharing with the others.

As the two-month strawberry-picking season progressed, Danuta's level of spoken and written English improved remarkably. Renata and Margorzata, on the other hand, made little effort to improve their spoken English and thus, relied on Danuta (or Marcin) to translate Polish into English. Every day, she (Danuta) would attempt to converse or communicate with Charlie and other native English-speakers. Meanwhile, he (Charlie) continued to learn new Polish words and phrases, but at a much slower rate than Danuta learning English.

Besides her native tongue, Danuta was also a fluent speaker of Russian and German. She was also reasonably proficient with the Swedish language. Years later, Danuta would learn to speak Italian as well. Before coming to the United Kingdom, Danuta had lived in Germany for the past five years and in Sweden for two years. She had learned how to speak and write Russian throughout her schooling years. English would be her fifth spoken language!

At the converted stables, meanwhile, the behaviour of the Polish students could be quite *bothersome* at times. Charlie and Marcin mostly ignore their childish antics but Danuta clashed with them frequently – especially with several of the male students. One Sunday afternoon, halfway through the strawberry-picking season, she became involved in a heated exchange with one of the Warsaw students (Michał) in the laundry room.

What started as a verbal slanging match quickly transformed into a physical altercation. In an attempt to intimidate her, Michał decided to stand right in front of Danuta, practically standing on her toes. She responded by kneeing him in the testicles! Next, Danuta struck him in the face with her left forearm. As he recoiled backwards, she punched him in the jaw with her fist, sending him to the ground. Sighting a nearby broom, Danuta grabbed it and whacked Michał on the head several times. At that point, Renata and Margorzata (who were also in the laundry room at the time) finally decided to move her away from him. Several of the students came to the laundry room to investigate the noisy commotion. Charlie and Marcin, however, stood in the doorway and prevented them from entering the laundry room.

When the strawberry-picking season ended, Charlie returned to Broadacre Wood Farms (West Malling) for the upcoming apple-picking season. He had worked on this orchard in previous seasons. During the apple-picking season, however, Charlie met up with the Konin Sisters and Marcin every Sunday. After the completion of the apple-picking season, Charlie kept in contact with Danuta and Marcin (via handwritten letters or postcards) for the next several years. He never heard from Renata or Margorzata though.

Two years later, Charlie travelled throughout Poland for six weeks. During that time, he caught up with Marcin in his hometown of Piaceszno (16 kilometres south of Warsaw) and stayed with his family for a few days. Although Charlie never saw Danuta again, he did manage to contact her by telephone, three weeks after catching up with Marcin. Charlie, at the time, was staying at a friend's place in the city of Poznan: 107 kilometres west of Konin. Danuta had been staying at her mother's place (in Konin) for several days; she was about to return to the German capital of Berlin. Eight months later, he received a postcard from her. Danuta had relocated to northern Italy. The postcard was the last piece of correspondence between the two.

The following year, Charlie decided to seek employment at another strawberry farm (part of Tick Tock Orchards) in the Maidstone area. A few months earlier, he had been living and working on the Greek island of Crete and one of his fellow itinerant workers (Gareth) had provided him with the address of Tick Tock Orchards. He assured Charlie that the orchard's strawberry-picking season would be financially profitable for him.

Before the commencement of the strawberry-picking season, Charlie had already been back in England for nearly two months. After staying with a friend in Ilfracombe (a seaside resort and civil parish in the county of Devon) for two weeks, he hitchhiked to Broadacre Wood Farms (West Malling, Kent). For the next six weeks, Charlie was employed to cut asparagus. Instead of pitching his tent in the camping area, he was offered accommodation in what could best be described as a child's cubby-house placed on top of a towable trailer. Charlie, however, regarded the basic accommodation as being quite homely.

When the asparagus-cutting season was completed, Charlie relocated to Tick Tock Orchards the following day. Laden with a full-sized backpack (with a small tent attached to the base of it) and a medium-sized carrier bag, he walked a distance of five miles (eight kilometres) before arriving at the entrance of the orchard. After having a brief discussion with the orchard manager, Charlie was directed to the spacious camping area. In this area, there were twelve small tents, five caravans and one large camper van. Next to the camping area, there was a large tract of land that contained ten brightly green-coloured demountables (portable housing) – all of them occupied by Eastern European students.

Charlie stayed on Tick Tock Orchards for the next six weeks and saved over five hundred pounds sterling. Throughout the strawberry-picking season, employment was available for six or seven days each week. The typical working day was six to eight hours. He rarely left the orchard, except for grocery shopping and to patronise the nearby hotel on just three occasions.

Although there were over eighty people in the accommodation area, the atmosphere within the large group was mainly one of harmonious bliss. The 'community' was comprised of many different nationalities: English, Scottish, Irish, South Africans, Polish, Bulgarians, Ukrainians, Hungarians, Czechs, Slovaks, etc. Charlie was the lone Australian. The accommodation facility also boasted of a large and well-equipped communal area. It contained a spacious kitchen area (along with several large refrigerators and numerous food storage cabinets) and a large dining area (comprising five long tables with matching long-bench seating). The communal area was widely used for social interaction between the strawberry pickers.

A large caravan, situated in the middle of the camping area, was primarily used as the 'television room'. Besides the large antiquated television, there were several well-used lounge chairs and several small coffee tables. Charlie entered this caravan – once. Upon entering, he was instantly met with an *intolerable haze mixed in with indescribable odours*. Numerous empty plastic apple-cider bottles, dozens of empty beer cans and overflowing ashtrays were strewn across the carpeted floor space.

This particular strawberry-picking season coincided with the 1994 World Cup Football tournament. As a result, the television room was a constant buzz of 'hysterical activity' during the televising of any football match. When the prestigious football tournament had whittled down to the final sixteen teams, the caravan was largely occupied by the Bulgarian male students. One of the students informed Charlie that the Bulgarian national team had never won a match in their previous five World Cup encounters. Although the team lost their first match (3-0), they bounced back with four consecutive wins.

Eventually, Bulgaria would lose to Italy in the semi-final. In their previous match (the quarter-final), however, they played against Germany. Late in the second half of the match, Germany led 1-0 but the Bulgarians equalised in the 75th minute. Three minutes later, they scored again and held on to win the match 2-1. When the referee blew the final whistle, a *deafening roar of pandemonium* instantly erupted inside the caravan. The overzealous, decibel-breaking commotion even gained the attention of the orchard manager residing more than a hundred metres away from the campsite. In response, he decided to venture to the campsite to further investigate the fracas – possibly fearing that a wild out-of-control brawl was taking place.

When the strawberry-picking season ended, Charlie boarded a London-bound train the following morning. Whilst staying in London, he purchased a one-way ticket to Sydney (Australia). Originally, Charlie had planned to return to Broadacre Wood Farms for the apple-picking season. During the strawberry picking season, however, he had been in contact with several fruit-picking itinerant workers in Australia. Charlie was informed that the tomato-picking season in Bowen (North Queensland) had, so far, been financially lucrative. Furthermore, the remaining months were forecasted to be even more financially rewarding, largely due to two key factors: bumper tomato crops were being harvested throughout the year and, there was a severe shortage of tomato pickers due to officials from the Australian Immigration Department (accompanied by police officers) *raiding* most of the tomato farms within the Bowen region on several occasions. A large number of employees (both tomato-picking and shed hands) were arrested and later deported.

Charlie boarded an Aeroflot airlines flight at London's Heathrow Airport late one afternoon. After several stopovers, the aircraft landed at Sydney (Kingswood Smith) Airport. He stayed in Sydney that night and the next day, Charlie drove along the Pacific Highway in a northerly direction. He had borrowed a friend's VW Kombi van (which he would later purchase) for the four-day road journey. Before Charlie had even arrived in the town of Bowen, there had been *intense negotiations* between the itinerant workers and tomato growers. As a result, there was a significant increase in the piece-rate being paid for each bucket of tomatoes picked. Over the remaining three months of the tomato-picking season, he would push his body beyond his 'normal limits' and, thus, earned (and saved) a considerable amount of money.

9

The Twelve Days of Guinness

As the cherry-picking season came to a close, so did the month of August. The commencement of the apple-picking season was still two weeks away. As there was no employment during this time, Charlie thought, 'Do I indulge in a do-nothing period of relaxation or should I opt for something more invigorating?' He decided to do something more invigorating – a 'Guinness-fuelled' hitchhiking tour of Ireland.

On a mild and sunny Friday mid-morning, Charlie boarded a train from Maidstone East railway station, bound for London's Victoria railway station. From Victoria railway station, he caught another train (District Line, London Underground) to Chiswick Park railway station. After arriving at Chiswick Park station, Charlie alighted from the train and he immediately walked towards a multi-road junction: the start of the M4 motorway.

At the junction, Charlie held a thin white cardboard sign (with Bristol written on it) and a protruding left thumb. He did not have to wait long for his first lift. After receiving several lifts along the M4 motorway, mainly from a motorway service area to another one, Charlie eventually arrived at the northern outskirts of the city of Bristol. By now, it was late evening. As he casually strolled along a byway (minor road), the darkness of night slowly crept in. Charlie decided to seek 'accommodation' for the night.

Upon coming across a 'comfortable-looking' paddock, partially fenced off with tall shrubs, Charlie laid his tent and sleeping bag on the ground. Within ten minutes, he was in a state of restive slumber. Two hours later, however, Charlie was woken up – by the sound of hooves. Several cows had wandered perilously close to his overnight campsite. In an instant, he gathered his belongings and relocated to another nearby paddock: one that, hopefully, was free of livestock. Charlie laid awake for over an hour, but he eventually drifted into another period of quality slumber.

Early the next morning, Charlie was 'back on the road' again. Using a hand-held map, he decided to walk towards the nearest M4 road junction, located more than five miles away. After arriving at the road junction and with a new sign (Swansea), Charlie waited patiently for his next lift. He soon realised that most of the traffic was most likely going in a north-easterly direction (along the M5), instead of a north-westerly direction. After waiting for several hours, Charlie obtained his first lift for the day.

The motorist was going to the Welsh city of Newport via the M4 route. This motorway also continued onto the city of Swansea. Charlie was dropped off at an M4 road junction. At the time, the only way into southern Wales (via crossing over the Severn River) was by driving on the Severn Bridge. The final construction of the Second Severn Crossing Bridge would be several years later. The M4 was, subsequently, re-routed over this bridge. The section of road that went across the Severn Bridge was renamed the M48. After receiving several more lifts, he arrived in central Swansea. Charlie then walked to the Port of Swansea Queens Dock Ferry Terminal. It was now 6.00 pm. A ferry to Cork (Ireland) was departing in two hours.

The ten-hour voyage across the Celtic Sea that night could best be described as *rough*. Although most of the seafaring passengers were in the ferry cabin berths that night, a few people were in the communal lounge area. The lounge area contained a refreshments bar. Charlie would make several trips there before it closed at midnight.

On this particular night, the volatile Celtic Sea posed a major challenge for any individual wishing to walk across the floorboards, especially if one was carrying a drink (or several drinks). The constant rocking motion of the wooden floorboards presented an effect where one would feel that their feet were about to leave the floorboards one moment and, in the next moment, felt like your feet were being dragged into them!

After downing several pints of Guinness stout beer, Charlie slept soundly on a wooden bench seat, using his medium-sized luggage bag as a pillow. A few hours later, Charlie was awoken by the bright glare of the new day beaming through the windows. One hour later, the ferry arrived at the port of Ringaskiddy: a village 15 kilometres from the city of Cork.

Upon disembarking from the ferry and making his way through the customs area (there was no passport check), Charlie immediately walked to the outskirts of the village. As the city of Cork was fifteen kilometres away, he was soon 'thumbing it' on the N28: a road that linked Ringaskiddy directly to Cork. After waiting for just a few minutes, a kind-hearted motorist gave Charlie a lift to the centre of Cork. He would stay in Cork for the next two nights at a Caravan and Camping Park.

During his two-night stay in Cork, Charlie planned his travel itinerary around Ireland. He was also an active participant in Cork's then-thriving pub culture. As Charlie ventured from hotel to hotel, he realised that the city (at the time) had a very high ratio of hotels and bars, compared to the overall population of the city!

On the morning of the third day, Charlie walked in a south-westerly direction towards the N22 national road. Deciding not to use a sign, he casually stood by the side of the road with just a protruding left thumb. Charlie's main goal was to explore the vibrant pub culture of Ireland – in any village, town or city. Receiving numerous short-distance lifts, he hitchhiked along the N22, via 'Guinness stopovers' in several villages and the town of Killarney as well. After arriving in the town of Tralee, Charlie downed two more pints of beer. Feeling somewhat 'socially inebriated' by now, he hitchhiked along the N69 towards the city of Limerick.

Charlie's initial plan was to just have one or two pints of Guinness beer at any particular hotel before proceeding to move on to his next destination. As soon as he moved his lips, however, the *strange accent* immediately caught the attention of the friendly and chatty local patrons. They, in turn, ensured that Charlie would be staying inside the hotel longer than he intended! Over several pints, various topics were discussed, but one particular subject would dominate all others: Irish ancestry. Charlie readily informed the inquisitive local patronage that there was Irish ancestry on his mother's side of the family – equating to a free pint (or two) of Guinness stout beer.

Probably the main highlight of Charlie's 'self-managed tour' of Ireland was the *privilege* to have patronised Ireland's oldest pub – on several occasions. With enthusiastic pride, patrons or bartenders would explain 'sincerely' to Charlie, why their hotel establishment was the oldest in Ireland! Each hotel establishment would have, at least, several large framed newspaper articles (courtesy of the local press) and a few of them even had *genuine certificates* placed on the wall – as evidence – in a vain effort to convince the unsuspecting traveller of the vociferous claim.

After leaving a hotel, Charlie would stroll (albeit, a little unsteady at times) towards the outskirts of the village or town. Patiently waiting for his next ride, he would once again extend his left arm and with a protruding thumb, tried to be steady as possible. Charlie would rarely have to wait more than thirty minutes for a lift: the easily-visible Australian flag on the front of his backpack practically ensured that he received regular lifts. Once inside a vehicle, it could be quite a challenge for Charlie to stay awake at times! Fortunately, most drivers were quite chatty and, thus, would discuss with him a wide array of topics: local history; localised customs and traditions; religious issues; and, general politics.

Throughout his *Guinness Tour* of Ireland, a major problem for Charlie involved the ability to comprehend the various localised accents. A typical example of this problem occurred one afternoon when he was inside a vehicle travelling along the N69 towards Limerick. The conversation between the three young male occupants was largely unintelligible to Charlie. One of them, however, attempted to converse with him using a 'more refined' level of English.

Charlie, nevertheless, persevered with the 'language barrier' and still managed to have some form of communication with them. At one point in the conversation, he was asked if he had visited the Blarney Castle (located eight kilometres from Cork) and whether he had kissed the Blarney Stone or not. To both questions, 'No' was the response from Charlie.

'Yeah… good thing you never kissed the Blarney Stone… locals piss on it regularly!'

Charlie stayed in a paddock that night, just outside the northern outskirts of Limerick. He slept quite well – undisturbed by inquisitive cows. Early the next morning, Charlie was back on the road again and obtained a lift in less than ten minutes. A few kilometres later, he was dropped off near a roundabout. A hundred metres away, there was a service station and an adjoining café. Inside the café, Charlie consumed a scrumptious 'protein-laced' breakfast. Afterwards, he wandered to a nearby bus bay and attempted to thumb his next ride.

Several minutes later, a scruffily-dressed child (probably aged 10-12 years old) casually approached the bus bay and immediately attempted to initiate a conversation. Charlie had earlier passed a campsite near the roundabout, one that was inhabited by Irish Travellers (also known as *Minkiers* or *Pavees*). The campsite was a cluster of old run-down caravans with plenty of dogs and cats roaming freely, along with piles of rubbish/waste material. The young Irish Traveller then tried to persuade him to purchase some grocery items from the Service Station (for his family). Although the youngster was quite persistent, Charlie steadfastly refused to become involved with *local politics*. He had already learnt that there was a lot of ill-feeling towards the travellers by the local population. Numerous communities simply didn't want the Irish Travellers dwelling in their local area. Most businesses, furthermore, refused to provide any service to this largely ostracised group. Despondently, the young lad wandered back towards the campsite.

A few minutes later, a black-coloured (and late-modelled) Volvo vehicle with dark-tinted windows stopped beside Charlie. Inside the vehicle, he was coolly greeted by an elderly pipe-smoking Catholic priest! Initially, *Father* was not overly talkative. With a certain degree of smugness, he seemed to be quite content to just puff away on his pipe. Eventually, Charlie decided to break the aura of the hazy silence, 'Where are you going?'

'Off to another bloody funeral!'

An undeterred Charlie then attempted to foster further conversation by declaring to the priest that he had some Irish ancestry on his mother's side of the family.

'My mother's maiden name is Carman.'

'Spanish name… lot of Carmans in Ireland, though.'

Then Charlie mentioned the surname 'Thornberry': a surname that was prominent on his mother's father side of the genealogical tree.

'Northern Irish… they're probably Protestants!'

From that point, however, the discussion between the pair was far more harmonious but Irish 'issues' dominated the general conversation though. An hour later, the priest arrived at a village church where he would conduct a requiem mass. Afterwards, the burial ceremony would take place at the cemetery: next door to the church. For the rest of the day, Charlie edged his way towards Dublin via numerous short-distance lifts and several hotel stopovers.

Just after 6.00 pm, he walked out of a village hotel and a short time later was attempting to obtain his next lift. There was a scarce amount of traffic travelling along the R445 and to make matters worse, Charlie soon had *competition*. An elderly and obnoxious gentleman was staggering along the road, trying to thumb a ride as well. When he was just a few metres away (from Charlie), the elderly gent attempted to initiate a conversation – standing in the middle of the road. As a car swerved around him, he swore and cursed at the driver. The elderly gentleman was absolutely 'pickled' and struggled to remain upright! Charlie then decided to walk a further hundred metres or so down the road. A few minutes later, he obtained a lift with three women: a middle-aged woman and her two daughters. They were heading home to the small town of Kildare.

One of the daughters informed Charlie that the elderly gentleman was well known in the area and his drunken antics were a regular occurrence. He lived in a farmhouse, located between two nearby villages. She further stated that the elderly gent often slept in a bus shelter or on a comfortable patch of grass near the roadside (if he was unsuccessful in obtaining a lift from anyone). The local police officers, in particular, were quite content to just let him sleep for a few hours. When he woke up, they would drive him back to his farmhouse.

Half an hour later, Charlie was dropped off at the eastern outskirts of Kildare. Within ten minutes, he obtained another lift: one that took him to the western outskirts of Dublin. By now, nightfall had settled in. After walking for several kilometres, Charlie came across a public park. After making his way through the park, he laid out his tent and sleeping bag on a patch of ground, well concealed by several large shrubs. The next two nights, however, Charlie decided to stay in a hostel in central Dublin.

Several months previously, when Charlie was living in London, his English co-workers stated to him that Dublin was practically a *miniature version* of London. He soon realised this line of thought was largely incorrect! Charlie felt that Dublin was far more relaxed than London and the general pace of life here was noticeably slower. On the fourth day, Charlie walked from the hostel and towards a road junction that connected with the M50. He obtained a lift at the junction within half an hour; one that took him along the M1, towards the town of Dundalk (84 km from Dublin). Charlie was hoping to catch up with a former work colleague: Maggie.

The pair had worked together in London. Several months earlier, Maggie had moved back to her former hometown of Dundalk to commence a business studies course. Whilst in Dublin, he attempted to contact her by telephone but was unsuccessful. After being dropped off in the centre of the town, Charlie sought Maggie's place of residence. Fifteen minutes later, he stood outside the house only to be informed by a neighbour that she had ceased her studies and returned to London! Two months later (in London), however, Charlie did manage to catch up with her.

Instead of staying in Dundalk, Charlie decided to hitchhike back to Dublin. He arrived at the northern outskirts of the city just as dusk was creeping in. After walking for about a kilometre, Charlie came upon a new housing estate. There were several partly-built houses, without any doors or windows. He slept in one of these buildings that night.

Early the next morning, Charlie walked to a nearby road junction (M50). With a new sign (Waterford), he patiently waited for his first lift for the day. Forty minutes later, a sedan stopped beside him; the driver was going to Kildare. After being dropped off at the southern outskirts of the town, Charlie attempted to hitchhike along the R415 which would connect with the M9. This motorway went all the way to Waterford (*Waterford Crystal* is named after the city). He arrived in the city just after midday and walked to the nearest hotel. As Charlie sipped on a pint of Guinness, he conversed with several patrons. During the conversation, they claimed that Waterford was Ireland's oldest city, dating back to the year 853 when Viking raiders established a settlement there. King Henry II of England arrived at Waterford in 1171 and declared Waterford as a royal city. Dublin was declared a royal city a short time later.

After consuming several pints of Guinness, Charlie casually strolled towards the N25. After receiving several lifts along the N25, he made it to the south-eastern outskirts of Cork just as nightfall was creeping in. Charlie soon discovered a block of land which contained an unoccupied and partly-ruined dwelling. Instead of sleeping inside the dwelling, he decided to set up a makeshift camp in the front yard. As it contained numerous bushy shrubs, Charlie was able to hide from public view relatively easy.

Just after 4.30 am the next morning, Charlie rose from his night of slumber and was soon walking (in near-darkness) towards the start of the N28. This particular road went to the port of Ringaskiddy. After a ten-minute wait, the first vehicle that came along stopped next to him. The motorist, a middle-aged and white-bearded gentleman, was also going to the ferry port. He was the captain of the ferry going to Swansea!

Throughout the ferry crossing, Charlie was reminiscent of his 'Guinness tour' of Ireland. During his twelve-day adventure, he had only paid for four nights of accommodation. Charlie calculated that the low-budget tour had only cost him the equivalent of a little over 150 (English) pounds sterling. The currency used in Ireland at that time was the Irish Pound (also known as the Punt). He further estimated *two-thirds of the total cost* was spent on the 'soup-like' stout beverage.

Charlie deemed his hitchhiking experience in Ireland as being unique, in comparison to other European countries that he had previously hitchhiked in. This was largely due to the diverse types of people who had offered him lifts: farmers, priests, a mum with offspring, white-collar employees, blue-collar employees, the young, the elderly, lone females, couples, etc.

The ferry departed from Ringaskiddy and after a relatively smooth ten-hour crossing over the Celtic Sea, Charlie arrived in Swansea in the early evening. After spending an hour in a hotel, he walked to the outskirts of the city. Charlie soon located a 'comfortable-looking' paddock, separated by a row of hedges from the roadway. A quick scan of the area ruled out the presence of any cows in the immediate proximity!

The following morning, Charlie walked to a roundabout: a road junction that led to the M4 motorway. Somewhat ambitiously, he held out a sign: 'London'. Less than half an hour later, a delivery van stopped beside him. The motorist was going all the way to the county of Kent (southeast of London). Indian-born Raj (who had a partial-Cockney accent) was returning to his hometown of Sevenoaks: twenty kilometres from the town of Maidstone.

An amiable character, Raj chatted throughout the journey. The pair would keep in contact for the next few years. Charlie would send postcards (from outside the United Kingdom) to him and, on several occasions, boarded a Sevenoaks-bound train to visit Raj and stayed at his family home for a night or two.

Charlie arrived back at the orchard in the late afternoon. The next morning he was picking apples. Two days later, however, Charlie relocated to another orchard: Broadacre Wood Farms. He had previously been employed there. During the next six weeks, Charlie worked hard and saved hard. When the apple-picking season came to a halt, he boarded a London-bound train the following day. Two days later, Charlie was on board an Aeroflot aircraft. After holidaying in Singapore and Malaysia for two weeks, he continued his air journey to Sydney (Australia).

10

Kerikeri Kiwi Fruit

After a three-hour flight, the Thai Airlines jet landed on the tarmac of Auckland Airport (New Zealand). It was a glorious autumn afternoon. Charlie was feeling a lot better now, compared to the start of the flight when he felt 'under the weather' – largely due to excessive consumption of alcohol the previous night. During the flight, however, he still drank three glasses of brandy and dry!

Charlie collected his luggage from the carousel and was looking forward to breathing in the fresh outdoor air again. He was hoping to pass through the customs area relatively quickly. It would be well over an hour later, however, before Charlie was able to pass through the large glass doors of the Arrivals complex. As an Australian passport holder, he thought that the procedure of customs clearance into New Zealand would be a relatively swift and simplified process. Charlie soon found himself in a lengthy queue where 'progress' was practically at a snail-paced level. Eventually, he made it to the desk. The peroxide-blonde female customs officer was quite pleasant initially. But that soon changed. She soon began to ask a series of questions and some of them were quite bizarre. For example: 'Will you be working in New Zealand?'

A perplexed Charlie stated that he will indeed be working and reminded her that he held an Australia passport (Australian citizens can work in New Zealand without a work permit).

'Do you indulge in illegal substances?'

Charlie sarcastically retorted, 'Doesn't everyone?'

She snappily replied, 'I'm only doing my job.'

Charlie casually explained to her that he 'wasn't into drugs' but did admit that he *probably* drank too much.

'Yes, I can smell the alcohol on your breath!'

After several more questions, the customs officer then noticed the small tent attached to the bottom of Charlie's backpack.

'Is it clean? Have you used it recently?'

Charlie hadn't used the tent for several months. Quite sarcastically, he stated that his tent had recently been *professionally cleaned* (which was a lie). Unperturbed, the customs officer then directed him to the 'tent inspection' area where ten other passengers were also waiting to have their tents inspected. Forty-five minutes later, his tent was returned – with a large school-like sticker on it that read: PASS. Charlie walked through the exit doors of the Arrivals lounge and had only taken a few steps into the fresh outdoor air when, suddenly, he was swarmed upon by vulture-like hostel 'touts'. Charlie followed them to a section of lawn near a bus bay, joining a group of recently-arrived backpackers. He was immediately inundated with pamphlets promoting several backpacker hostels: all located in central Auckland.

The frantic attempts to put pamphlets into Charlie's hands reminded him of election days, where numerous individuals (from various political parties) engaged in treacherous and frenzied behaviour – forcibly trying to make people vote for the political party that they belong to. He casually responded, 'I will be boarding the first bus that arrives!'

Twenty minutes later, a hostel minibus arrived. All eighteen newly-arrived backpackers boarded it! Three of the hostel touts, however, would not be easily discouraged and they continued to rant about how *their* hostel was better, further stating that the respective buses would be arriving within the next few minutes. The minibus, however, drove off – with eighteen passengers.

Charlie stayed in Auckland for the next three nights. On the fourth day, he left the hostel and boarded a bus which travelled to the northern side of the Auckland Harbour Bridge. After alighting from the bus, Charlie walked to a road junction: located near the M1 (Northern Motorway/Auckland-Waiwera Motorway). With a protruding left thumb and a sign (Kerikeri), he attempted his first experience of hitchhiking in New Zealand. Ten minutes later, a motorist stopped beside him and Charlie was on his way.

Throughout the rest of the day, Charlie received several more lifts and late in the afternoon, arrived in central Kerikeri: 240 kilometres north of Auckland. Whilst staying in the Auckland hostel, he had pre-arranged accommodation via a telephone call to Hidden Lodge hostel (Kerikeri). Inside the town's lone hotel, Charlie consumed a jug of Speights lager (it was cheaper to buy a jug of beer instead of several glasses separately). Eventually, he rang the hostel and half an hour later, a minibus arrived.

Charlie climbed into the front passenger seat of the minibus. In the driver's seat, sat a portly gentleman; his large stomach *comfortably rested* on the bottom part of the steering wheel. After introducing himself as Melville (the hostel manager), he drove off. The fifteen-minute journey to the hostel, however, was mostly one of eerie silence. Charlie attempted to initiate a conversation (twice) but was met with a single-word answer each time.

Once inside the hostel office, Charlie paid a week's accommodation and was soon led to a small room with two double bunk beds. He would be sharing the room with three other males: a New Zealander, a Frenchman and a Japanese chap. Charlie would stay at Hidden Lodge for the next three weeks. Later in the evening, he learnt that 'Big Mel' (Melville) rarely spoke to any of the hostel residents and rarely left the confines of the building that housed the administration office during daylight hours. It soon emerged that Melville tended to be more like a prison warden than a hostel manager!

Every evening, just before 8.00 pm, Melville would emerge from the administration office and proceeded to *patrol* the area within the Hidden Lodge perimeter. He was largely looking for 'undesirable aliens' (non-residents) and in quite a tactless manner, ordered them to leave the hostel environs immediately. At 10.00 pm, Melville would close the main common room and close the smaller common room a few minutes later. On Friday and Saturday nights, the 'curfew' in both common rooms commenced at 11.00 pm. In quite a 'bullish' manner, he ordered everyone to return to their rooms immediately.

Charlie wasn't overly happy with the cramped room conditions but he still got on quite well with his roommates. Whilst Leon, Pierre and Charlie were able to converse with each other easily, it was a struggle for young Yoshiaki at times. Although his English vocabulary was at a reasonable level, he regularly struggled with basic sentences and the pronunciation of certain words. Fortunately, hostel residents (including his roommates) would patiently converse with him regularly and, as a result, his level of spoken English steadily improved over the next several months.

Before seeking employment in the Kerikeri area, Charlie needed to obtain a New Zealand IRD (Inland Revenue

Department) number. The nearest IRD was in the city of Whangarei: 85 kilometres south of Kerikeri. Instead of catching a bus, Charlie decided to hitchhike on State Highway 10, near the junction with Kerikeri Road. Ten minutes later, a motorist stopped and gave him a lift. After being dropped off in central Whangarei, he soon located the IRD office building.

Two hours later, Charlie had an IRD number. His day was going smoothly – until he tried to hitchhike back to Kerikeri. After walking to the northern outskirts of Whangarei, Charlie stood on the side of the road and attempted to thumb a ride. Without a backpack and a sign, however, he would have to wait quite a while before obtaining a lift. After waiting for over three hours, a vehicle finally stopped. It was an antiquated school bus that had been converted into a motorhome. Charlie entered the bus and was politely greeted by its occupants: two ladies aged in their late sixties. The two retirees had been travelling around both islands of New Zealand for the past few months. They had completely refurbished the interior of the bus. Several minutes into the journey, the driver casually remarked to Charlie, 'Hope you're not in a rush!'

The bus drove smoothly along the flatter sections of the highway and at a leisurely pace, travelling at a speed of 70–80 kilometres per hour. Driving uphill, however, was an entirely different story! The vehicle *crawled* noisily up the steep inclines in first gear and at a speed barely above walking pace. Just over two hours later, the converted motorhome arrived at the road junction of State Highway 10 and Kerikeri Road. Charlie farewelled the travelling retirees and in near-darkness, proceeded to walk along Wowoha Road. Ten minutes later, he was in the main common room at the Hidden Lodge hostel, proudly showing his new IRD card.

The next morning, Leon and Charlie sought employment for the upcoming kiwifruit picking season. They contacted a local fruit-harvest contractor (Neil). Although Neil mostly hired local people or residents staying at the Harangue Backpackers hostel, he was quite happy to employ the pair. Employment would commence three days later and would last for nearly three months.

After two weeks, Leon and Charlie decided to relocate to the Harangue Backpackers hostel. During the first two weeks of employment, it had been quite a hassle for them to get to work each day from the Hidden Lodge hostel. Every morning, they would either have to walk the entire distance to the Harangue Backpackers hostel (a 40-minute walk) or, on the odd occasion, manage to obtain a lift part of the way (but only along Kerikeri Road and after crossing the highway junction intersection). On most afternoons, however, Charlie and Leon managed to obtain a lift: either to Hidden Lodge hostel or to the highway junction.

On the first day of the kiwifruit picking season, Charlie worked with fourteen other people as one large group. Initially, he *detested* the idea of group labour as he had mostly picked fruit (or vegetables) previously on his own. Instead of being paid an hourly rate, the large group were paid piece-rate. This meant that the total number of full bins of kiwifruit was divided evenly amongst the number of fruit pickers who worked on a particular day. For example, if sixty bins had been filled by a group of fifteen, each fruit picker would be paid for four bins of kiwifruit (multiplied by the piece-rate).

Financially, this was a poor deal for Charlie as he was one of the faster fruit-pickers within the group. But the camaraderie and the *co-operative harmony* within the group did provide an enjoyable employment experience for him. His weekly earnings would easily cover all living expenses and social life activities.

Despite the friendly camaraderie within the working group, the contractor (Neil) still insisted that everyone worked at a reasonable pace. During the second week, Neil informed two employees that 'their services were no longer required' as he felt that they were letting the rest of the group down. The rest of the group supported his action. Throughout the kiwifruit picking season, most of the group would either race against one another or try to keep pace with the two fastest pickers: Charlie and Martin (a Swiss national). By the third week, the group were filling bins of fruit at a much faster rate than the first week: from four bins to six or seven bins each per day.

Throughout the kiwifruit-picking season, the sporadic winter weather conditions were a constant problem. Light showers of rain frequently fell on a near-daily basis, resulting in temporary employment stoppages. The kiwifruit, generally, would only be removed from the vines in dry or near-dry conditions. Late starting times were commonplace – even as late as 2.00 pm on some days. If the day's employment hadn't commenced by 10.00 am, a large number of kiwifruit pickers would soon congregate at Kerikeri's lone hotel. If there was going to be any kiwifruit picking on that day, Neil and other contractors would drive their vans/minibuses to the hotel. The majority (or all) of their employees would be there!

Each individual was responsible for bringing food (e.g. sandwiches) and containers of water to the orchard. Afternoon tea, however, was provided by the orchard owners. Neil had negotiated with them to include this 'kind deed' as part of contractual arrangements! Afternoon tea consisted mainly of homemade sweet savouries, pastry-based food items or small sandwiches, along with hot or cold beverages.

Most of the kiwifruit orchards within the Kerikeri district only operated on a relatively small scale or as a part-time business. Thus, it was more convenient for the kiwifruit growers to just use the services of a contractor to provide labour needs for their annual fruit harvest (lasting from a couple of weeks to several months).

On the weekends, the centrally-located hotel was filled with a mix of local inhabitants, New Zealand itinerants and backpackers. Although most patrons were quite amicable towards each other, certain individuals would be involved in alcohol-fuelled 'fisticuff moments' – especially on Friday and Saturday nights. The bar manager (aged in his mid-fifties and an ex-professional boxer) would be amidst these *pugilistic disagreements* and would often be sporting a black eye or minor facial bruising (or both) the following day!

At the Hidden Lodge hostel, most residents regularly involved themselves in a variety of evening activities in either of the common rooms: card games, board games, pool/snooker and table tennis or just simply watch the television. Charlie watched his very first episode of *The Simpsons* during this time. Several residents tried to get Melville to socialise with them but to no avail. The amicable atmosphere within the hostel facility should have been an ideal situation for him to thrive socially. Strangely though and for reasons unknown, Melville decided to adopt a hermit-like existence. Aforementioned, he rarely left the office building.

Whilst the social vibe within the hostel facility was mainly a positive one, numerous repairs were urgently required with most of the building structures. In short, extensive renovations needed to be carried out. The main issue, however, evolved around the everyday use of water.

The showers would frequently run out of hot water. Even worse, water would barely trickle out after more than five minutes of usage. The *colour* of the water was another major problem. It came out of the taps quite frothy and with a distinct off-white colour! Fortunately, there was a rainwater tank at the side of the main common room which provided cool, clean and crisp drinking water. The water issues were raised with Melville several times and he robotically responded each time, 'The owners of the hostel will rectify the situation!'

During Charlie's three-week stay at Hidden Lodge, the problematic water situation would not be resolved and the 'mysterious' hostel owners were nowhere to be seen.

One Saturday afternoon, there was a mass exodus from the Hidden Lodge hostel. At least half of the departing residents relocated to the Harangue Backpackers hostel. Although the accommodation facility was much larger than the Hidden Lodge hostel, it was managed much better. The owners of the hostel (Pete and Rose) took great pride in maintaining the facility, frequently interacting with the residents in a friendly and civil manner. Every Saturday night, Pete and Rose would organise a friendly get-together in the ultra-spacious common room, primarily to promote an atmosphere of 'goodwill'. A vast array of finger delicacies and savouries was laid out on two large tables. The social function provided an opportunity for hostel residents to get to know each other better.

When the kiwifruit-picking season came to a halt in late-August, Pete and Rose allowed contractor Neil to organise an end-of-season function for his employees. It took place in a section of the common room. As a token of appreciation, he provided his crew with an array of savoury finger-food delights and alcoholic/non-alcoholic beverages. In a short speech, he expressed his sincere gratitude towards the group as his contractual obligations with the kiwifruit orchardists were easily met.

Charlie deemed the past three months in Kerikeri as a wonderful experience and he was momentarily sad when the picking season came to a halt. Within the next three days, the vast majority of backpackers left and moved onto their next adventure. Charlie had made numerous new friends and he kept in contact with a large number of them in the ensuing years. A few weeks later, Charlie was reunited with several people from the Harangue Backpackers hostel in northern Australia, courtesy of the tomato-picking season in the town of Bowen (Queensland). The following year, he met up with a few more people in several areas of the United Kingdom.

With a laden backpack, Charlie walked from the hostel to the highway junction. With a protruding left thumb and a sign (Auckland) held in his right hand, he patiently waited for his first lift for the day. Charlie arrived in central Auckland in the late afternoon and stayed in a hostel the following two nights. On the third day, he boarded a Thai Airlines flight, bound for Sydney Airport. Charlie, at the time, was hoping to return to Kerikeri for another kiwifruit picking season but this would never eventuate.

11

Vive La France

After a sixteen-hour flight from Seoul (South Korea), the aircraft touched down at Charles De Gaulle Airport (Paris). The *highlight* of this tedious trip for Charlie was the viewing of the Siberian landscape. Courtesy of a window seat, he stared at the white desert – for hours and hours. Two years had passed since Charlie had last been on French soil.

After collecting his luggage from the carousel, Charlie made his way towards the Customs Clearance area. He had his Australian passport ready for inspection, but the customs official was only interested in seeing the disembarkation card. Charlie was then ushered through to the next section of the Arrivals terminal: Luggage Inspection. In this area, customs officials were only selecting a few people (at random) for a luggage inspection. The majority of the horde, including Charlie, just shuffled slowly through and several minutes later, they walked through an automatically-opened glass double-door. He was now in the passenger lounge of the terminal. Despite requiring a visa to enter France, Charlie had not been subjected to any form of passport inspection or luggage search!

After staying in a youth hostel that night, Charlie boarded an Orléans-bound train the next morning (Orléans is 132 kilometres south of Paris). After leaving the railway station, he walked to the southern outskirts of the city. The next phase of his 'life on the road' adventure was about to commence. Over the next four days, Charlie hitchhiked through the central regions of France, mostly in a southerly direction. His intended final destination was Ceret. Nestled in a valley, the commune (of Ceret) was located on the northern side of the Pyrenees Mountains, close to the Spanish border.

Similar to his hitchhiking adventures two years previously, Charlie slept out each night. The first night, he slept out in a paddock; the second night in a forest; and, the third night in an uninhabited hut. From Orléans to Ceret, Charlie obtained numerous lifts; the most memorable ones were from would-be *Grand Prix* drivers. He encountered the worst of them on the second day of hitchhiking!

Just after 1.00 pm, Charlie was hitchhiking near a large roundabout, on the outskirts of a small commune. A sports car manoeuvred through the roundabout at a relatively high speed and then veered towards Charlie. The motorist slammed on the brakes right beside him. As soon as he entered the vehicle, Charlie could only smell one thing: alcohol.

The middle-aged driver was of a burly build and sported a hairstyle similar to that of an Elvis Presley fan. Charlie suspected 'Elvis' had just left a nearby tavern. Due to too much sudden pressure being applied to the accelerator, the wheels of the sports car spun on the gravel surface and didn't stop until they made contact with the tar-sealed main road. A few seconds later, the vehicle was travelling over the allowable speed limit. Fortunately, the driver was only going to a village, 20 kilometres away.

Still travelling well above the speed limit, 'Elvis' overtook numerous cars until he came upon a line of seven vehicles. For the next several kilometres, the road was quite windy and there was no overtaking lane. The driver became increasingly agitated with being caught up behind traffic and Charlie was hoping that the alcohol-fuelled gentleman wouldn't do anything stupid!

Eventually, the line of vehicles entered a straight stretch of road which also contained a middle overtaking lane. Several vehicles moved into the middle lane to overtake the first vehicle. However, *Mr Impatient* decided to move into the far lane (three vehicles abreast) and overtook EVERY vehicle. Charlie turned his head to the right and briefly caught a glimpse of each vehicle being overtaken in both the middle and right lanes. When the vehicle returned to the correct side of the road, he turned his head and recommenced viewing the picturesque scenery in front of him and not a car in front of him. With a wide cheesy grin, 'Elvis' turned his head towards Charlie and uttered gravelly in English, 'No problem!'

Several minutes after the near heart-stopping incident, Charlie happily alighted from the vehicle. For the rest of the day, he obtained numerous short-distance lifts. In the late afternoon, Charlie obtained a lift with a police officer who had just finished his shift of employment. He was returning home, driving an early-1960s model Renault. Despite the occasional 'cough' and 'splutter', the vehicle still managed to move along the autoroute at a reasonable speed. The driver's physical appearance (his moustache, in particular) reminded Charlie of a well-known fictional character, *Inspector Clouseau*: the central character in The Pink Panther movie series.

Similar to his previous hitchhiking experiences in France, motorists enthusiastically pointed out to Charlie the various key landmarks in local areas, such as large, antiquated castles and historical buildings (e.g. churches/cathedrals). Once again, he was also treated to spectacular landscape viewing: notably lakes and mountains.

Instead of taking a relatively direct route to Ceret via the A75, Charlie decided to hitchhike along the D806 and then onto the N106: a scenic and mountainous route through the Cevennes region. Obtaining lifts along both roads was quite difficult at times. On several occasions, he had to wait several hours and the lifts he received tended to be of a short distance only. The breathtaking scenery throughout this mountainous region, however, greatly outweighed the slow progress of his hitchhiking efforts. It would take two days for Charlie to reach the outskirts of Montpellier from the commune of Saint-Chély-d'Apcher: a distance of 202 kilometres.

Interestingly enough, motorists automatically assumed that Charlie was English. Despite his inability to speak at a level of conversational French, he would still find a way to convey to the driver that he was Australian. Charlie had memorised the phrases, *Je suis Australien* ('I am Australian') and *Je viens d'Australie* ('I am from Australia'). Their excitable response each time led Charlie to believe that they were probably saying, 'You are a long way from home' or 'Australia is far, far away!'

One afternoon, just past the commune of Alès, Charlie received a lift from a middle-aged male. He was going to the city of Nimes, 45 kilometres away. The chatty motorist occasionally spoke a few words of English but mostly attempted to converse in French. Ten minutes into the journey, Charlie felt a sense of uneasiness, deeming the motorist's persona as somewhat 'odd'. His suspicions were confirmed a few minutes later. At one point during the conversation, the driver *insisted* that he should stay at his place for the night. An equally insistent Charlie, however, informed him that he would continue onwards to Montpellier. Then, the motorist *complimented* his 'nice blue eyes'. Memories of a similar incident, two years earlier, suddenly flashed back to Charlie!

The motorist then decided to play a cassette tape in the vehicle's audio system. The first English-sung song was basically about homosexual love! Charlie was now quite irate and soon had his 'trusty' flick-knife (fishing knife) in his right hand and was ready to inflict serious injury to the driver if he wasn't dropped off at a road junction near the outskirts of Nimes. Then, without warning, the driver turned into an industrial yard and drove behind a small warehouse. Charlie glared at him – and was ready to knife him. Nervously, the motorist stammered, 'Non-problem, non-problem' and alighted from his vehicle. Moments later, he was talking to several employees standing outside the warehouse. Judging by the puzzled expressions on the faces of the warehouse employees, Charlie thought to himself, 'What the hell is this clown doing?'

Several minutes later, the driver returned to his vehicle with a piece of cardboard (a torn flap of a cardboard box). Using a black texture, he wrote on the cardboard: 'Montpellier'. Charlie thought to himself, 'This guy has got a few screws loose up top!'

Ten minutes later, Charlie was dropped off at a road junction near the autoroute (A9). After waiting for a couple of hours, he eventually obtained a lift: one that took him a few kilometres south of the city of Montpellier. Charlie slept in a paddock that night. In the early afternoon of the following day, he arrived in the picturesque commune of Céret: located in the foothills of the Pyrenees Mountains. The view from the centre of the commune was simply breathtaking, dominated by the background setting of the (Pyrenees) mountains. Charlie soon located a nearby camping ground and pitched his tent. He would stay there for a week.

The next day, Charlie spent most of his time trying to locate cherry orchards which were within five kilometres of the camping ground. On one of the cherry orchards, there were five small huts and several Polish-registered vehicles. He approached a Polish couple, who was conversing with an elderly gentleman. Charlie politely enquired to whether there was any cherry-picking employment available on the orchard. The Polish woman spoke in French to the elderly orchardist and then relayed to Charlie in English that employment positions were still available. The cherry-picking season, however, wouldn't be starting until two or three weeks. The limited accommodation on the orchard, however, had already been filled. Céret is the first locality in France to harvest cherries. Recent cooler-than-average temperatures had delayed the commencement of this cherry-picking season.

Back at the camping ground, Charlie had befriended an elderly English couple. The retirees had been coming to Ceret every year for over a decade and usually stayed in the area between May and September. They confirmed that this year's cherry-picking season would commence later than normal. As a result, Charlie decided not to wait for the commencement of the cherry harvest as he knew the strawberry-picking season in the county of Kent (United Kingdom) would be commencing in 7-10 days.

Charlie stayed at the camping ground for a further five days, exploring the picturesque local environs and the *artistic* history of Ceret as well. The elderly English couple explained to him that Ceret had been a popular haven for numerous artists over the years; especially in the first half of the twentieth century. Pablo Picasso, Georges Braque and Chaim Soutine had lived in Ceret at one time. Other artists such as Henri Matisse, Aristide Maillol and others had formerly used Ceret as a meeting place.

On the day of his departure, Charlie walked to the north-eastern outskirts of Ceret and attempted to thumb a ride to the nearby city of Perpignan. After waiting for over an hour, a vehicle finally stopped to give him a lift. In Perpignan, he was drinking a shot glass of brandy and a large mug of coffee inside a café/tavern (near Perpignan Train Station), when the 'heavens' opened up well and truly. One of the patrons informed Charlie that torrential rain was forecasted in southern France for the rest of the day. Not wanting to stay in Perpignan, Charlie decided to purchase a train fare to Lyon: the third-largest city in France.

Just after 1.00 pm, Charlie boarded a Lyon-bound train. The first part of the rail journey was dominated by the rain pelting hard against the train's windows. Any view of the scenic countryside was thwarted by the inclement weather. After the train departed from *Gare d'Avignon Centre* (Avignon Railway Station) the treacherous weather conditions began to ease. A clear blue sky eventually emerged, albeit containing a few mild-mannered clouds. In stark contrast to the train journey between the cities of Perpignan and Avignon, Charlie was able to view the picturesque countryside throughout the rest of the rail journey.

Charlie stayed in a centrally-located youth hostel in Lyon that night. The next morning, he walked three kilometres to the north-western outskirts of the city and attempted to hitch a ride at a road junction which joined the autoroute (A6). Charlie soon obtained a lift but was only taken a few kilometres before being dropped off in front of a péage. Holding a sign (Paris), he waited for his next lift, along with five other hitchhikers. Just over half an hour later, a small vehicle displaying British number plates stopped beside Charlie. The driver was going all the way to northern Paris. English-born Lisa was returning to the French capital after spending the past few months working in a ski resort in the French Alps (near the French–Italian border).

Lisa's home base was in the commune of Saint-Denis, located in the northern suburbs of Paris. She dropped Charlie off at a road junction which was linked to the A15. By now, nightfall was slowly creeping in and he decided to seek nearby shelter. As Charlie casually strolled along a roadway, he passed through what could be best described as an 'affluent neighbourhood'. Mansion-filled estates dominated the landscape. As Charlie continued walking, he espied a suitable resting place for the night: a partially-hidden garden shed. It was nestled between several trees and high shrubs. The door of the garden shed was unlocked, so Charlie went inside. He placed his sleeping bag on top of the flattened two-person tent (on a concrete floor). Although Charlie slept fairly well, he was twice woken by bizarre and unfamiliar insect noises.

Just after 5.00 am the next morning, Charlie was on the road again. He had also written a new sign: Le Havre. His first lift of the day took him to the city of Rouen. From the south-western outskirts of Rouen, Charlie obtained several more lifts along autoroutes 13 and 131 and arrived at the port of Le Havre just after midday. A few hours later, he boarded the ferry bound for the port city of Portsmouth (United Kingdom). The ferry arrived at Portsmouth Port just after 9.00 pm. As the passengers passed through the customs area, Charlie would be the *only* person who would have to endure extensive questioning by customs officials as he didn't have a 'European' passport!

A customs official carefully perused through the pages of Charlie's 'well-used' passport and eventually noticed an expired work permit. After being asked what his travel plans were and how he was going to fund them, Charlie presented two wads of travellers' cheques: £2000 worth (in £20 denominations). However, only £1000 worth of traveller's cheques were legitimate! Before he left Australia, Charlie reported his original set (of traveller's cheques) as having been 'stolen' and, subsequently, they were replaced with a new set. Although the first set of travellers' cheques were worthless, he kept them – solely as a ploy to present to customs officials.

Twenty minutes later, Charlie passed through the exit door of the port terminal. After walking through the dark of the night for about forty minutes, he made his way down an embankment with the use of a small torch. Once on levelled ground, Charlie laid out his tent, placed the sleeping bag inside it and covered everything with the tent fly. The grassy area was well concealed by numerous shrubs. He slept well that night.

The next morning, Charlie walked towards the A27. After waiting for nearly two hours, he managed to obtain a lift. The vehicle travelled along the A27 and later along the M27, before dropping Charlie off at the northern outskirts of the city of Southampton. After walking through several villages (where each one bordered the next one), he eventually came upon a suitable place to recommence hitchhiking. For the next two days, Charlie hitchhiked along numerous A-roads and B-roads, eventually arrived at his final destination: the seaside resort of Ilfracombe (county of Devon). He would stay at Mal's place for the next eight days. The pair had worked together in New Zealand, two years previously.

12

The Bonnie Raspberries of Scotland

On a cool summer afternoon, Charlie arrived in the sleepy Scottish town of Blairgowrie. He had been hitchhiking from the northern outskirts of London the past two days. Blairgowrie is the larger of the former twin burghs: Blairgowrie and Rattray. A burgh is a former 'autonomous municipal corporation' in Scotland and Northern England.

By now, Charlie had less than twenty English pounds sterling left in his pocket. The need to obtain employment quickly was of the essence. At his previous place of employment (in the English county of Kent), one of Charlie's Polish co-workers provided him with the address of a raspberry farm located near Blairgowrie. Upon being dropped off in the centre of the town, he immediately walked to the farm: a journey of ten minutes.

After a brief discussion with a middle-aged Scottish local, a permanent employee of the raspberry farm (although other fruits were harvested there), Charlie was informed that all raspberry-picking positions had been filled – entirely by Eastern European students. The pleasant gentleman, however, informed him that there were still plenty of other employment opportunities within the area. He further added that licenced hotel premises in Blairgowrie would be excellent sources of information, regarding the upcoming raspberry-picking season.

With an aura of confidence, Charlie strutted back towards the town centre and entered the first hotel that he saw: The Unicorn. As Charlie ordered a beer, the barman uttered inquisitively, 'You're not from around here… are you!'

As Charlie sipped on a pint of Tennent's lager, he casually discussed the upcoming raspberry-picking season with the barman (George). After Charlie had purchased another pint, George decided to make a phone call. Several minutes later, Charlie was informed that he could commence employ-ment at a nearby raspberry farm the next day. Caravan accommodation was also provided for the raspberry pickers.

When he finished the second pint of lager, Charlie walked to the raspberry farm: a distance of less than half a mile (equivalent to about 800 metres) from the hotel. The raspberry farm was owned by an elderly spinster, Mrs Willis. As he arrived at the farm, two elderly women were engaged in an earnest conversation. Charlie introduced himself to Mrs Willis and he, in turn, was introduced to Lena: a local woman aged in her mid-sixties.

Lena was in charge of all the raspberry-picking operations. After a brief discussion, she directed Charlie to one of the caravans. At that stage, he had the caravan to himself but it was likely that he would be sharing with another person (or two people) within the next couple of days. This would be his home for the next two months. Although he would see Lena every day, Charlie rarely crossed paths with Mrs Willis, who tended to live a mostly-reclusive lifestyle.

The next morning, a large group of people gathered at a patch of raspberries, nearly 100 metres from the accommodation site. The patch consisted of numerous rows of relatively dense raspberry bushes. Each individual raspberry-picker was assigned two half rows: one made their way in between these two rows, picking ripened raspberries (only) on the first half of each line of bushes. After *plucking* the ripened raspberries off the bushes for an hour, Charlie realised that raspberry-picking was not going to be financially prosperous for him!

At the end of the first six-hour working day, Charlie had earned just over £8. To make the employment situation even worse, Lena had been trying to get everyone to pluck the raspberries off the bushes – gently. As she had small delicate hands, it was much easier for her to remove the raspberries properly from the bushes. Charlie quickly pointed out to Lena that his hands were much larger than hers and *plucking them off gently* was quite an unfair challenge. Lena replied with a wry smile, 'Charlie… just try your best!'

Although raspberry-picking would be 'financially challenging', the camaraderie that soon developed within the raspberry fields amounted to a mostly-enjoyable experience. By the second day, Charlie had decided to accept this experience as *paid outdoor exercise*. Lena, fortunately, was a lovely-natured woman who also possessed a sharp sense of humour. It appeared that she endeavoured to make each individual's experience on the raspberry farm an enjoyable one or at least a memorable one.

Lena's younger sister, Rita, was in charge of the 'weigh-in' area. The raspberry-pickers would bring their punnets of raspberries on a tray to the weighing station. Once a tray met the minimum weight condition, she would pay the individual in coins. Each raspberry-picker had been provided with a Bank of Scotland money bag: ideal for holding a substantial amount of coins. At the end of each working day, Charlie would empty the coins from the money bag onto his bed in the caravan and tally the day's earnings.

Similar to her sister, Rita was friendly and also had a keen sense of humour. Charlie would regularly share a laugh with her – especially when he was having his trays of raspberries being weighed. Rita would often quip, 'Are we having fun today?' Before Charlie could even respond, she would add, 'Now… can I please see your hands!'

Charlie's fingers were constantly red: a consequence of squashing some of the raspberries (which he tried to hide at the bottom of each punnet). On top of *every* tray, he would place a small amount of foliage (mainly leaves and the occasional small flower) on top of the punnets. A smiling Rita would 'scold' him as she gently brushed the unwanted foliage to the ground. Charlie, nevertheless, was paid for each tray delivered, providing it passed the 'weigh and presentation' test.

Being paid in coins instead of notes, however, soon irked the majority of the raspberry pickers – especially the Eastern European students. The students were trying to save money and were quite annoyed with all the coins! In stark contrast, Charlie had no qualms about being paid in coins. He routinely disposed of them at several places: at the supermarket, at takeaway food outlets and inside hotel establishments.

During the two-month raspberry picking season, none of the Eastern European students patronised any of the local hotels. The students would only part with some of their hard-earned coins at the local supermarket. As there were no refrigerators inside any of the campsite caravans, most individuals ventured to the supermarket at least three times a week.

At the supermarket checkouts, it was easy to tell who the raspberry-pickers were: grocery items were purchased with coins only. A large number of one-penny, two-penny and five-penny coins were unceremoniously dumped onto the counter for the checkout operator to count! Some checkout operators, however, would count the coins with astonishing speed and accuracy – plenty of previous experience – especially during the raspberry-picking season.

The grocery purchasing habits of the Eastern European students were uncannily similar to the 'low-budget' backpackers that Charlie had encountered on previous travelling adventures. Generic brands of bread, instant noodle packs, baked beans and bargained-priced vegetables dominated the shopping list. Any type of meat products (except spam) was generally regarded as a *luxury* item and were seldom purchased.

As the raspberry-picking season progressed, being paid in coins became a major issue and the Eastern European students (in particular) began to pressure Lena into exchanging large collections of coins for banknotes. On Wednesday afternoon, during the sixth week of the season, Lena calmly announced to the raspberry pickers that a designated time for a 'coin-to-note swap' had been approved: 2.00 pm on Friday. But there were several conditions though: coins could only be swapped for £5 notes; each individual had to write their name on the list within the next twenty-four hours; and, state how many £5 notes they required.

The next afternoon, Lena noticed that Charlie's name was absent from the list. With a stern look on her face, she exclaimed to him: 'I better put your name on the list… you'll miss out!'

Charlie responded, 'No need to… if I don't spend all my coins at the supermarket, I'll spend them at the hotel!' An undeterred Lena, however, still added his name to the list – and four £5 notes.

At precisely 2.00 pm on Friday, Mrs Willis (in one of her rare public appearances) drove to the entrance of the campsite – in a Rolls Royce. The elderly spinster then took out a well-used, school-like brown port and two large plastic buckets from the boot/trunk of her vehicle. The port contained the banknotes and the buckets were to be used for the *coin collection*. The Eastern Europeans, in particular, had been eagerly awaiting her arrival! Lena's first task, however, was to organise them into that great British tradition – the queue.

Initially, Charlie decided to just loiter peacefully in the background. With arms folded, he was enjoying the priceless entertainment unravelling before his eyes – the concept of queuing seemed to bamboozle most of the Eastern Europeans. Visibly frustrated, Lena and Rita urgently required assistance. Several raspberry-picking families from the Scottish town of Airdrie were also residing on the campsite. Three middle-aged and heavily tattooed Airdrie males (along with Charlie) stepped in to provide *security* for the two ladies.

Mrs Willis, meanwhile, was inside her vehicle and (presumably) with the doors locked! After a fair amount of 'jostling and jockeying' for positions, the queue was finally established. Several Ukrainian males had made the situation more difficult than it needed to be: they tried to push their way towards the front of the queue – even attempting to shove their way in front of several female students. The Airdrie lads and Charlie, however, soon intervened and 'physically encouraged' the errant males to move to the end of the queue.

Within an hour, the 'coin-for-note exchange' frenzy was over. The two buckets were now nearly filled with coins and were soon placed in the boot of Mrs Wallis' Rolls Royce by two of the Airdrie males. She hastily drove off. It would be the last time that Charlie would see her.

The two-month raspberry-picking season would not be financially rewarding for Charlie. He still, nevertheless, enjoyed the pleasant camaraderie on the strawberry fields and outside work hours, Charlie experienced a thriving social life. Throughout the season, employment was quite sporadic at times. The unpredictable Scottish summer weather resulted in a few days being 'washed out' and late starting times were a regular occurrence. The raspberries, in general, needed to be dry before being plucked off the bushes. Throughout July and August (of this particular year) there was an overall lack of sunshine. Welcome to summer in Scotland!

Life in the raspberry fields, aforementioned, was mostly of a relaxed and harmonious nature. The actual work itself was not physically taxing. Charlie would regularly converse with his fellow raspberry-pickers as he 'gently' plucked the fruit from the bushes. All-day long, Lena would wander up and down each row, ensuring that a minimum standard of raspberry-picking *etiquette* was met. She would also pick a punnet (or two) of raspberries for each raspberry-picker.

The repetitive nature of raspberry-picking would create a level of intolerable tedium at times and especially for the younger raspberry-pickers. Local teenagers and the youngsters from Airdrie attempted to alleviate the monotonous nature of the work via a *raspberry war* where raspberries were casually lobbed over the bushes and the aim was for the fruit to harmlessly land on someone's head. Then the situation would escalate and within a relatively short period, the 'raspberry war' had attracted more participants. A much larger volume of raspberries was now being hurled back and forth over the bushes. The escapade, however, was short-lived. Lena's booming voice would soon be heard. 'Ok, that's enough… back to work!'

Lena would then casually stroll up to the main instigators and exclaim, 'Having fun are we… not long to go now!' The defiant youngsters, however, denied that they were the instigators – even attempting to blame the Eastern European students. With a glint in her eye, Lena would just gaze and smile at them. For the next 10-15 minutes, though, she would stay nearby, keeping a firm eye on the restless youngsters.

At the end of the second week of the season, Charlie still had the caravan to himself. Several campsite dwellers, however, would visit his temporary abode on an almost daily basis. One of them was a young Spanish student: Conchita. One Friday evening, he met up with several people (including Conchita) inside the Unicorn Hotel. Later in the evening, in a separate room, a DJ was playing music. On several occasions, Conchita tried to coax Charlie to dance with her. He detested dancing but once Charlie had reached a certain level of 'social inebriation', he finally gave in and thus, danced with her for several songs.

After the hotel had closed, the group made their way back to the campsite. A slow-walking Conchita chatted incessantly with Charlie and they soon lagged well behind the rest of the group. As the pair approached a raspberry field, a hundred metres from the camping area, she grabbed his arm and swung Charlie around so that he was facing her directly. Moments later, the pair was enthusiastically engaged in a 'kiss and cuddle' session between two of the rows of the raspberry field! Ten minutes later, Charlie suggested to Conchita that they should go back to his caravan. Inside the caravan, the kissing and cuddling soon evolved into a session of *jig, jig, push, push*. The next day, she moved into the caravan and stayed with him for the next six weeks.

Throughout the raspberry-picking season, around 8.00 am each morning, Lena would knock on the door of each caravan. She would inform the occupants to whether they would be working that day or not and a possible starting time. On numerous occasions, the picking wouldn't commence until at least 10.00 am. If there was persistent rainfall in the morning, however, the day would be declared a 'washout'. Conchita and Charlie relished any days off and didn't leave the caravan.

In the last week of August, the raspberry-picking season came to a halt. Two days later, Charlie farewelled Conchita. She was returning to Spain. He remained in Scotland for a further week. Nine months later, Charlie met up with her in the northern Spanish city of Zaragoza. Three weeks earlier, he had received a financial boost: an Australian tax refund cheque worth just over £400. The windfall improved Charlie's financial position significantly as he had only saved £20 from the two-month raspberry picking venture!

As the commencement of the apple-picking season in the English county of Kent was still two weeks away, Charlie decided to spend a week exploring other regions of Scotland. After bidding farewell to Conchita, he boarded a Perth-bound bus the next morning. Charlie stayed in a youth hostel for the next two nights. On the third day, he walked to the north-western outskirts of the city and commenced hitchhiking at the start of the A85. His intended destination was the village of Crianlarich: 85 km west of Perth. After several lifts, Charlie arrived in Crianlarich in the late-afternoon.

After staying in the SYHA youth hostel overnight, Charlie hitchhiked to the town of Fort William: the gateway to Ben Nevis (the highest mountain in the British Isles). In the centre of Fort William, scores of tourists had practically 'flooded' the area. He entered a hotel and ordered a meal. An hour later, Charlie was attempting to hitch his next ride with a protruding left thumb and holding a sign which read 'Inverness'.

Charlie arrived in the city of Inverness in the late afternoon. After a short stroll from the CBD, he located a campsite dominated by a large number of tent-dwellers. At the entrance of the campsite, read a large sign: 'Tent Area is full'. An annoyed Charlie decided not to seek any other type of accommodation and instead walked in a northerly direction towards the Kessock Bridge. After walking across the bridge (also part of the A9), he came across a woodlands area on the eastern side of the roadway. As nightfall was creeping in, Charlie disappeared into the woodlands and set up a makeshift camp for the night.

The next morning, just after 6.00 am, Charlie was on the side of the A9 attempting to hitch his first ride for the day. Five minutes later, a vehicle stopped beside him and he was on his way to the northern region of Scotland. After several short lifts on the A9, a travelling vacuum-cleaner salesman (Angus) stopped to give Charlie a lift. Angus would eventually take him to the coastal village of Tongue.

Along the way, Angus stopped in the towns of Wick and Thurso (and in the village of John o' Groats as well). In both Wick and Thurso, he dropped Charlie off at a hotel and returned half an hour later. In the village of John o' Groats (one of the most northerly points of Great Britain), the pair had a luncheon meal in one of the hotels. After lunch, Angus had an appointment with a potential client, so Charlie filled in his time by wandering about within the local area. One of the landmarks that he viewed was *Journey's End* signpost. Angus eventually returned and he drove Charlie to the village of Tongue.

After farewelling Angus, Charlie went looking for Tongue's lone youth hostel, only to discover that it was closed. As he consumed a couple of pints inside the village's only hotel, he discovered that there were no other budget accommodation options. Charlie left the hotel and casually strolled away from the village in a southerly direction. Less than a mile outside Tongue, he decided to ascend an area of hilly terrain.

Halfway up the hill, Charlie came upon a flat piece of terrain, partially surrounded by several trees. He set up camp for the night by unravelling the sleeping bag and placing it inside the tent which was laid flat on the ground. After getting inside his sleeping bed, he next had to contend with a large swarm of highland midges! Waving his arms frenetically, Charlie eventually managed to clear the swarm and then covered everything with the tent fly. Somewhat surprisingly, he managed to sleep right through the night undisturbed. Early the next morning, Charlie emerged from beneath the tent fly – instantly 'greeted' by a swarm of midges. He thought, 'These patient little bastards have been waiting all night for this moment!'

Charlie quickly loaded his backpack and proceeded to make his way down the hill. On the roadway, he attempted to thumb his first lift for the day. For the next several hours, Charlie tried to hitchhike away from Tongue along this road (it had no name) which passed by the historical Ribigill Farm. His original plan was to hitchhike along various roads in the northwest regions of Scotland, eventually returning to the town of Fort William. Whilst he waited patiently for several hours, only five cars drove past – all with 'continental' number plates.

Succumbing to an obvious defeat, a reluctant Charlie trundled back through the village of Tongue and onwards to the A836. He decided to hitchhike back to the town of Thurso. Grey clouds were rapidly becoming darker and the light of the day was now much dimmer. Near the A836, Charlie noticed an abandoned hut and he hastily made his way there. Several minutes later, the skies well and truly opened up and heavy torrential rain immediately followed.

The torrential rain persisted for several hours. Charlie passed the time away by reading one of several books he had in his backpack. The sunshine eventually broke through the clouds and Charlie once more, attempted to thumb his first ride for the day. Twenty minutes later, a motorist stopped and gave him a lift. The middle-aged driver, however, was only going to the nearby village of Strathy. He stopped in front of the Strathy Inn and invited Charlie to join him inside the hotel.

Several pints later, Charlie was on the road again, trying to thumb his next lift. The copious amount of alcohol, though, had made him quite sleepy! Half an hour later, a vehicle with Polish number plates stopped and gave Charlie a lift. The three occupants were two siblings (brother and sister) and their mother. They were going to the town of Thurso. Charlie chatted incessantly to the siblings – mainly as a means of trying to stay awake. The siblings were living and working in the English county of Kent. They were on a holiday break and thus, providing a guided tour for their mother throughout Scotland and England. The pair spoke fluent English and regularly translated to their mother in Polish. As Charlie was sharing his employment experiences in Kent with them, the siblings' mum was curious to know why he smelled strongly of alcohol! Charlie was sharing the back seat with *matka*. She also wanted to know why he was in this particular area.

An exuberant Charlie recounted his previous night's battles with the highland midges on the side of a hill near the village of Tongue. Then, he discussed today's events: the unsuccessful attempt to hitchhike southwards from Tongue; sheltering in an abandoned hut during the morning torrential downpour; and, the several inebriating hours at the Strathy

Inn. The bemused siblings were trying not to laugh but when they translated Charlie's anecdotes to their mother, her tearful laughter soon triggered a similar response!

After Charlie was dropped off in Thurso, he immediately sought a café. Charlie hadn't eaten since the moment he woke up. It was now 4.00 pm. In front of the café entrance, a car with Belgian number plates was illegally parked on the footpath. The two occupants of the vehicle were sitting at a table, located just inside the café. Charlie ordered a meal and sat at a table. As he waited for his food to arrive, the Belgian male suddenly decided to light up a cigarette. There were several large signs within the café clearly stating: 'No Smoking'. An irate female staff member immediately confronted him about the *no smoking* policy within the café. He tried to ignore her and continued to puff away on his cigarette. In an instant fit of anger, she yanked the cigarette out of his mouth and extinguished it on the table in front of him!

Less than five minutes later, a police officer placed a *parking violation* ticket under the windscreen wipers of the illegally-parked vehicle. Then the officer entered the café and politely asked the Belgian male if he wanted to pay the fine now. Visibly irate, he shook his head angrily and steadfastly refused to move his illegally parked car. Three minutes later, a tow truck arrived and towed the vehicle to a vacant parking spot, across the road from the café. A contemptuous, smug smirk instantly appeared on the Belgian man's face but that quickly vanished when a wheel clamp was affixed to one of the wheels of his vehicle!

Charlie arrived in Inverness in the early evening. In fading light, he pitched his tent up inside the camping ground that was 'tent-full' several days earlier. After staying in Inverness for two nights, Charlie hitchhiked (for two days) on the A9 and several motorways, heading towards the English coastal town of Blackpool. He arrived there in the late afternoon. Two hours later, Charlie was in a hotel conversing with three women: Jill, Betty and Lisa. Two years earlier, he had worked with them in the northern New Zealand town of Kerikeri.

During his one-week stay in Blackpool, Charlie stayed at Betty's place. At the time, the tourist season (in Blackpool) was in full swing. The *tackiness* of the carnival-like seaside resort was of little appeal to him; especially along the promenade. He did, however, enjoy the coastal town's thriving nightlife scene. Charlie socialised with the three ladies and their friends every night during his stay.

On Sunday, Charlie was given a guided tour of the nearby historical city of Lancaster. He was accompanied by the three ladies and two of their friends in Lisa's minivan. Firstly, they stopped at Clitheroe castle. Next stop: a view of the outside of Lancaster Castle (it was still being used as a prison at the time). After consuming a traditional hotel Sunday Roast, the group then ventured into the Lakes District, exploring the

Cumbrian towns of Windermere and Ambleside. They returned to Blackpool in the late evening.

After bidding farewell to his Blackpool friends on Wednesday morning, Betty dropped Charlie off at a road junction near the M55. The apple-picking season in Kent was to commence within the next several days. With a sign (M6) and a protruding left thumb, he received his first lift after waiting for about forty minutes. Staying mostly on the motorways (M6, M1, M25 and M20), Charlie arrived at Broadacre Wood Farms in the early evening.

Just outside the office, he was greeted by the orchard manager (Colin). After a brief chat, Charlie pitched his tent in the camping area in dwindling daylight. The area was largely occupied by New Age Travellers, dwelling in their refurbished 'ice-cream' vans. By now, his finances had dwindled to less than £20. Fortunately, the apple-picking season was commencing in two days.

13

East of Amsterdam and
The Polska Expedition

After staying overnight in a Christian-run hostel, located just outside Amsterdam's red-light district, Charlie casually strolled towards the outskirts of the city the next morning. It was the third week in October. Just over an hour later, he attempted to hitch a lift along a roadway which, in turn, would take him onto the *autosnelweg* (A1). After waiting for a quarter of an hour, Charlie obtained a lift that would take him towards the Netherlands-German border.

Charlie was attempting to hitchhike to the northwestern Polish city of Szczecin, via the German city of Lübeck. In Lübeck, he would meet up with Geoff, who had been residing in the city the past three years. The former friends had known each other from their 'institution' days in Sydney (Australia). Charlie arrived in the city on the third day of hitchhiking.

On the first night (before arriving in Lübeck), Charlie had slept out near a village, a few kilometres from the Netherlands-German border. On the second night, he camped out in a woodlands area, 40 kilometres south of the large

German city of Hamburg. After hiding his luggage and camping gear, Charlie walked to a nearby autobahn (Bundesautobahn 1) services centre. Before entering the services centre café, he had to walk past a group of leather jacket-wearing Neo-Nazis. The inebriated and obnoxious individuals leered at Charlie and, in a gruff manner, started talking to him. He politely responded (using basic German) that they speak to him in English.

A rotund, bespectacled and leather-cladded *Neanderthal* with several swastikas on his leather jacket, then responded to Charlie (in English), immediately enquiring to why he was in this particular area. Unperturbed, Charlie falsely replied that he was staying at a friend's place in a nearby village. Even before any verbal exchange had taken place, Charlie sensed that they were wondering whether he was a Turkish migrant or not. At that particular time, there had been numerous horrific crimes committed towards the Turkish community by extremist far right-wing groups. For example, many houses had been torched – even with the occupants still inside.

Charlie decided to stay in the café until the *uncouth barbarians* got back in their cars and left the vicinity. Afterwards, he cautiously made his way back to the woodlands. Charlie gathered his belongings and decided to relocate further into the forested area. By now, the temperature had dropped significantly. When he woke up the next morning, the ground was covered with a mild frost. A short time later, Charlie was at the services centre, attempting to obtain his first lift for the day. Five minutes later, he was in a vehicle travelling along the autobahn. The motorist, upon learning that Charlie had slept out in the woodlands the previous night, informed him that the overnight temperature had dropped to a minimum of -2 degrees!

Charlie arrived in Lübeck just before midday. He obtained a local map from the *Touristen-Informationszentrum* (Tourist Information Centre) and soon located Geoff's place of residence. Over the next few days, Charlie spent a good part of his time exploring the sights of Lübeck and its nearby environs on one of Geoff's (several) bicycles. Throughout the city and surrounding areas, bicycle paths were abundant. On the sixth day, Charlie farewelled Geoff and walked to the south-eastern outskirts of Lübeck. Half an hour, he obtained his first lift for the day. Just a few kilometres to the east of Lübeck was the former East German border. As the motorist drove along the A20, he sarcastically quipped to Charlie, 'Guess where the border with East Germany used to be!'

It was easy to determine where the wire-fenced borders use to be – the landscape revealed everything. An invisible line divided the luscious green fields (former West Germany) from a landscape that could be best described as *downtrodden* (former East Germany). On the western side of the divide, the landscape was well-organised (evidently worked with high-tech modern farm machinery) and quite picturesque. The eastern side, however, was in a pitiful state of dilapidation.

An hour later, Charlie was dropped off in a small town, still largely impacted by the scarred remnants of the ex-communist state legacy. Grey and drab-looking cement buildings (many in a ruinous state of decline) were plentiful. In stark contrast, **Lübeck** was largely dominated by picturesque and *cheerful* modern styles of architecture. Charlie walked through the town until he came upon an entrance road to the Bundesautobahn 20 (A20). As Charlie patiently waited for his next lift over the next two hours, he was quite intrigued by the numerous antiquated East German-made (and the occasional Soviet-made Ladas) cars that passed by – especially the Trabants. Eventually, a vehicle did stop in front of him: an early-1960s model Trabant station wagon.

Throughout the day, Charlie did manage to obtain several more lifts along the A20. A major problem, though, was communication difficulties between the motorist and himself. Each driver's level of spoken English was quite limited at times. Charlie's level of spoken German, unfortunately, was even worse! In former West Germany, fluent English was widely spoken.

Charlie slept out that night in an area best described as a large block of 'communal allotment gardens' (at least a hundred in total). These wired-enclosed *miniature orchards* were just outside the town of Prenzlau (located sixty kilometres south-east of the city of Neubrandenburg and forty kilometres away from the German-Polish border). After climbing over two wired-fences and passing through two gated entrances, he set up a makeshift-camp between several small fruit trees. In future travels, he would encounter numerous communal allotment gardens (mostly throughout Poland), numbering in the hundreds or even more than a thousand.

Just after midday the following day, Charlie arrived at the Germany-Poland border on the A11. This particular border was located about ten kilometres west of the Polish city of Szczecin. There was a long queue of motor vehicles waiting to enter Poland. However, the line of trucks/lorries queue was *much* longer. He would later learn that truck/lorry drivers could wait up to two days before being allowed to enter into Poland from Germany!

An hour and a half would elapse before the vehicle that Charlie had hitched a ride in was allowed entry into Poland. The Polish military officials controlling the border were satisfied with his Polish visa and correctly-filled entry card, completed in *both* English and Polish. A short time later, Charlie was dropped off in central Szczecin. At the railway station, he purchased a rail fare to the city of Gdynia. The train was going via the city of Koszalin. Before boarding, Charlie decided to buy food and a drink from a kiosk. He gave the peroxide-blonde, middle-aged woman a 500,000 złoty note (now equivalent to the new 50 złoty banknote). She attempted to give him change only for a 50,000 złoty note!

A calm Charlie held his hand out and speaking in limited Polish, insisted he had been short-changed. The woman pretended she didn't understand what Charlie was trying to say to her. A suit-wearing gentleman standing nearby, however, intervened and started yelling at her. She promptly returned the correct change and Charlie thanked the man. *"Dziękuję Bardzo"* (thank you so much) and the gentleman replied in English, 'You're very welcome!'

Half an hour later, Charlie was standing on the platform waiting for the Koszalin-bound train. A sign, attached to the roof read 'KOS' but the time of departure was three minutes earlier than what was printed on the rail ticket. After the train had stopped, he politely asked the train guard, *'Pociąg do Koszalin* (train to Koszalin)?' In a pitiful response, the agitated train guard just nodded and then looked away. From the moment the train left the platform, Charlie had the uneasy feeling that he was on the wrong train: it should have been going in an easterly direction – not in a southerly direction.

Charlie's suspicions were soon confirmed when the ticket inspector, fifteen minutes later, requested to see his train ticket. The train was going to Kosztryn! At the next stop (fifteen kilometres from Szczecin), he alighted from the train. For the next two hours, Charlie walked back towards

Szczecin. Eventually, he came across a *przystanek autobusowy* (bus stop) and a short time later, boarded the *autobus* (bus). Fortunately, it was going directly to the central railway station in Szczecin.

In the late evening, Charlie boarded an overnight Koszalin-bound train. Just after midnight, he alighted from the train at Koszalin railway station and, subsequently, waited several hours for the connecting Gdynia-bound train. Charlie managed to gain a couple of hours of sleep on a wide, wooden bench. Other people were either waiting for a train or were homeless. Several military personnel (armed with sub-machine guns) patrolled the railway station.

The Gdynia-bound train eventually arrived at the platform. As all the carriage compartments appeared to be full, Charlie spent the next several hours in the corridor, along with many other passengers. He sat on top of his backpack the entire trip. Alas, no more sleep for him that night! Young military personnel regularly walked up and down the corridors of each carriage. The train arrived in Gdynia just as dawn emerged. As Charlie hadn't eaten for the past twelve hours, he quickly located an opened kiosk and purchased two *zapiekankas* (an open-faced sandwich with various toppings). Two hours later, Charlie was aboard a bus, bound for the town of Kartuzy. He was meeting up with Tadeusz (Taddy), who he had previously worked with on an orchard in the English county of Kent. At the bus stop in central Kartuzy, Charlie was greeted by Taddy and his wife, Janina (Jane).

Fifteen minutes later, Charlie was inside a large two-storey house and was being introduced to Taddy's extended family: his young daughter (Barbara); his two younger sisters; his mother; and, his grandmother. During his ten-day stay, he spent a fair amount of time in the nearby city of Gdansk (33 kilometres from Kartuzy) as Taddy worked in the city from Monday to Friday. Each working day, Charlie would be a passenger in his *samochód* (car/automobile). He spent most of these daily trips just gazing through the passenger-side window, eyeing the countryside and village architecture. Charlie avoided looking straight ahead as Taddy was quite an erratic driver and had scant regard for road rules. He drove well over the speed limit, overtook car after car and, constantly swore at slower-driving motorists in front of him. And then there were the pedestrians. If people were crossing a pedestrian crossing, Taddy would blast the vehicle's horn and not slow down or stop. He emphatically explained to Charlie, 'Roads are for cars… not people!'

Taddy further insisted that pedestrian crossings should be re-named *road decorations*. During Charlie's five-week stay in Poland, he would regularly witness the overzealous practice of a motorist flashing the vehicle's headlights/high beam and overuse of the vehicle's horn at people who dared to cross these 'road decorations'! He felt sorry for the elderly who often had to scurry across a pedestrian crossing. A standard reaction of the elderly (or hapless) pedestrians commonly involved the raising and shaking of fists at the ill-mannered motorist, accompanied with quite a few 'colourful' Polish swear words and phrases!

The city of Gdansk, at the time, was largely a sad remnant of the time-warped Communist regime. It was one of a distinct and depressing grey colour, largely dominated by concrete buildings and cemented paths. The gloomy, wintery, grey skyline further exacerbated the overall scene. The shipyards were even less inspiring. As a tourist, Charlie felt that the city offered little except for the numerous bustling coffee houses. He filled in most of his day with long bouts of ambulation and numerous visits to coffee shops. By the late afternoon, Charlie looked forward to the return trip to Kartuzy.

Charlie was still in the town of Kartuzy when *Dzień Zaduszny/Zaduszki* (All Souls Day) was celebrated on the 2nd of November. Throughout Poland, the deceased are remembered in a solemn festival-like manner. Packed with large crowds, the local cemeteries are aglow with thousands of candles. In Kartuzy, there was a distinct silent and sombre mood throughout the streets and in the cemetery on this day. It was a time of silent prayers and thoughts of positive reminiscence. All business activity was closed on this day.

On the day of his departure, Charlie was farewelled by Tadeusz and Janina at *Gdańsk Główny* (Gdansk's main railway station). Five hours later, he arrived at *Warszawa Centralna* (Warsaw's Central railway station). After alighting from the *pociąg* (train), Charlie walked along the station platform and then up a flight of stairs. As he trundled slowly up the stairs with his unique-styled backpack (one that was noticeably different from the standard Polish backpack) and a medium-sized sports bag, he was harassed (along with other train passengers) by over-eager Russian immigrants. Occupying a single step, each middle-aged or elderly Russian desperately tried to sell a range of wares: typically shawls, scarves and ties.

Halfway up the stairway, Charlie made the mistake of responding to several of the Russians in Polish and they immediately seized upon his non-Polish accent! As he made his way up the remaining set of steps, Charlie was aggressively jostled – especially by the tactless, ageing *babushkas* (grandmothers). He managed to keep moving albeit with a lot of help from the *Varsovians* (Warsaw natives), eventually making it to the top of the stairway and onto the thoroughfare/street of *aleje Jerozolimskie* (Jerusalem Avenue).

Situated along aleje Jerozolimskie (al. Jerozolimskie) and close to the central railway station, stood a sizeable market area comprising mostly of food kiosks. Newly-arrived capitalism at the time was quite evident in central Warsaw.

As Charlie walked along the thoroughfare, Americanism dominated the general panoramic view. Large and flashing neon billboards advertised many well-known American companies: Taco Bell, McDonald's, KFC, etc. He would stay in Warsaw for two weeks at a budget-priced hostel where the cost of accommodation was much less than what one would pay in Western Europe (e.g. Germany).

Charlie, initially, adopted a cynical approach to the over-supply of food kiosks near the central railway station. Nevertheless, he soon became a frequent visitor and developed quite a healthy 'addiction' to the different types of *zapiekankas* (open-faced sandwiches) available. During his stay in Warsaw, Charlie never ate at any of the American-styled food outlets; he preferred the local cafes, restaurants and kiosks instead.

Whilst staying at a *Schronisko Młodzieżowe* (youth hostel), Charlie was informed by fellow backpackers of the popular and thriving (and cheap) university-owned 'soup kitchens' throughout Warsaw. Every morning, he would have a breakfast meal inside one of these eateries. Although the menu (typically posted on a large blackboard) was written in Polish, Charlie translated the food items into English, courtesy of a Polish-English phrasebook. As the mostly middle-aged/elderly soup-kitchen staff did not speak any English (or only a limited amount), he *always* ordered his meal in Polish. If Charlie's pronunciation wasn't correct, he would be instantly corrected by some staff members, in a (mostly) pleasant and light-hearted manner. These experiences in the soup kitchens enabled Charlie to learn the proper pronunciation rules of written Polish. The strange letter combinations of many Polish words now made more sense to him.

Charlie spent a sizeable portion of most days by walking throughout the suburbs of Warsaw viewing numerous landmarks and exploring numerous eateries (along with coffee shops and bars). Although the city provided an extensive tram service, he rarely used it. Not far from the *Stare Miasto* (old town), Charlie even discovered a tavern that sold imported Australian Foster's beer!

Whilst staying in Warsaw, Charlie reacquainted himself with several people who he had worked with in recent fruit-picking seasons in the county of Kent (United Kingdom): Agnieszka, Tomasz and Marcin. He met up with Agnieszka and Tomasz on two separate occasions. Marcin, however, lived in the town of Piaseczno: 16 kilometres south of Warsaw. Charlie managed to catch up with him one day using a tram service to and from the town.

At the youth hostel, Charlie soon struck up a temporary friendship with a few of the other backpackers. Together, they explored various landmarks and frequented eateries/cafes/bars. Inside a soup kitchen one morning, two female backpackers (an American and an Australian who were travelling together) recounted a harrowing experience to Charlie that had occurred to them several days earlier.

The hapless ladies had been victims of luggage theft on one of the 'tourist' trains: an overnight rail journey from Berlin to Warsaw. The pair had a carriage compartment to themselves. The compartment comprised of two long bench seats which meant that each of them had a 'comfortable bed' to sleep on. Their luggage was chained to these bench seats. In the morning, just as the rays of sunlight began to beam through the small compartment windows, they both woke up feeling 'heavy-headed' – and their luggage was gone. The chains had been cut; probably with bolt-cutters. The pair soon realised that they may have been 'chloroformed' (a cloth pressed against their faces) during the night. The American woman, with the assistance of military personnel at Warsaw's Central Railway station, managed to locate some of her clothing (but not her backpack). The Australian woman, unfortunately, lost everything.

Both of the women, fortunately, still had their passports and money belts secured inside the clothing they were wearing. The pair were soon arranging for replacement backpacks and clothing items to be sent over by relatives or friends. In the meantime, they decided to purchase basic items of clothing (underwear, socks, etc) at one of Warsaw's daily open-markets.

Inside the youth hostel, Charlie shared a room with five others, including two young American males who were former school friends. As he conversed with them, Charlie soon realised that the pair seem to be quite naïve when it came to 'global travelling'. They complained about being harassed as they walked along the streets; especially by Russian peddlers/hawkers and Romanian gipsies (the latter were generally begging for money).

One afternoon, the three of them were walking about in central Warsaw. The American lads each carried a camera attached to a cord around their neck and wore money belts *outside* their clothing. Standing in front of a landmark, the pair 'gawked in amazement' and took numerous photographs. Charlie, meanwhile, tried to adopt a more conservative approach to sightseeing and attempted to 'blend in' with the local population. He suggested to the pair that they should refrain from speaking in English when in the presence of peddlers/hawkers or begging gipsies. Their booming American accents instantly attracted unwanted attention from these groups of people!

One morning, Charlie managed to persuade the young American males to join him for a breakfast meal inside one of the soup kitchens. Upon seeing the breakfast menu written in Polish, however, the pair wanted to go to a McDonald's restaurant! Charlie quickly reassured them that he had *mastered* the translation process. With his trusty Polish-

English phrasebook in his hand, Charlie soon translated all the menu items into English. Somewhat reluctant, they decided to stay. After finishing their respective meals, the pair admitted they were quite impressed with the quality of the food and at a much cheaper price (compared to the American-based fast-food outlets).

As they ate their breakfast meal, the pair discussed with Charlie their upcoming travel plans. In two weeks, they were planning on hitchhiking throughout Sweden and Norway. It was mid-November! Gobsmacked, he calmly informed the novice travellers that this was the wrong time of the year for extensive outdoor travelling as the weather conditions would mostly be less than ideal. Another important aspect they had not considered was the significant reduction in daylight hours, especially in the northern regions of these Scandinavian countries. Charlie sensed that the two lads were well 'cashed-up' but the phrase *too many dollars but not enough sense (cents)* soon entered his mind!

Charlie departed from Warsaw's central railway just before midnight, boarding an economy-fared train to *Kraków Główny* (Krakow Main) railway station. At Krakow's main railway station, he would meet up with Helena who he had previously worked with on an orchard in the county of Kent (United Kingdom). Charlie was the sole occupant of a carriage compartment for a good part of the journey and sat upright on the bench seat. With his right foot positioned behind one of the sliding doors, he would close his eyes and drift off into a partial slumber. If someone moved the sliding door, Charlie would be woken up. For extra personal security, he also dozed with one hand in a coat pocket, clutching his trusty 'flick' knife in readiness for any possible assault.

Halfway into the train journey, a passenger entered the compartment. Before sitting down, he turned up the heater temperature. Charlie alighted from his bench seat and turned the temperature back down to its former position and informed the passenger, '*Jest zbyt gorąco* (it's too hot).' Several minutes later, the passenger alighted from his seat and turned the temperature back up. Charlie responded immediately and turned the (temperature) dial back down again. The temperature inside the compartment was already quite warm. He suspected that the passenger may not be Polish and was well aware of Russian criminals robbing people on trains. For the next few minutes, the young, wiry-built passenger would regularly peer and smirk in Charlie's direction. Eventually, a tired and irritable Charlie eyeballed him and took the knife out of his coat pocket and blurted out, '*O co chodzi* (What's the matter)?' The passenger's attitude suddenly mellowed and he didn't dare touch the temperature control for the remainder of his trip!

Charlie arrived at *Kraków Główny* railway station just after 6.00 am. Alighting from the train, he walked on the platform and through the lone exit. A few metres away, stood a quirky and diminutive lady: a smiling Helena. The petite young woman (with a physical stature of 1.45 metres tall) had also brought two female friends with her. Putting down his luggage, Charlie lifted her off the ground and the pair embraced passionately – much to the amusement of her two companions. He would stay in Kraków for the next nine days.

Helena was studying at Jagiellonian University, majoring in English literature. On several occasions, Charlie accompanied her to the English language/grammar tutorials. The tutorials were solely conducted in English. He was quite intrigued by the verbal discussion between the students and their tutor: a mixture of Polish, English and American accents. Edyta, the class tutor, spoke fluent English but with a localised accent. Charlie, along with Helena, had several discussions with her after each tutorial. At one point, Edyta even asked him if he would like to work as a tutor at the university; she could easily understand his 'refined' Australian accent. Charlie politely declined as he was en route to Greece where the weather would be much warmer.

Jarek (one of Helena's male friends) would be Charlie's 'tourist guide' for the duration of his nine-day stay in Kraków. He was close to completing his degree and only attended the university two days a week. The pair soon discovered that they had a mutual fascination for general history. Jarek's detailed historical knowledge of Kraków's landmarks was extensive and Charlie was quite grateful for his intrinsic insights. The city emerged at the end of the Second World War virtually unscathed. Kraków boasted numerous museums, art galleries, churches/cathedrals and castles; many of them centuries old. Throughout the day, the guided tour would be interrupted several times, courtesy of visits to coffee shops. By the late afternoon, Jarek and Charlie had met up with Helena (and other student friends) either in a coffee shop or a quirky low-cost eatery.

For the first several days of his nine-day stay, Charlie drank a lot of coffee. Jarek, however, occasionally opted for a large mug of lemon or rosehip tea – mixed with a shot (or two shots) of vodka. On the fourth day, Charlie decided to try a cup of lemon tea with a shot of vodka and he took an instant delight to the unusual tasting beverage. This particular moment was the beginning of a lifelong affinity: lemon-flavoured tea mixed with a 'healthy' amount of vodka. It would become one of his favourite beverages!

Aforementioned, Charlie was quite impressed with Jarek's in-depth historical knowledge of Kraków. At times, however, he (Jarek) seemed to be 'trapped' in a delusional world of academia. Largely engrossed in hypothetical theories, Jarek appeared to be clueless in understanding how the *average* person thinks. Charlie believed that he needed to be more involved in the practical elements of everyday life, instead of being heavily influenced by theoretical academia.

One night, a group of students and Charlie went to the cinema to view an 'alternative-themed' movie – Jarek's choice. When the movie ended, Charlie felt it was one of the weirdest movies that he'd ever seen! Even during the movie's screening, Helena whispered to him several times. She didn't understand the plot or the point of the movie. Charlie glanced at several of Helena's female friends. In unison, they smiled wryly and gently shook their heads. At one point, Charlie suggested (in a loud whisper) that the scriptwriters must have been on mind-altering substances when they wrote the screenplay. Jarek, however, continued to watch the movie with *intense* interest.

After leaving the cinema, the group congregated inside a coffee shop. The movie soon dominated the discussion; the consensus was that it was senseless and without a recognisable plot. At this point, a slightly-irritated Jarek intervened and tried to explain to the rest of the group that the movie had many intertwining plots. He then diagnosed the suppose relevance of *each* major scene, even justifying his sentiments with word-for-word dialogue. It all made sense to him! The rest of the group, however, was still perplexed.

Two nights later, Charlie boarded an overnight economy-fare train, bound for the city of Poznań: 458 kilometres north-west of Kraków. Helena, Jarek and several others bid him farewell on the railway platform. The train arrived at *Poznań Główny* (Poznan's main railway station) just after 5.00 am.

Charlie had pre-arranged to meet Ivana at the railway station at 8.00 am. The pair had previously been employed on an orchard in the county of Kent (United Kingdom). For the next three hours, he patiently waited at the railway station, dividing his time between reading a book and casually observing his immediate surroundings.

As with other railway stations in Poland, young military personnel with sub-machine guns patrolled the precinct. Throughout the station, a large number of homeless people had slept there during the night on flattened cardboard boxes and well-used tattered blankets. Sadly, more than half of them were elderly and empty vodka bottles lay near most of these makeshift sleeping quarters.

Just after 7.00 am, a family of six (2 adults and 4 children) sat down at a table, several metres from an opened kiosk. As Charlie sipped on a cup of coffee at a nearby table, he presumed the family unit was also homeless. They were eerily quiet as they consumed a breakfast meal. Ten minutes later, each family member produced a money bag. Coins and notes were emptied onto the table, directly in front of them.

Based on their dress sense, Charlie surmised that the family unit wasn't Polish. The father of the clan then started yelling at one of his sons in a non-Polish language. He (Charlie) stopped reading his book and was now more intrigued by the behaviour of the family. Charlie suspected that they were probably Romanian gipsies. The money that was being put on the table was most likely from begging throughout the night and, perhaps, the previous evening as well. Papa wasn't happy with the number of coins and notes that the boy (who was probably aged between ten and twelve years old) had put on the table in front of him.

He slapped the side of the boy's head and continued to yell at him. The boy started crying and received another slap to his head. In an instant, the youngster stopped crying. The mother and her other offspring, meanwhile, were silent – and with heads bowed. Papa was now quite agitated. Twenty metres away, stood three military personnel. One of them looked like he wanted to intervene but his colleagues physically dissuaded him from doing so. Several of the elderly homeless had now wandered close to the family. Silently, they stood a few metres away and just glared at the father. One felt that they probably wanted to give him a good beating! Two minutes later, however, the family group arose from the table and left the railway station precinct.

At 8.10 am, Ivana arrived at the railway station. It had been over two years since Charlie last saw her. The pair boarded a tram and half an hour later, they were inside her parent's high-rise unit. Charlie was introduced to Ivana's parents. An hour later, they left the unit and boarded a tram that took them back to central Poznań where Ivana's place of employment was at a sports store. Her hours of employment were 10.00 am - 4.00 pm, five or six days per week.

For the past two years, Charlie and Ivana had stayed in contact with each other by exchanging letters only. Her parents were still waiting to have a telephone connected to their unit – having been on the waitlist for more than eight years. With each letter written to him, he had noticed a steady improvement in Ivana's written English levels. Her level of spoken English, however, had improved dramatically compared to the last time the pair had spoken to each other.

Charlie accompanied Ivana to the sports store every morning. Overall customer activity within the sports store was generally quite minimal. The pair, therefore, was able to chat with each other throughout the day frequently. Ivana, occasionally, would alight from her comfortable chair to assist a potential customer. More often than not, however, she would direct one of her young male colleagues to assist the person!

Westernised countries often provided customer service along the line of the well-known cliché: *the customer comes first* or *the customer is always right.* Charlie, however, soon realised that the retail situation in countries like Poland was very different! Despite the collapse of the Communist political system, an 'old mentality' still prevailed. For example, in a westernised economy, a staff member would approach a customer and politely ask, 'Hi (or hello)… can I help you?'

Throughout his stay in Poland, Charlie witnessed quite a *different* approach: the customer would advance towards a staff member and ask (or plead) for assistance. They, in turn, would be met with a typical response like '*co chcesz*' (what do you want)? Words such as 'polite', 'assistance' or 'tact' were not part of customer service at the time! This attitude was quite evident inside the sports store. In fairness to the staff, however, they didn't own the store and they were also paid a paltry monthly wage (in comparison to wage levels of westernised nations). Additionally, employment was in abundance at the time and it was easy to obtain another job. When Charlie queried to the owner's whereabouts, Ivana stated that they were in the south of Poland on a skiing trip. Elaborating further, she informed him that they were frequently on a 'holiday'.

Charlie and Ivana were engaged in an earnest conversation one afternoon when a woman (aged in her sixties) approached them. She wanted to know the range of beanie hats, scarves and gloves that were available in the store. The conversation, initially, began in a light-hearted and cordial manner but it soon evolved into a 'verbal war'. A barrage of Polish swearing words soon followed, along with frantic hand movements and arm gesticulation!

The volatile and animated theatrics lasted for several minutes. Ivana, eventually, ordered one of her young male colleagues to deal with the 'obnoxious' woman. Agitated, she sat beside Charlie and exclaimed, 'I'm not serving that *old bag...* she's complaining about the lack of colours available in the scarfs. Is she blind?'

Charlie looked at the clothes rack and saw that the scarfs came in three colours: grey, black and white. He thought to himself, 'The customer is right!'

Throughout his five-week journey in Poland, Charlie observed a distinct disdain between the older and younger generations. The 'rivalry' seemed to be mostly between the *old communists* versus the *new capitalists*. He sensed that Ivana was caught somewhere in between the opposing mindsets. Whilst largely welcoming the advent of capitalism, she still possessed high regard for numerous aspects of communism.

Charlie stayed in Poznań for ten days. Although Ivana's behaviour could be quite volatile at times, he enjoyed her company. One night, they started conversing (as they drank red wine and ate chocolates) in a light-hearted fashion but the amicable chit-chat soon transformed into one of a more serious nature. Charlie sensed that Ivana was trying to tell him something! Eventually, he confessed that he had taken a 'liking' to her and quickly added that she was quite *cuddly-looking*. She rose and sat on Charlie's lap. The pair was now face-to-face and so it began: a night of 'sexual frolicking'.

On the day of Charlie's departure, Ivana accompanied him to the inter-city bus stop, located beside the main railway station. He boarded the Poznań-Opole minibus amidst a light fall of snow. A tearful Ivana bid Charlie farewell but nine months later, they would meet again.

As the bitter cold Polish winter was nearing, Charlie was happy to be returning to Greece (after a two and a half year absence). In the city of Opole, he boarded a larger bus destined for Rome, Italy. After arriving in the Italian capital, Charlie boarded a train, bound for the port city of Brindisi. He boarded a ferry (in Brindisi) that sailed along the Adriatic and Ionian seas, eventually arriving in the Greek city of Patras. Charlie would reside in Greece for the next five and a half months.

Charlie returned to Poznań in August of the following year. After living and working in the United Kingdom for three months, he travelled to Amsterdam (The Netherlands) via a bus-ferry-bus service from London. Charlie stayed in Amsterdam for two nights before hitchhiking to the German capital of Berlin. In central Berlin, he boarded an overnight train, bound for Warsaw via Poznań. The first part of the rail journey took him to the Polish town of Rzepin. Charlie shared a compartment with another male. He assumed, initially, that the gentleman was a Polish national. Fifteen minutes into the journey, the man attempted to initiate a conversation with Charlie, who quickly realised that he was most likely a Russian national. His accent, along with the use of several Russian words, immediately aroused Charlie's suspicions!

The Russian male attempted to initiate a conversation via the use of several languages. English, however, was not one of them. He seemed to be quite proficient with the German and French languages though. Charlie's level of spoken German was quite poor but he did have a reasonable French vocabulary at the time. Speaking in a mixture of French and Polish, Charlie managed to converse with the Russian national. The Russian man had recently been employed in a Berlin restaurant for the past two years and had previously worked in vineyards in both France and Germany. On several occasions, Charlie was offered a biscuit but declined each time – he still remembered the warnings from his previous visit to Poland.

Just after the train departed from the city of Frankfurt an der Oder (not to be confused with the major city of Frankfurt), German military custom officials inspected passports. After crossing the German-Poland border, Polish military custom officials also checked passports. After viewing Charlie's Polish visa and correctly-filled entry card, his passport was promptly returned to him. The Russian national produced a *Polish* passport. The customs officials, however, practically interrogated him for the next ten minutes or so. Nevertheless, his passport was eventually returned to him.

Just after 10.00 pm, the train arrived in the Polish town of Rzepin: 20 kilometres east of the German-Polish border. Most passengers (including Charlie) alighted from the train to purchase another train fare. Charlie purchased a ticket to Poznań. It was much cheaper to buy two separate tickets instead of purchasing just the one ticket (in Berlin) from Berlin to Poznań. At the ticket booth window, he paid for the train fare in Deutschmarks but received the change in Polish złoty. Charlie spoke to the woman in Polish. She, however, immediately seized upon his accent and attempted to short-change him. He counted the notes and coins but realised that he had only been short-changed a minuscule amount. With a smirk on his face, Charlie replied, '*Wiem – ale, żaden problem* (I know – but, no problem)!'

Twenty minutes later, Charlie reboarded the train but chose to sit in another compartment, sharing one with an elderly Polish couple. Several hours later, the train arrived at *Poznań Główny*. Little had changed in nine months: a sizeable number of young military personnel were still patrolling the railway station perimeter and the homeless were still there. For the next several hours, Charlie sat on a bench seat, occasionally falling asleep. He felt quite safe as patrolling military personnel were always nearby.

Just after 7.00 am, Charlie boarded a tram along *Ulica Grunwaldzka* (Grunwaldzka Street) and alighted at a tram stop near Ivana's parent's place. He rapped on the eleventh-floor apartment door and was greeted by a sleepy Ivana. An hour later, the pair travelled together by tram to her new place of employment: a clothing boutique in central Poznań. During his three-week stay in Poznań, he would accompany her to the small shop each working day. Ivana was minding the boutique for an old school friend who was on holidays for several weeks.

The boutique was one of ten 'speciality' boutiques, all housed inside a small arcade-like complex. Each day, people (nearly all were female) would wander in and out of the boutiques but rarely purchased anything. Polish wages, at the time, were no match for the 'westernised' price tags. Virtually, the costs of all items were equivalent to at *least* two weeks' worth of wages.

As (profitable) retail activity was barely existent, a typical day for the female boutique employees could be best described as boring. The ladies, however, soon got to know each other quite well and they conversed with each other regularly; mostly in the arcade's central walkway. Up to several times a day, Ivana would try on a dress that was for sale in the boutique. Instead of changing clothes in the shop's change-room, she opted to strip to her underwear – in the middle of the shop. Ivana would then seek Charlie's 'expert' opinion. His standard response went along the lines that she looked beautiful, regardless of what dress she was wearing!

The boutiques were owned by wealthy locals who were more interested in the ever-increasing value of property in Poznań's CBD. At some point, they intended to sell the prized real estate at a significant profit. The only people who purchased the expensive items (clothing, footwear, jewellery, etc) tended to be the city's wealthy elite, well-paid professionals or foreign nationals (Germans in particular).

Each working day, Ivana used the time to improve her English writing and conversational skills. Charlie was her tutor. As there was only one chair inside the shop, the tutoring was mostly conducted with Ivana sitting on his lap! If a well-dressed or 'wealthy-looking' woman (or couple) entered the boutique, she would instantly stand up and offer assistance. The *window-shoppers*, however, were largely ignored by her: a practice that was also mirrored in the other boutique shops. There was also an elaborate sound system inside the boutique. Ivana would mostly play dance or house music. If the arcade was void of customers, she would turn the volume up several notches and start dancing inside the shop or in the arcade walkway, much to the amusement of the other boutique employees. Sasha and Renata, who 'minded' the boutique directly opposite, would also dance with Ivana as well.

Despite Ivana being 'friends' with Sasha and Renata, she informed Charlie that the pair were also *working girls* (prostitutes). The pair provided 'services' on weekends (pre-arranged inside one of the local nightclubs) at a residence, owned by a Turkish-born German national. Mehmet was much older than them and he was also their 'agent' (pimp).

Charlie met him several times inside the boutique arcade. Mehmet spoke English quite fluently and boasted to Charlie that he owned several businesses in Poznań, including the boutique that was being tended to by Sasha and Renata.

After staying with Ivana for three weeks, Charlie departed from Poznań and boarded a Berlin-bound train. In Berlin, he boarded a Hamburg-bound train. In central Hamburg, Charlie boarded an overnight bus that took him to London via a ferry service and another coach service. He arrived in London early the next morning. Ten hours later, Charlie boarded an Aeroflot flight, bound for Sydney (Australia) via several stopovers. He remained in contact with Ivana and six months later, was reunited with her – in Sydney.

14

He Came, He Saw, He Conquered...
But He Returned

After an absence of two and a half years, Charlie returned to Greece, via a sea voyage from the city of Brindisi (Italy) to the city of Patras (Greece). He stayed in a Patras hostel for one night only. The next morning, Charlie walked to the northern outskirts of the city. For several hours, he attempted to hitchhike to the ancient city of Corinth but, alas, no joy. Succumbing to an obvious defeat, Charlie walked back to the central intercity bus station.

Just after midday, Charlie boarded a bus, bound for Corinth. In the central part of the city, he waited in a bar (near the bus terminal) for a bus to Nafplio: a seaport town in the Peloponnese region. Charlie arrived in the town just as dusk was creeping in. There was a *kafeneío* (café/bar) not far from the bus stop. He entered the premises and came upon a group of people huddled around a table speaking in English to each other. Within half an hour, Charlie was discussing local employment opportunities with his 'new-found' friends. The group, however, was not looking for any employment as they were about to travel to several of the Greek islands. Charlie did learn, though, that most of the orange orchards were located in and around the villages of Tolo, Assini and Drepano.

A few minutes after 9.00 pm, Charlie decided to seek accommodation for the night. As this time of the year was outside the traditional tourist season, the majority of the hotels/pensions were closed. As he walked away from the town centre, Charlie noticed several partially-built buildings and was considering whether to just 'squat' or not for the night. However, a pension displaying a large bright neon sign, *Vacancies*, soon caught his eye. Before knocking on the door, he decided he would not pay any more than 2000 drachmas (equivalent to less than £7 sterling at the time) for a night's accommodation.

Charlie knocked on the door and a few seconds later it was opened. The middle-aged male stated (in fluent English) that the price for one night was 3000 drachmas. Charlie responded by declaring that he could only afford to pay 1500 drachmas. For the next few moments, there was an eerie silence of a stalemate. Charlie began to move slowly from the door. The pension owner then quizzed him to where he was going to stay for the night and was met with the response, 'In one of those partially-built buildings!' Sensing that the owner was probably interested in earning some extra cash, Charlie commenced the negotiation process. Eventually, 2000 drachmas were agreed upon.

After consuming a sumptuous breakfast the next morning, Charlie decided to walk to the village of Tolo: a distance of 11 kilometres. Over two hours later, he was inside one of Tolo's tavernas. As Charlie sipped on a coffee, he struck up a conversation with the lone staff member: Margorzata (a Polish national). They were soon discussing employment opportunities and accommodation options within the local and surrounding area.

An elderly English gentleman, sitting at a nearby table, soon joined the conversation. Margorzata made several telephone calls and relayed back to Charlie that virtually all pensions/hotels were closed at the moment; they were only opened during the tourist season. For the next two nights, he camped in an orange orchard, located several kilometres from Tolo.

Over the next several days, Charlie wandered in and around the villages of Tolo, Assini and Drepano. Inside a Drepano kafeneio, one late afternoon, he discussed local employment opportunities with several Polish and Czech males. Using a mixture of Polish and English (and a few Greek words), Charlie managed to engage in some form of communication with them. At one point, they even invited him to join their (working) group but he preferred to work with mostly English-speaking people.

The following evening, Charlie was casually strolling towards the village of Tolo when he came upon an elderly English couple. They were residing in a spacious homestead, located between the villages of Tolo and Assini. At the front of their yard, the couple was engaged in a friendly conversation with a younger English gentleman. As Charlie walked passed he said hello to them. The thirty-something Englishman instantly introduced himself (Andy) and the elderly couple (Boris and Margaret) as well. For the next half an hour or so, the trio chatted amicably with him. When the conversation ended, Andy and Charlie walked to Tolo.

As they walked along the edge of the road leading into the village, Andy stated that he had been living in the Tolo region for the past four years in a rented house: two kilometres from the village. He further explained to Charlie that he had driven from England to Greece (except for the ferry trip between Italy and Greece), six years ago, in an old Austin Morris 1100 (a mid-1960s model). Before deciding to settle in Tolo, Andy had travelled throughout mainland Greece and the island of Crete for two years. The pair entered a taverna and inside there was a large group of English-speaking people clustered around two tables.

Andy introduced Charlie to another English chap (Chris) who was attempting to organise a group of 'potential and willing' orange pickers. Employment options soon dominated the discussion. Ten minutes later, the owner (Marius) of the taverna approached Chris, Charlie and several others. Marius was also a contractor, providing employment (or fulfilling labour needs) to the upcoming orange harvest. Over the next half an hour or so, he discussed with the group the terms of employment: start and finish times, rates of pay, meal breaks, etc.

By the end of the discussion, Charlie sensed that he (Marius) wasn't being entirely honest with them. Marius stated that he paid the best piece rates in the area for orange picking and also claimed to have a plentiful supply of employment for the group over the next two to three months. Marius further *promised* that the orange-picking crew would be 'well looked after'. But his general appearance set off alarm bells for Charlie (and others in the group). He was immaculately dressed and seemed to have a penchant for anything gold: a gold watch, several gold rings and an expensive gold chain worn on the outside of his silk shirt. Charlie viewed him as a 'slick and dodgy' salesman – one that had probably never worked in an orange orchard.

For the rest of the evening, Charlie enjoyed the social chatter and light-hearted banter with other individuals within the English-speaking group. He learnt that a 'team' of twenty-five was commencing orange-picking employment in the morning. With exuberant enthusiasm, most of the group was quite excited by the concept of group labour. Charlie, however, viewed the concept of a large group of people working together (and each individual getting paid the same amount) would be a short-lived exercise, lasting one or two days perhaps.

Charlie learnt that night that only a handful of people had even worked on an orchard (or a fruit/vegetable farm) before. He suspected that the majority were only in the area for the travelling *experience* and to write about in their travel diary. Charlie further learnt that at least half of the group had never been outside the United Kingdom before! Aforementioned, this

'Socialist' concept of group labour practically meant that total earnings would be divided by the total number of workers. Everyone gets paid the same – regardless of how much work each individual does. For the past six years, Charlie had mostly worked by himself and was paid by piece-rate, instead of an hourly or daily rate of pay. His daily earnings were solely based on the number of bins, buckets, etc he had picked.

Charlie firmly believed that the upcoming employment venture was most likely to fail within a day or two. Nevertheless, he was quite happy to provide any assistance to Chris if required. Charlie's finances, by now, had severely diminished – immediate employment was now of the essence for him. Chris and his partner (Mary) offered Charlie to sleep in their large campervan. He accepted their offer. They were residing in a three-room homestead. Accommodation in the campervan would be a pleasant change for Charlie as he had just spent two chilly nights in an orange orchard!

Early the next morning, the group of twenty-five huddled together inside the large campervan. The converted campervan had formerly been a medium-sized truck/lorry. Chris drove the group to the orange orchard: a journey of about twenty minutes. The general mood throughout the short journey was mostly one of an eerie silence – a far cry from the enthusiastic chatter that had taken place in Marius' bar the previous night.

At the orange orchard, the group alighted from Chris' vehicle and soon displayed a positive level of eagerness for the big day ahead. The orchard owner, along with two Czech males (who would be loading the full crates of oranges onto a truck) met them. Marius, however, was nowhere to be seen. The group was informed that they would have to wait for him to arrive before any orange picking could commence. He arrived nearly an hour later.

For the next fifteen minutes, Marius and the orchard owner casually chatted away. More time being wasted. Eventually, the following equipment was issued to the group: large wooden ladders (old enough to be classed as antiques); metal buckets with wooden hooks attached to the handles (to be attached to a ladder rung or a tree branch); *kloovers* (plastic crates); and, *karótsis* (metal-framed wheelbarrows) used to transport full crates of oranges. No canvas fruit-picking bags were provided. A day of comedic hilarity was about to commence!

Chris, unfortunately, was clueless about how to organise this large group of mostly novices. When prompted for 'direction', he told everyone to *scatter* and to just fill the crates with oranges. The crew, initially, literally wandered about and picked oranges from any random tree – and mostly from the lower sections of the trees. The middle and top sections of the orange trees were mostly untouched. Fifteen minutes later, Charlie decided to intervene and strongly suggested to Chris that this large group of 'orange-harvest warriors' needed to split up into five groups of five people. He further suggested that each group should only work together on one row of orange trees at a time. Without hesitation, Chris readily agreed with Charlie's 'intuitive' line of thinking!

Charlie, Chris and three other males (two Englishmen and a South African) each grabbed a wooden ladder and proceeded to remove the oranges from the top of the trees. Marius, meanwhile, had already left the scene of *disorganised pandemonium* and had probably gone to the comfort zone of his taverna.

By lunchtime, aspirations within the large group had diminished significantly. The jovial enthusiasm, several hours earlier, had all but disappeared. The luncheon break, however, did lift spirits a notch or two. The orange pickers were provided with what may be best described as a banquet: a large array of differing salami pieces; several varieties of olives; generous servings of feta cheese; dried flavoured tomatoes; and, slices of fresh bread (accompanied with olive oil). An ample supply of homemade wine (both red and white) was also provided.

During the luncheon feast, the mood within the group was notably quiet, only to be interrupted with periodic murmurs of sporadic chit-chat. Charlie sensed that the majority of the group was on an emotional downward spiral: mentally and physically. Most of them were *not* enjoying the experience.

The mostly-downhearted group returned to the orange orchard for the afternoon orange-picking session. A short time later, Marius returns. After a brief chat with the orchard owner, he confronts the group over their 'pitiful' morning effort, lambasting them for working too slow! The majority of the orange pickers, however, just stood there and folded their arms. An irate Charlie retorted, 'So, Marius… your point is?' Somewhat surprisingly, an exasperated Marius was suddenly lost for words. Moments later, he turned around and walked back to his vehicle. Marius left and probably heading back to his taverna again.

During the luncheon break, Charlie managed to quietly discuss with the two Czech nationals (Jan and Tomáš) the *diabolical* morning session. The pair picked up the crates of oranges and later loaded them onto a lorry. Once the lorry was laden with full crates, they would then accompany the (lorry) driver to the weigh station, ensuring that the total volume of oranges was being weighed correctly. Charlie informed them that he was going to look for another contractor. They suggested to him to directly approach one at the weigh station: located between the town of Nafplio and the village of Assini. He also learnt that many of the contractors also drove the vehicles to the weigh stations.

Compared to the morning session of orange picking, the afternoon session was more productive. More crates of oranges were filled. A perplexed Charlie, however, tried to explain to several of the group that they could work much quicker if they used *both* hands at the same time. He further reminded them that they were being paid piece-rate, not by an hourly rate. Charlie further explained to them that they don't need to *inspect* the oranges before putting them in the crate. He further suggested to them to just throw or hurl them into the crates as fast as you can! And then there was Ivan.

Ivan was the only male in his group. He was the 'designated' ladder-user as the four females insisted that they would *not* be scaling the ladder. The other ladder-users generally emptied the wooden-hooked bucket of oranges (attached to the ladder) into crates that were close to the tree that they were working on. Ivan, bizarrely, would regularly walk 10-20 metres with the bucket of oranges to an empty or partly-filled crate! It was much easier and *quicker* to fill a nearby crate.

Within the first few days, Charlie had developed an attitude of dislike towards Ivan. Ivan's *snake-like* eyes were disconcerting but there would be other reasons to why he didn't particularly like him. Ivan constantly rambled on about being a 'diehard Brit' and often used the catchphrase: 'We Brits must stick together!' His idea of 'Brits' included *all* native English-speakers.

Charlie explained to Ivan, several times, that he did not have any known British ancestry. His ancestry was a mixture of Swedish, German, Irish and Spanish. Largely as a retaliatory measure, Charlie decided to irk him, stating that Australia barely had any ties to Great Britain any more. He cited two key periods in history: the *Fall of Singapore* (or Battle of Singapore) in 1942 where British troops practically deserted their Australian counterparts and when Britain joined the EEC in 1973, effectively ending most economic ties between the two nations. Charlie further added that Australia was now, primarily, a diverse multicultural country as it was largely built on significant periods of past immigration. He added, just to *add fuel to the fire*, the country will probably become an independent republic in the future.

Over the next several weeks, Ivan was quite 'charming' towards most of the females within the group through a façade of pleasantness, friendliness and gentlemanly behaviour. The majority of the males, however, disliked him and like Charlie, basically regarded Ivan as a 'snake'. It soon emerged that he had an unhealthy disdain towards the *colonials*: Australians, New Zealanders, South Africans, etc. A sarcastic Charlie, on several occasions, suggested to him that he should visit Australia someday. Upon learning of Ivan's obsession with English cricket, Charlie gleefully ribbed him of England's under-performing test cricket team at the time; especially in the test matches against Australia.

In the orchard, meanwhile, the 'orange-harvest warriors' persevered with the afternoon fruit-picking session. Although the general spirit within the group was still in a state of decline, the lunchtime banquet had provided a revived aura of light-heartedness and *light-headedness* during the first couple of hours. Within the last hour of the working day, the motivational levels of the 'battle-weary' labourers had, once again, largely evaporated. It all became too much for one of the English ladies (Misty). An eerie atmosphere of silence was sliced apart by Misty when she suddenly blurted out in a distinct east-Londoner cockney accent,

'This is bullshit... I'll be struggling to make the equivalent of ten pounds today. Back home, I could easily make the same amount of money with a ten-minute blowjob!'

Aged in her late twenties, Misty was a freelance journalist and writer. Primarily on a working holiday, she was using the experience to write a series of articles for a publishing company. Misty had already published numerous travel-related articles. Over the next couple of weeks, she attracted quite an amount of 'attention' from the males within the group who were probably motivated by her blowjob comment! Misty, however, ended hooking up with the youngest male in the group: nineteen-year-old Aidan.

At the end of the day, the experience had largely proven to be quite a negative one for most of the group. Nearly half of them didn't want to return to the orchard the next day. The orchardist, however, didn't want them either and he terminated employment for the entire group. Inside the tavern that evening, an unfazed Marius calmly informed Chris (and others) that the group could commence employment at another orchard in the morning. Charlie felt that he was only offering employment to the group, primarily as a means to encourage them to keep purchasing meals and beverages in his taverna!

After leaving the taverna, some of the group went to Andy's house. Along the way, large plastic bottles of homemade wine and half-litre bottles of ouzo were purchased. Inside his house, the events of the day were discussed in earnest. Andy, initially, was notably silent. He listened to the general conversation intently – and with a smirk on his face. Eventually, Andy spoke up. He stated that he had avoided the past two orange harvests, largely due to the pitiful wage one was paid earn for this type of employment.

During the past four years, Andy had become friends or acquainted with a large number of people within the local communities of Tolo, Nafplio, Assini and Drepano. He had mostly survived, financially, by doing *odd jobs*. Andy had set up a business and marketed himself as 'Handy Andy – where no job is too small or too large.' He would advertise his services either through the local newspaper or directly to residents and businesses via printed business cards.

Most of Andy's income was derived from landscaping/gardening employment (especially for northern and central European ex-pats) and 'plumbing' jobs. During the tourist season, in particular, the majority of these plumbing jobs involved receiving phone calls from the mostly Greek-owned hotels/pensions/villas – to unblock the drains. He explained to the group that tourists were supposed to put the toilet paper in the small garbage bins (located next to the toilet bowl) instead of trying to flush it down the toilet. Andy only needed two tools for these jobs: a plunger and a stretched-out wire coat hanger.

Before the group departed from Andy's abode that night, he warned the young females to beware of *Greeks that bear gifts.* The women responded with dismissive bouts of giggling. The next day, however, his 'words of wisdom' would come to fruition for one of these hapless ladies!

The group gathered inside the campervan the next morning. Enthusiasm was at low ebb and there were ten fewer people than the previous day! Twenty minutes later, they arrived at the orchard. The smaller group would be joined by several other people that day: two French ladies (Louisa and Russian-born Ivanka), Daniel (a Luxembourger) and George (a Swedish national).

The two French ladies resided in the village of Tolo. The two males, on the other hand, were *outdoor dwellers*. Daniel, for the past three and a half years, had been living in one of the above sea-level caves, located about one-kilometre north-east of Tolo. 'Caveman' George, however, had been habituating the cave system for more than seven years!

Charlie worked and chatted near George for a good part of the day and soon learnt a few things about him: the Swedish national had acquired his American accent from living in the USA for nearly ten years; he was approaching his fiftieth birthday; had been travelling since he was sixteen years old; had been married three times; wasn't sure how many kids he had fathered (but at least ten); and, he had previously lived in numerous countries (USA, Canada, Mexico, France, Sweden, Norway, Denmark, etc).

Financially, the day would be more 'fruitful' than the previous one. The camaraderie within the group had noticeably improved and the elderly orchardist was quite happy to see all his fruit being properly removed from the trees (and at a decent pace). Yet again, the luncheon interval was another scrumptious banquet. All was going well but that was about to change!

Half an hour after the luncheon break, the elderly orchardist was wandering throughout his orchard. Then he approached one of the young females: Annika (a Dutch-born British national). The elderly gentleman attempted to make conversation with her in badly-broken English. With a wry smile, he extended his right arm out and offered Annika an orange. As she extended her left arm to grab the orange, the orchardist extended his left arm and gently grabbed her right breast!

A shell-shocked Annika instantly retreated. Charlie, who was working nearby, descended from his ladder. However, instead of him being sympathetic to her plight, he casually remarked, 'Now, what did Andy say last night?'

A now-embarrassed Annika burst out laughing.

'I know… I know… shut up!'

In the evening, a large number of people were inside Andy's abode and the 'Annika Incident' soon dominated the general conversation. A bemused and mostly-silent Andy just shook his head from time to time!

The next morning, the group gathered at yet another orange orchard, patiently waiting for the orchardist and Marius to arrive. A group of Serbian males were also waiting. Charlie would later learn that most of them were 'army deserters' (from the Bosnian War happening at the time). A large number of young Serbian males had relocated to Greece to avoid military conscription; many believed they faced harsh prison sentences if they returned to their country. A spokesperson for the group, who spoke fluent English, assured the 'westerners' that the Serbian group would not be working with them.

As everyone waited for the orchardist and Marius to arrive, an argument between the two French ladies and Daniel broke out. The conversation between them started mildly enough but soon developed into a heated one, with both women gesticulating wildly with their arms. Each time Ivanka said Marius' name, she spat on the ground! Louisa's source of agitation, however, was mostly directed at Daniel. She spat at his feet several times and, at one point, raised her fist at him. He tried to talk calmly to both hot-headed ladies but without success. Exasperatingly, Daniel threw his arms in the air and walked away from the vicinity.

As Daniel disappeared into the distance, the two women soon regained their composure. Charlie, casually, enquired to what was happening between the pair and Daniel. Ivanka explained to him that Marius had promised them (Louisa and her) that they would each be paid 4500 drachmas for the eight-hour working day, instead of piece-rate. Daniel, however, had asked Marius the previous night to what the payment method would be to which he replied that all orange-pickers would be paid by piece-rate. Daniel had only relayed this information to the pair fifteen minutes earlier. Ivanka then added that Louisa and he were currently in a relationship: a 'love-hate' one. It was quite evident that the relationship was now in a *hate* phase.

When Marius finally arrived, Ivanka and Louisa immediately confronted him. Within seconds, a heated argument erupted. Marius tried to argue with them in French but Ivanka (now screaming hysterically) replied to him in English: largely for the benefit of the English-speaking employees. Meanwhile, the Serbian spokesman translated the *volatile* and *entertaining* discussion back to his 'comrades'. Both ladies were now quite irate and their faces reddened with anger. As they 'roared' at Marius, both of them started stomping their feet on the ground and practically took turns at spitting on his clean polished shoes!

Marius responded with a 'barrage of profanities' (a selection of well-known Greek swearing words) and lots of arm-waving. Then, he was silent and refused to talk to them anymore. Marius walked away and sat in his vehicle. The dejected women left the vicinity and walked towards the village of Tolo. The Serbians approached Marius in an attempt to negotiate a more favourable employment outcome but to no avail. They, too, decided to leave.

The twelve remaining orange pickers chatted amongst themselves and decided whether to stay or go. All four females in the group decided to leave. Charlie, Chris and

George then stated to Marius that they would pick oranges for the whole day but only on the condition that they would be paid in the evening for today's (and yesterday's) employment. He readily agreed. The rest of the day went by without any further incidents. In the evening, Marius duly paid Chris for the two days of employment. A large wad of notes was counted on a large table and it was the correct amount. Besides Marius and Chris, there were five other males seated at the table: Charlie, Kane, George and the two Czech lads (Jan and Tomáš).

After receiving the sizeable amount of cash, Chris admitted that mathematics was 'not one of my strong points'. Using a large sheet of paper, Charlie (with some assistance from Jan) constructed a handwritten graph which indicated how much each individual would be paid. Most of the group that had worked the past two days (or just for the one day) was remunerated that night.

The next day, the two French women and Daniel were paid. Daniel's share was given to George as he knew which cave Daniel was residing in. Charlie was able to locate both Ivanka and Louise inside a taverna in Tolo. The pair was not pleased about being 'underpaid' but they, nevertheless, were grateful that Charlie ensured they got paid something. As a token of thanks, Ivanka invited him back to her humble abode (which she also shared with Louisa) for a home-cooked evening meal. He brought a bottle of wine and a bottle of vodka with him. In the late-evening, Ivanka and Charlie were consuming vodka; Louisa was still drinking wine. He stayed there that night – sharing Ivanka's bed.

Over the next few days, most of the westerners were unemployed. Ivanka and Louisa left the Tolo region to seek 'greener pastures' elsewhere. The lack of employment opportunities during this period, however, fostered an abundance of social interaction and the overall spirit within the group lifted significantly.

Charlie had been residing in Chris and Mary's campervan for three weeks when two Irish women (Judith and Anita) asked him if he would like to move into a large house which they were renting. Two other people were also living in the house: Hannah (an American woman) and Paul (a South African male). They were residing in the upstairs section of the house which comprised of three bedrooms (with four single beds and a double-bed). The downstairs section comprised of two bedrooms. Giorgio, the owner of the house, occupied one of these bedrooms. The other bedroom was occupied by a Russian couple, who were aged in their forties.

For the first three nights, Charlie shared a bedroom with Paul. On the fourth day, he was strolling on one of Tolo's beaches in the evening when he crossed paths with Hannah. This particular beach was located near a caravan/camping ground (northeast of Tolo) and it was also close to a series of caves where George and Daniel dwelled. The pair stopped walking and chatted with each other.

After engaging in idle chit-chat for several minutes, Hannah suddenly requested a hug from Charlie. He duly obliged and gently declared, 'Hannah, you are very cuddly!'

With a glint in her eye and a cheeky smile, Hannah replied, 'You can sleep with me if you like!'

Without hesitation, Charlie gleefully accepted Hannah's offer and for the next six weeks, he enjoyed a healthy sex life with her. Hannah (after these six weeks) returned to the United States. Although they kept in contact for the next few years, the pair would never see each other again.

Meanwhile, after four days without employment, Charlie's financial situation had reached a point of critical despair. Along with Kane, he decided to walk to the weighing station, located between the town of Nafplio and the village of Assini. The pair approached numerous contractors as they patiently sat in their lorries/trucks in a lengthy queue: one that extended well past the weighing station entrance and along the side of the main roadway.

The weighing station was primarily the location where a lorry/truck would come to have the total volume of oranges weighed. When it was his turn, the driver would place his vehicle onto the weighbridge. The total weight of the oranges was calculated by the following formula: the total weight minus (the weight of the truck + the total weight of empty crates/bins). There was only one weighbridge.

Activity within the weigh station could best be described as 'hilariously chaotic': a comical spectacle that amused Kane and Charlie immensely. *Traffic controllers* (and there were several of them) tried their best to keep the traffic moving and, thus, avoid traffic jams. Vehicles would swerve, dodge or be carefully manoeuvred around each other as they were directed to one of several packing sheds. Inside the sheds, crates or bins of oranges were unloaded from the vehicle.

The noisy and vibrant buzz of activity within the weighing station area made it quite difficult for the traffic controllers to communicate verbally to the drivers. Instead, wild gesticulation (mixed in with some interesting miming techniques) was the prevalent form of communication. Charlie sarcastically quipped to Kane, 'I wonder if these traffic controllers are all graduates from the Marcel Marceau School of Mime!'

As Charlie and Kane's level of spoken Greek was still quite minimal, attempts of communication with contractors were largely fruitless. Their persistence, however, would eventually pay off. After attempting to seek employment for over two hours, they came across a burly contractor who spoke English fluently.

Twenty-six-year-old Petros was seeking another small crew (six to eight people) of orange pickers to work for him over the next few weeks. He further added that he may even need more people on the larger orange orchards. Petros informed Charlie and Kane that a crew of six people could commence employment in the morning, starting at 8.00 am. He would provide the transport to and from the orange orchard each working day. Petros then suggested to Charlie that he should be his subcontractor: a person who would be responsible for organising daily labour needs and paying each employee at the end of the week (the subcontractor would be paid a lump sum of cash every Friday afternoon). Charlie accepted the role.

Once employment conditions were finalised with Petros, Charlie walked to Nafplio. Kane headed back towards Tolo. At Nafplio's general post office, he collected an envelope (via poste restante from Australia). Besides containing a letter, the envelope also contained an American Express cheque. Within the space of a few hours, Charlie's financial position was now in a much healthier state!

Charlie would be Petros' subcontractor for the next two months. At the end of each working day, he would reconfirm with Petros the total number of full crates picked. Aforementioned, Charlie would be paid a lump sum of cash every Friday afternoon. A vital aspect of his role as a subcontractor was to keep accurate records each day, ensuring that each employee was paid correctly at the end of the week. The size of the group generally consisted of six to eight people but on some days, there were as many as fifteen people.

Throughout these two months, the westerners would occasionally pick oranges near another group of people: Albanians. The group of Albanians worked in a different section of the orange orchard and their tally of full crates was kept separate. At Petros' insistence, both groups would join together for the one-hour luncheon break. In an attempt to foster communication between the two groups, he would take on the role of translator. Most of the Albanians could speak a reasonable amount of Greek but very little English.

Charlie, in particular, was quite keen to know more about the Albanians and their way of life. They, on the other hand, struggled to understand why the westerners would want to work in Greece! Charlie (via a translation from Petros) attempted to explain to the Albanians the concept of *travelling*: focusing mainly on the basic differences between a traveller and a tourist. In response, they still regarded westerners as *tourists* who were primarily in Greece to do only three things: spend lots of money; spend a lot of time partying; and, to drink a lot of alcohol each day. Petros explained to Charlie that the Albanians understood what he was trying to say but they were still perplexed to why westerners would want to work in Greece, instead of much wealthier nations where earnings were potentially much higher.

The travelling (or touristy) westerners travelled to the Peloponnese region by one or more of the following methods: aeroplane, bus, train or by a motor vehicle. The vast majority of the Albanians, however, had travelled to this region – on foot. It was quite common for the entire or near-entire male population (aged from 14 to 65) of villages and towns to walk across the Pindus mountain range. A section of this mountain range stretched for about 160 kilometres along the Albanian-Greece border. They would walk across the mountain range to the northern Peloponnese. Then, they would continue walking or board a bus (in the city of Patras) to Nafplio. The journey would typically take two or three weeks to complete.

The vast majority of Albanians had only one goal whilst working in Greece: to save as much money as they could. Most of them would return to Albania via conventional means (bus, train, etc). At the border, however, many of the Albanians would often have to deal with roguish Greek border officials who, at times, attempted to confiscate some of their hard-earned cash by imposing an 'overstay' monetary fine. Charlie would later learn of several unsavoury incidents that occurred within the Greece-Albanian border region in previous years. Serious allegations centred on the claim that some Albanians had been shot (or shot at) whilst they were crossing over the Pindus mountain range – especially when they tried to return to Albania. A further claim alleged that a large number of Albanians had been stopped, once they were on Greek soil, and forced to pay for a 'work permit': a practice that was officially outlawed in Greece.

For two months, Charlie relished his position of sub-contractor as he was able to provide consistent employment (four to six days a week) for a regular group of eight 'harvest warriors'. Occasionally, Charlie was able to employ other individuals (not part of the regular group) for one to three days per week. The majority of the (westerner) females, however, tried to avoid the orange orchards by seeking employment in one of Tolo's kafeneios/ tavernas. Several of them obtained employment in Marius' taverna – but not for long. The base hourly rate of pay was quite low. To supplement their income, a 'bonus' was paid if they could *attract* an increase in male patronage. Despite there being no official dress code, the women soon realised that pants/slacks/jeans were generally discouraged. Short dresses, nylon stockings and tops that displayed a fair bit of cleavage, on the other hand, were widely encouraged!

Inside one of the tavernas, a young English woman wore a short dress for her first two nights of employment. On the third night, she entered the taverna wearing a tidy pair of jeans and was tactlessly informed by the taverna's owner (before she even commenced her shift), 'your services are no longer required'. Most of the young females soon found themselves working in an orange orchard (or a packing shed) again.

Charlie, meanwhile, enjoyed Hannah's company; albeit for only six weeks. Instead of staying to the end of the orange harvest season, she decided to return to the USA and commence new employment in her home city of Atlanta, Georgia. The household saw a regular flow of visitors, especially in the evenings or on non-working days. Three weeks into the orange-picking season, the westerners had largely ceased patronising the tavernas in Tolo; except for the one owned by Dmitri (an Athenian) and his (French-born) wife Catherine.

Inside Charlie's household, meanwhile, the overall atmosphere was mostly a harmonious one, but that was about to change. Ivan would occasionally visit the two Irish ladies (Judith and Anita) and a friendship had developed between them. They largely deemed him as a *charming gentleman*. Charlie, on the other hand, regarded him more like a *snake*. One afternoon, he (Ivan) approached Judith and Anita with a sob-sob story about being 'desolate and forlorn'. Ivan had just been evicted from the camping ground where he had been staying the past several weeks; he had not paid any rent for the past three weeks. Ivan had also been struggling to find employment (he was 'blacklisted' by Charlie).

The empathetic Irish ladies were 'touched' by Ivan's current predicament and they allowed him to sleep in the hallway of the household – in his sleeping bag – and much to the annoyance of Charlie. Even worse, Ivan did not pay any rent. Meanwhile, word had got around that food had been mysteriously disappearing from the communal fridges at the camping ground for the past several weeks. Several residents (at the camping ground) stated that Ivan was the most likely culprit. Charlie confronted him with this newly-learnt accusation but he, steadfastly, denied any responsibility.

After residing in the house for two months, Charlie moved back into Chris and Mary's campervan. He was planning to leave the Peloponnese region within the next week and, therefore, did not want to pay another fortnight's rent. Employment with Petros had come to a halt and the orange-picking season was nearing the end. Charlie, however, did manage to find another two days of employment: unloading crates of oranges from trucks/lorries.

Three days before his departure, Charlie crossed paths with the Irish ladies and Alan (a retired English gentleman aged in his early sixties) one morning near the Tolo post office. As the four of them were engaged in an earnest conversation, Ivan emerged from the post office. With several opened envelopes in his hand, he walked straight past them after uttering a casual hello to Anita and Judith. A grinning Ivan was in quite a jovial mood.

A minute later, Charlie turned to Alan and, with a smirk on his face, quipped, 'Do you think Ivan will do a runner within the next couple of days?' Alan replied, 'I presume he has just been sent some money… yes, it's highly probable!'

Judith and Anita were unimpressed with Charlie and Alan's presumptions of Ivan. They bid farewell and quietly walked away from them. Alan, who was holidaying in the camping ground with his wife (Florence), stated to Charlie that he didn't trust him as he firmly believed that it *was* Ivan who had been stealing food from the campground's communal refrigerators.

During the evening of the next day, Charlie visited his former housemates. At one point, it was just Ivan and himself in the kitchen. A silent Charlie sat at the table reading an English newspaper and casually sipped from a 500ml bottle of ouzo. Moments later, a contemptible Ivan attempted to initiate a conversation. An agitated Charlie then grilled him to whether he had paid all his debts yet and angrily asked him, 'So, how much money do you owe Judith and Anita?' He was met with stony silence.

Glaring at Ivan, Charlie sarcastically asked him, 'What time in the morning are you leaving?' Ivan smugly replied, 'You don't trust me... do you?'

Using a well-known cliché, Charlie responded, 'I wouldn't trust you as far as I could kick you!' and then added, 'Ivan... you are slimy and you're scum. If you have a problem with that, let's go outside and sort out our differences... physically.' The smug smirk quickly disappeared from Ivan's face and he cautiously walked out of the kitchen. Charlie resumed reading the newspaper and continued drinking ouzo.

Early the next morning, Charlie was woken up by loud knocking on the campervan door. Gingerly, he made his way to the door and opened it. A red-faced Anita was in a state of bewilderment and exasperatedly blurted out, 'Ian… his belongings and his bicycle are gone!'

Ivan had sneaked out in the early hours of the morning and rode off on his bicycle into the eerie darkness of the night. An upset Anita soon explained to Charlie that he had indeed borrowed a substantial amount of money from Judith and her. Anita, annoyingly, repeatedly stated that she didn't think the *charming* Ivan would do something like this. Eventually, she decided to take a deep breath. A stone-faced (but smug) Charlie aptly replied, 'Now you know why I never trusted him!'

Woken by the outside commotion, Chris came out of his homestead to investigate. Anita informed him what Ivan had done. A short time later, he was driving the campervan (accompanied by Anita and Charlie) along the main road to Nafplio. After no sighting of Ivan in the town, Chris decided to continue driving along the road to the city of Corinth. The search, however, would be fruitless; he was long gone. Charlie suspected that Ivan may have only cycled as far as Nafplio and then caught an early train to Athens.

Two days later, Charlie left the Peloponnese region. Chris (accompanied by Mary) drove him to the city of Corinth. They bid farewell to Charlie at the bus station. He arrived at the

Inter-city bus station in Athens a couple of hours later. Later in the day, Charlie was at the port of Piraeus. Several hours later, he boarded a Souda-bound ferry, taking him to northwest Crete. Before boarding the sea vessel, however, Charlie had waited in a nearby bar and had noticed a highly inebriated George (the Swedish-born cave dweller).

Charlie boarded the large ferry before George and was hoping to avoid him during the entire overnight crossing. Later, out on the high seas, he located him in one of the lounge rooms, highly intoxicated and muttering incomprehensively to himself. No-one was sitting close to George! Charlie made himself comfortable in another lounge room.

Early the next morning, the large ferry docked into the port of Souda. An hour later, Charlie boarded a Chania-bound bus. Somewhat surprisingly, George was nowhere to be seen. He (Charlie) would stay on the island of Crete for the next three months. Charlie suspected that George was somewhere in the Chania region but the pair would never cross paths.

15

The Magnet of Kriti

For three weeks, Charlie stayed in a centrally-located pension in the city of Chania (Crete). The accommodation facility was above a taverna and access to the rooms was by a stairwell. On the cobbled pavement in front of the taverna stood a large sign, *Les Testicules de Porc*. Within the itinerant/travelling community, the taverna was better known as 'Pigs Balls'.

Charlie rarely ate a meal in the taverna, deeming the quality of the food as mostly sub-standard. He would, however, consume alcohol inside the taverna every late-afternoon and regularly converse with several other travellers: two English males (Mack and Derek) and two French males (Marko and Christo). Charlie had known the French guys two years previously. All four of them no longer participated in the olive-picking and orange-picking seasons. Occasionally, they would be involved in other forms of employment but their main source of income was from *begging*. A dishevelled-dressed Mack always wore a well-used and crumpled suit. Similar to the other three, he spent most of his 'begging income' on alcohol. Charlie soon had a collective name for the four of them: *The Beggars Quartet.*

Begging in Chania was only tolerated by the local authorities outside the main tourist season. Before the main tourist season (commencing the first week of June), the local and tourist police would 'round-up' the beggars and place them in police vehicles. Beggars and other 'undesirables' would then be driven well away from any tourist areas and told not to come back to the area until November. Non-compliance often resulted in a beating and/or a lifetime ban from the region.

Two years previously, the rooms inside the Pig's Balls pension were mostly filled with English-speaking or French-speaking travellers. This time, however, most of the rooms were occupied by Serbian army deserters. Several of them could speak English quite fluently and Charlie would converse with them on an almost daily basis. It soon emerged that none of them wished to return to Serbia any time soon. Tensions had built up significantly within the former Yugoslav Republic as the Bosnian War (1992-1995) was in progress at the time. The majority were hoping to stay in Greece indefinitely. Several years later, Serbia would once again be involved in another armed conflict: the Kosovo War (1998-1999).

For the first three days, Charlie remained in Chania. On the fourth day, he boarded a bus, one that took him to the village of Alikianos: 13 kilometres southwest of Chania. After alighting from the bus, Charlie walked to the *Καφενείο Ευφτίσια* (Eftesia Kafeneío). The premises had been renovated during his two-year absence. He casually strode past a group of boisterous English-speaking males and headed inside the kafeneío. 'Uncle' Eftesia emerged from a small adjoining room. Charlie cheekily declared, 'Hi, Eftesia… I'm back!'

Charlie attempted to converse with Eftesia in Greek, but the elderly gentleman responded in broken English. He was keen to demonstrate how his spoken English had vastly improved over the past two years: an excellent achievement for someone aged in their mid-sixties! A few minutes later, a smiling Maria (Eftesia's wife) emerged. Charlie tried to converse with her in Greek but was constantly interrupted by Eftesia – thoroughly enjoying his role as translator.

Eventually, Charlie purchased a half-litre bottle of Amstel beer and proceeded to the outside beer garden section of the taverna. Reading an English newspaper, he sat alone on a table, several metres away from the boisterous English-speaking group. Charlie was quite content to peruse the newspaper peacefully and occasionally sip on his bottle of beer. However, one of the English lads (on several occasions) glanced towards him.

A few minutes later, the same gentleman suddenly blurted out to Charlie, 'Is that today's newspaper?'

'No… yesterday's paper.'

The English male then uttered, 'I detect a bit of an accent… an Aussie, perhaps?'

Then an Irish male joined the conversation, 'You've been here before… haven't you?'

The two males then came over to the table and introduced themselves. Englishman Paul and Irishman Seamus then chatted with him for the next half hour or so. Charlie soon learnt that there had been significant changes within the Chania region over the past two years. The cost of living (e.g. food and accommodation) had increased substantially. Even bottled beer had doubled in price. The daily wage (based on an eight-hour working day) for picking oranges, however, was still 5000 drachmas!

Paul and Seamus soon informed Charlie that the availability of work had substantially diminished over the past two years. Similar to his recent experience in the Peloponnese region, most fruit-picking employment was now supplied by contractors. The practice of working directly for an orchardist had largely eroded. Contractors did not supply any food or drink to their employees which meant that banquet-like luncheon meals were rarely provided by the orchardist's family anymore.

Charlie resided on the island of Crete for the next two and a half months. Employment opportunities during this period could be best described as *sporadic*. Large groups of Albanians were not the only non-westerners within the Chania region. An influx of Serbians, Kosovars/Kosovans, Bulgarians, Romanians, Russians, etc were also seeking employment.

For the first several weeks, however, Charlie managed to obtain a steady flow of employment through Eva (a local) who was aged in her early forties. Eva's father was the actual contractor but as she spoke English fluently, all work-related communication was with her. Orange-picking employment, unfortunately, was only for two to four days per week. Charlie, however, secured other forms of employment (via assistance from Eftesia) from time to time: mainly the loading/unloading of trucks containing crates of oranges or packaging material.

Eva would regularly work with her small crew of 'orange harvest warriors'. A friendly and pleasant woman, she was also quite a fast orange-picker. Eva soon realised, however, that Charlie could remove the oranges from the trees just as quick (if not quicker) than her. On the second day, she casually asked him if he had undertaken any fruit picking previously. Charlie explained to her that he had been an itinerant fruit-picker over the past few years, mainly within the eastern states of Australia. He further added that he had been picking fruit in several other countries as well. Charlie then informed Eva that he had recently been picking oranges in the Peloponnese region and had also been living (and working) in this area two years previously. She shook her head and started laughing, fascinated that people like Charlie were able to eke a living all year round from various fruit/vegetable harvest seasons in different geographical regions.

Charlie stayed in Chania for several weeks and it was an enjoyable time for him. Every evening, he would have a sit-down meal in one of the local tavernas or restaurants. Charlie, however, rarely purchased any food or drink within the overpriced tourist precinct of the city. The menus of these 'over-rated' eateries were often written in English (and Greek) and to a lesser degree, in French or German. Outside the tourist precinct, however, the menus were mostly written in Greek (i.e. using the Cyrillic alphabet). Charlie, by now, could translate most of the Cyrillic-written menu items and, thus, was able to speak a certain amount of Greek when ordering food and beverages. His favourite food dish was ποικιλία (poikilia): a mixed grill of meat (or seafood) and vegetables.

Charlie's three-week stay in the pension could best be described as 'interesting'. The first week was a relatively quiet and uneventful one. The second week, however, would be far more *vibrant*. During this second week, one of the rooms that neighboured Charlie's room was occupied by a Greek 'couple'. For the first few days, he never saw them, but he would certainly hear them – especially the female – every night.

For five nights, and in the early hours of the morning, Charlie would be awoken by frantic sexual activity happening inside the neighbouring room. The wall separating the two rooms was *paper-thin.* The sound of squeaky and bouncing bedsprings, intertwined with loud orgasmic grunts and groaning, echoed effortlessly through to other rooms as well! Most of the orgasmic sound effects were coming from the Greek woman. Charlie soon named the room the 'honeymoon suite' as he presumed the occupants were newlyweds.

On the third night, however, Charlie thought that the male's voice sounded different compared to the male occupying the room the previous two nights. Plus, his groaning was louder and more frequent. Charlie sensed that she was on top of him, *giving his bones a real good rattle* – her groaning was still much louder than her 'submissive' though. On the fifth night, it appeared that the room was occupied by yet another male. Having already dismissed the 'newlywed' theory, Charlie thought that she might be *on the game.* Although there were no males inside her room for the next two nights, he (Charlie) was still woken up when she returned in the early hours of the morning: the room's door-lock made loud clicking noises and the hinges squeaked when moved.

At the start of the third week, Charlie crossed paths with the Greek woman in the hallway between the rooms. Taller than Charlie, she had a physique best described as voluptuous, along with thick and shoulder-length black hair. He smiled and politely greeted her. The woman smiled back and reciprocated the greeting. Introducing herself as Sula, she began to chat with Charlie in fluent English.

Sula was a resident of Athens and had come to Chania for a two-week holiday. Charlie informed her that he was in one of the next-door rooms. At one point, during the conversation, he casually asked Sula what the nightlife was like in Chania. Responding, somewhat cheekily, she informed Charlie that she enjoyed drinking and dancing – and had met several lovely guys in the previous week. He tried to keep a straight face as the conversation continued but moments later, Sula burst out laughing. Ogling him amorously, she said, 'I know what you're thinking.' Sula, playfully, grabbed Charlie's shirt collar and with a cheeky smile, demanded, 'Come with me!'

After leading Charlie into her room, Sula pushed Charlie onto the bed – and five days of sexual bliss was about to commence for him. Outside of her room, the pair enjoyed each other's company, filling in the days by exploring the sights and frequenting several tavernas/bars within the Chania region. Her vibrant outgoing personality and natural sexiness were like a *magnet* to Charlie. On the sixth day, Sula returned to Athens and Charlie resumed his life as an itinerant fruit-picker. The following morning, Charlie boarded an Alikianos-bound bus. As he approached *Eftesia's Kafeneío*, Charlie (jokingly) decided to walk bow-legged, taking short careful steps!

An inquisitive Paul soon asked Charlie, 'Where have you been the past week?'

'I've been busy!'

'Doing what?'

'Having close physical contact with a woman from Athens.'

Irish Seamus then abruptly intervened. 'Bullshit!'

As Charlie drank a small glass of Tsikoudia/raki (a spirit) with a coffee chaser, he explained to a now-captive audience his life for the past five days. Seamus was still sceptical until two Serbian lads (who were residing in the same pension as Charlie) confirmed the lustful tale.

A few days later, Charlie moved to a patch of land near the Rema Keritis River: a kilometre from the village of Alikianos. After pitching his tent, he automatically became a 'temporary member' of the *River Rats* community. This was home for Charlie for the next six weeks. Several of his fellow 'River Rats' was also living in tents. The majority, however, were dwelling in makeshift shelters. Several of them had ingeniously constructed bamboo structures and had strategically tied on measured thick sheets of plastic to the framework. These sturdy structures were even divided into separate rooms, along with a wooden-based floor, a doorway and several windows (made from thin measured sheets of plastic).

Charlie enjoyed living near the river and felt quite comfortable with this new lifestyle. He felt this new adventure, however, seemed to lack the same level of character, compared to his previous stay two years earlier. Seamus and Paul were certainly *entertaining* but Charlie regarded the rest of the group, except for Englishman Tim, as somewhat 'mundane' and 'colourless'.

Paul was quite a pleasant gentleman, despite having a major alcohol consumption problem. Fellow countryman, Tim, regularly referred to him as 'Captain Al' (as in Captain Alcoholic). Seamus, on the other hand, had a persona riddled with negativism and cynicism. Regardless of whether anyone wanted to listen to his views or not, he constantly moaned about how everything in the world was wrong. In drunken outbursts, he even attempted to upset Charlie by stating how bad Australia was, despite never having set foot in the country. An unfazed Charlie, however, chose not to respond to Seamus' drunken antagonistic antics by adopting an attitude of *no point adding fuel to the fire.*

Seamus would generally be ignored by everyone but eventually, he pushed his luck a bit too far one day with one particular gentleman: Eftesia's son (Thaddeus). On several occasions, Thaddeus had previously responded to his alcohol-fuelled antics with a fiery outburst in English. Then one night he snapped and punched Seamus flush on the side of his face. The antagonistic Irishman collapsed to the ground. Eftesia quickly intervened and broke up the scuffle. Charlie and others, meanwhile, practically ignored the fracas and just kept on drinking!

Aforementioned, Seamus' drunken bouts of antagonism were largely ignored by the itinerants, except for Englishman Tim. He managed to provoke Seamus on a fairly regular basis and the verbal exchange between the pair often provided a certain level of hilarity. Tim, firstly, would patiently wait until Seamus had consumed a copious amount of alcohol before engaging in any form of provocative discourse. Most of the discussion tended to focus on 'The Troubles' (also known as the Northern Ireland Conflict). Seamus, who was pro-Irish and a staunch Catholic, detested the sight of British troops in Northern Ireland.

Tim would regularly needle Seamus with the following statements:

'Northern Ireland needs the British presence';

'Northern Ireland should remain part of the United Kingdom'; and,

'There's more Irish living in London than Ireland!'

One day, Seamus made the mistake of telling someone that he was born in England! Tim was duly informed and he soon had a nickname for him: *Plastic Paddy*. From that moment on, Tim would never acknowledge Seamus by his Christian name again.

'Good morning Plastic Paddy.'

'How's Plastic Paddy today?'

'Plastic Paddy, yet again, you are wrong!'

Another individual who irked the itinerant community was Kevin. The Scottish national was also a negatively-minded character. Even worst, his behaviour at times was quite *weird*. Deeply religious, he often carried a set of rosary beads in his left hand, whilst holding a bottle of beer in his right hand! With a long straggly beard and thick (and greying) mangled hair, Kevin soon earned himself the nickname 'Jesus'. Charlie, however, thought he looked more like 'Catweazle': the central character in a 1970s television series of the same name.

One afternoon, several inebriated patrons inside the kafeneio were discussing the topic 'Myths and Legends'. The folklore of the Lochness Monster soon entered the discussion. Charlie, somewhat emphatically, stated that the creature was purely fictional. Kevin, who was sitting at a nearby table, overheard the conversation and quickly alighted from his chair!

In a visibly irritated manner, Kevin avidly declared, 'The Lochness Monster does INDEED exist.' Charlie responded, 'Bullshit.'

'If it exists… they would have found it by now.'

A now-flustered Kevin then responded by dangling his rosary beads in front of Charlie's face and vehemently declared, 'I swear on these rosary beads… that the Lochness Monster DOES exist.' He was now quite irate, with a reddened face and shaking with rage. Charlie, trying desperately not to laugh, decided not to antagonise him any further and casually responded, 'Yeah… whatever.'

Kevin turned around and went inside the kafeneio to purchase another beer. Quite audibly, Charlie quipped, 'Nutter!'

After this particular incident, most of the itinerant community rarely conversed with Kevin again. Strangely though, many individuals would still accompany him when they attended 'religious discussions' (two nights per week), held inside the local residence of a German-born couple: Klaus and Inga. Non-religious Charlie wasn't interested in attending these religious discussions. Surprisingly though, a relatively large group of people did attend.

Paul, on several occasions, attempted to entice both Charlie and Seamus in attending these *religious enlightenment* sessions. Interestingly though, he rarely mentioned to the pair what was discussed inside the house. His main point of persuasion mainly focused on the 'glorious' amount of food that was provided during the night. It appeared that the scrumptious feasting was the main drawcard!

Seamus and Charlie, however, did decide to attend one of these religious discussions one night. The first phase of the evening began with a short prayer session, followed by a half-hour session where 'modern' interpretations of several Bible passages were discussed. The second phase, primarily, involved a theatrical interaction between the German-born couple. Klaus, firstly, described his initial encounter with God. Speaking in German (along with plenty of arm waving and wildish hand gesticulation), he described the *rebellious and non-believing* period of his life: basically his teenage and early adulthood years.

Then suddenly (as if he had just been hit with a bolt of lightning), Klaus sees a bright light in the sky. He is instantly *empowered* by its beaming aura. The over-dramatic rant continues with how this 'enlightening' experience slowly but overwhelmingly, drew him closer to God's existence. Klaus then describes God as a *patient giant magnet.* During Klaus' performance, a stone-faced Inga, in a softly-spoken but passionate tone of voice, translated his over-the-top dialogue into English.

As the theatrical performance continued, an inebriated and agitated Seamus started to respond to Inga's translation with slurred words of sarcasm. An undeterred Klaus ignores the rude behaviour and soon reaches the pinnacle of his performance with a highly joyous (and relieved) expression on his face. In response, Inga and Kevin clap excitably and *loudly.* Out of sheer politeness, the rest of the attendees (except Seamus) also clapped but in a far more relaxed manner. Judging by the 'hopeful' facial expressions of most of the attendees, Charlie sensed that the food fest wasn't too far away!

The exuberant clapping, however, by Inga and Kevin had riled Seamus to a point where he had become even more disruptive. Bursts of unwarranted sarcasm were now flowing freely from his mouth. Paul and Charlie looked at each other and nodded in agreement. They stood up and grabbed Seamus by his arms and escorted him outside. Klaus followed them and calmly told Paul and Charlie that he would like to have a chat with Seamus.

Paul and Charlie went back inside the house and onwards towards the kitchen. The *gluttonous* banquet was about to commence. The large kitchen table was completely covered with food. Several of the attendees (notably Kevin and Paul) gorged heartily on the food as if they hadn't eaten for several days! Outside the house, Klaus' passive demeanour soon had a calming effect on Seamus and the pair soon rejoined the group.

An hour later, Charlie was chatting to Inga. She soon sensed that he appeared to have little interest in any religious discussion as the conversation constantly drifted to non-religious topics. Charlie informed her that he had resided and worked in the Alikianos area two years earlier. Charlie then casually asked Inga if she (and Klaus) had crossed paths with Gunther. There was a long silent pause. After taking a deep breath and with a wide smile on her face, Inga replied, 'Yes, I remember Gunther… how could Klaus and I forget him!'

Inga explained to Charlie that Gunther had been a regular attendee at their religious discussions. Initially, Klaus and she got on quite well with him but the friendship soured when Gunther *over-celebrated* his birthday. 'He completely lost the plot during his week-long birthday celebrations!' Inga further added that when Gunther left the local area, he left without saying goodbye and also owed them a substantial amount of money. The negative memories saddened Inga but Charlie soon cheered her up when he recounted Gunther's 'begging for cigarettes' episode (chapter six). After the night had passed, Charlie never attended another religious session and he never crossed paths with Klaus or Inga again.

By the end of the first week of May, the orange-picking season had come to a halt. It was time for Charlie to leave Crete. His next destination: the city of Zaragoza (northern Spain). For several weeks, he had been in contact with Conchita who he had met in the raspberry fields of Blairgowrie (Scotland) a few months previously. Charlie left the area, travelling with three other itinerants: Max (a German national), Lorraine (a French national) and Jorge (a Portuguese national). All four travelled together in Max's well-travelled VW Kombi van.

After arriving in the port of Piraeus, via a ferry trip from northwest Crete, Max drove his VW Kombi van to the port of Patras (western Greece). Whilst waiting in the queue to board the ferry to Bari (Italy), the quartet would be extensively questioned by military officials acting as border security. Upon inspection of the passports, the officials noticed that all four travellers had stayed longer than the standard three months.

Charlie sensed that the officials may attempt to impose a monetary penalty for 'overstaying'. The quartet, however, had anticipated beforehand to what questions they may be asked. Planned responses had already been well prepared. Firstly, the group was asked to why they overstayed, even though none of them required a visa to enter Greece. Max responded, 'We love this country. So much beauty and with wonderful people… it was very hard for us to leave!'

The quartet was then asked if they had participated in any form of employment. In unison, all four declared that they were *strictly* tourists and responded along the lines, 'engaging in any form of employment would have severely disrupted our wonderful experiences of this great country!'

The military officials, initially, intended to search Max's vehicle but changed their minds as there was quite a long queue of vehicles waiting to board the seafaring vessel. One of the younger khaki-wearing military personnel then decided to ask the same questions again to the quartet and all responses were identical to the previous ones. All four re-entered the VW Kombi van and Max drove the vehicle onto the large sea vessel. A short time later, they were all relaxing in one of the lounge areas, each with an alcoholic beverage in their hand. An hour later, the ferry departed from the port of Patras and Charlie's glorious Greek adventure had come to an end.

16

From Patras to Santander

After a sixteen-hour journey, the ferry docked in the Italian port city of Bari. An hour later, the four were in Max's VW Kombi van, leaving the city and heading towards the A14 Autostrada (now part of the E55 or European Route 55). Their final destination: Lyon (France). For the next three days, Max did most of the driving. For several hours (during the first night), however, Charlie drove the vehicle. He had an international driver's license whilst both Jorge and Lorraine did not possess a driver's licence. This would be the only occasion that Charlie drove a motor vehicle anywhere in Europe.

The first few hours of the journey were uneventful. Then the vehicle began to experience minor gearbox problems. Max brought the VW Kombi to a halt on the outskirts of an eastern coastal town. He knew what the problem was but stated to the others that the repairs may take two hours or so. By now, dusk was settling in. As Max repaired the gearbox, the other three just casually loitered nearby.

Half an hour later, a police vehicle drove past them –
slowly. Ten minutes later, the same vehicle drove past them
again. Five minutes later, the police vehicle returned and
stopped a short distance from where Charlie, Lorraine and
Jorge were standing. The driver alighted from the police
vehicle and, using the door as a shield, pointed a sub-machine
gun at the now-startled trio! At the time, the Italian
government had committed to a major crackdown on illegal
activities carried out by the *Cosa Nostra* (Mafia).

The second *Polizia di Stato* police officer (who was much
older than his colleague) cautiously alighted from the front
passenger side of the vehicle and slowly walked towards
them. At this point, Max ceased repairing components of the
gearbox and joined the other three. The police officer stopped
walking when he was about five metres away from the group.
Jorge and Lorraine, speaking in Italian, explained to him that
they were on their way to the French city of Lyon before
encountering a problem with the vehicle's gearbox.

Moving closer to the group, the senior police officer
requested to view all four passports. Upon examining the
passports (of four different nationalities), his mood lightened
significantly. Just over an hour later, the quartet was on their
way once more, with Max and Charlie driving throughout
the night to the north-western city of Torino (Turin).
Fortunately, there were no more mechanical problems with
the vehicle!

Before entering France, Charlie was required to obtain a travel visa. He was refused a visa at the French Consul in Athens due to him staying in Greece for more than three months and not having a resident visa. Telephone calls to several French Consuls in different parts of Italy proved to be fruitless as they only issued visas for *business* purposes.

Max's VW Kombi van arrived in Torino just before 3.00 am and, a short time later was parked in a supermarket car park. Just after 9.00 am, Charlie walked into the French consul in central Torino and three hours later, collected his passport. He had only been granted a *Limited Stay* Visa (a transit visa for three days). To be granted a three-month visa for France, Charlie could only obtain one at the French consul in Rome (690 kilometres away).

Two hours later, the group crossed into France via the Fréjus Road Tunnel. The tunnel is 13 kilometres in length and it runs under Col du Fréjus in the Cottian Alps between the commune of Modane in France and the town of Bardonecchia in Italy. For several kilometres and before the VW Kombi van entered the road tunnel, Charlie was entranced by the breathtaking mountainous scenery. When his wanderlust journey ended many years later, he regarded the close-up views of these particular picturesque panoramic views as being some of the most memorable! Nearly five hours later, the quartet arrived in Lyon: France's third-largest city after Paris and Marseilles.

The four of them stayed in a house owned by one of Lorraine's friends. In Greece, the quartet had originally planned to travel to Portugal via France and Spain. Jorge had promised the other three that he could secure employment for them in one of the Portuguese resort towns, located on the Atlantic Ocean coast. Unfortunately, 'personality clashes' between Lorraine and Jorge (which first emerged in Crete) had intensified by the time they arrived in Lyon. As a precaution, in case the Portugal-venture fell through, Charlie had been in contact with Conchita who resided in the northern Spanish city of Zaragoza. Nine months earlier, the romantically-linked pair had toiled together on the raspberry fields in Blairgowrie, Scotland. She invited him to stay with her for a while.

After staying in Lyon for several days, Jorge decided to board a train, bound for the Spanish city of Barcelona. Instead of boarding a train, Charlie decided to hitchhike from the southern outskirts of the city. His destination: Zaragoza. In Lyon, the four agreed to meet up at the central railway station in Zaragoza on a particular date and at a particular time. Max and Lorraine stayed in Lyon for a further week.

On the southern outskirts of Lyon, Charlie attempted to obtain his first lift for the day: one that would take him along the autoroute (A7) and towards the commune of Orange (Provence-Alpes-Côte d'Azur region). On the northern outskirts of Orange, he obtained a lift that would take him along the A9. Charlie hitchhiked along this autoroute to the southern French city of Perpignan.

To enter Spain, Charlie was required to obtain a visa. There was a *General Consulate of Spain* in Perpignan. Unfortunately, he arrived at the consul building half an hour after closing time! With dwindling finances, Charlie decided not to seek paid accommodation for that night and opted to camp out instead. He walked to the outskirts of Perpignan and came upon woodlands. A section of this area contained relatively dense scrub and, thus, made it easier for him to hide. A short time later, however, Charlie realised that there was a gipsy camp nearby. Although he couldn't see them, Charlie could hear voices. Smoke billowed from their campsite, which drifted over his makeshift camp. He was hoping his nearby presence wouldn't be noticed. It wasn't and Charlie slept through the night undisturbed.

The next morning, Charlie left his passport at the consul for several hours, stating that he required a transit visa to pass through Spain and onwards to Portugal. As Charlie had been in France for six days, he had used a thin black-coloured texture to alter the transit visa from three days to eight days.

Charlie's passport had been stamped with the date when he entered France via the Fréjus Road Tunnel. Although Charlie had previously been in and out of France, on several occasions, no entry (or exit) dates had ever been stamped in his passport. When he collected his passport from the consul,

Charlie had only been granted a three-day *limitado* (limited stay) visa and a small fee was charged for this 'service'. He asked why he wasn't granted a transit visa and the consul official bluntly (but untruthfully) stated that the Perpignan office doesn't issue transit visas. [Note: a transit visa was cost-free].

After leaving the consul's office, Charlie immediately walked to the southern outskirts of Perpignan. With a protruding right thumb and a sign (Zaragoza) in his left hand, he attempted to obtain his first lift for the day. Ten minutes later, a young French woman stopped beside him. A short time later, the pair was at the France-Spain border. Charlie's luggage was in the boot/trunk of her motor vehicle. The young woman talked to the Spanish customs officials for less than two minutes, before continuing to drive onto Spanish soil. There had been no passport checks.

After travelling along the autopista (AP-7) for half an hour, the young woman dropped Charlie off at a road junction, located northeast of the city of Barcelona. He then walked for several kilometres. That night, Charlie slept under an unfinished bridge but didn't sleep well; he was awoken several times by a persistent and torrential downpour.

Early the next morning, Charlie continued on his journey amidst rays of welcoming sunshine. His progress that day, however, would be frustratingly slow. For example, just before midday, he was dropped off near a road tunnel. The only solution for Charlie was to walk through the short-distance road tunnel – along the Autopista. When he emerged on the other side of the tunnel, Charlie was expecting to be greeted by the *Guardia Civil* (a military force with police duties). Fortunately, he was instead met by several road workers but one of the young males (who spoke fluent English) chastised him for walking through the road tunnel illegally! Nevertheless, they gave Charlie a lift to a more suitable place for him to hitchhike from.

During the late afternoon, Charlie walked through a forested area for several hours. He eventually espied a services centre on the Autopista (AP-7) in the distance. Charlie decided to camp in the woodlands, barely a hundred metres from the services centre. The next morning, he casually strolled into the services centre restaurant and promptly ordered a breakfast meal. Afterwards, he proceeded to hitchhike from a rest area, located near the services centre exit. Charlie thought that he should be able to obtain a lift fairly easily as there were plenty of vehicles (especially trucks/lorries) exiting – but he was wrong.

After patiently waiting for over two hours, Charlie decided to approach lorry drivers directly. An English lorry driver then informed him that the vast majority of the traffic was going *southwards* instead of westwards. Vehicles going to cities such as Zaragoza and Madrid would mostly be travelling on the A-2 (not the AP-7) before they got onto the

AP-2. Eventually, a motorist did stop beside him – four hours later. The young Spanish male was going to the Spanish capital of Madrid via the city of Zaragoza. Although the city (Zaragoza) was nearly 250 kilometres from the services centre, the vehicle arrived there an hour and a quarter later: it had been driven at a consistent speed of around 200 kilometres per hour!

Charlie was dropped off at the northern outskirts of Zaragoza and immediately walked towards the city centre. Less than an hour later, he located Conchita's place of residence: a two-bedroom unit (close to the city centre). Charlie was greeted by her parents who then informed him that she was currently at the main family residence: ten kilometres from Zaragoza. He stayed in the unit that night and the next morning (Saturday), Charlie was driven to the main residence. Conchita was waiting outside, sporting a wide grin; she embraced him for a substantial amount of time.

In the afternoon and throughout the next day as well, Conchita took Charlie on a guided tour throughout Zaragoza, highlighting the city's main landmarks. He had only intended to stay in Spain for less than a week but ended up staying for three and a half weeks. As a precautionary measure, Charlie had already pre-arranged to have an American Express cheque sent to him from Australia to Conchita's address.

Four days later, Charlie walked to the main railway station where he was to meet up with Jorge. Whilst staying in Lyon, the Portuguese national had provided Charlie with the details of a train journey from Barcelona to Zaragoza on that particular day (Wednesday). The train duly arrived at the designated time. A large number of passengers stepped onto the platform. Jorge, however, was not one of them!

Charlie left the railway station and returned several times during the day to check to see if Jorge was on a later train. He wasn't. The next morning, Charlie returned to the railway station and immediately noticed a familiar-looking VW Kombi van in the carpark! Max and Lorraine were already standing on the platform. Charlie greeted them and the trio waited for the next train from Barcelona to arrive. The train arrived but, alas, no sign of Jorge.

Realising that they had probably been 'hoodwinked' by Jorge, the three of them discussed their next course of action. Max and Lorraine decided that they would continue travelling to Portugal and onto one of the Atlantic Coast seaside resorts. Charlie, however, decided on a different plan. He would stay in Spain for at least two more weeks. Afterwards, he would board a Zaragoza-Santander coach bus and then board a ferry bound for Plymouth (United Kingdom). Charlie had also been in contact with an English friend (who resided in the north-Devon coastal town of Barnstaple), in case the 'Portuguese venture' fell through.

As the trio discussed their next moves, they were suddenly surrounded by numerous burly-built middle-aged males.

Attired in casual clothing, they immediately identified themselves as police officers and instantly demanded to see their passports. Max and Lorraine duly presented theirs. Charlie, however, had already overstayed his three-day *limitado* visa and tried to explain to the police officer that his passport was at an *amigo's* (friend's) place. It was actually in his possession but he didn't want to show it to them! Several officers tried to converse with Charlie in Spanish but he kept responding to them in English.

Several minutes later, Charlie was marched into a small room, located at the end of the platform. Before he entered the room, Charlie remembered that he had an International Driver's licence and an Australian (state of New South Wales) driver's licence in his wallet. Just after entering the room, Charlie immediately presented both licences to a desk-sitting police officer. Using a desk computer, the details of both licences were checked thoroughly: a process that lasted about fifteen minutes. Eventually, he was allowed to leave the room.

Charlie met up with Max and Lorraine in the carpark. They explained to him that the police officers' actions were directly related to several bombings that had occurred in Spain over the past several months. The Basque separatist group, *Euskadi Ta Askatasuna* (ETA), had been waging a violent political campaign against the government at the time. Fifteen minutes later, Max and Lorraine were on their way to Portugal. Charlie would never see them again.

Several months later, Charlie (whilst residing in the UK) received a letter from Max. The letter contained the following information: Jorge had 'disappeared'; the address of the Portuguese seaside resort was bogus; and, he had split up with Lorraine (who had returned to Lyon). Max further added that there was a plentiful supply of tourism-related employment within towns and cities situated along the Atlantic coast. He was quite content to stay in Portugal for a while.

Conchita's parents, meanwhile, had just begun a three-week holiday in the south of France. Charlie would stay with her in the unit/apartment for the next week. She was a student at the local university and was studying English and French literary works. At the time, Conchita had several major assignments to complete and the exam period was rapidly approaching. Charlie would assist her with two English literature assignments during the daytime. The evenings were reserved for 'red wine and romance' activities.

Before the commencement of the major exam period, Conchita had a week to prepare and study for her upcoming exams. She *needed* free time during this particular week. Charlie, therefore, decided to explore a section of the Pyrenees Mountains (mostly near the small city of Jaca) for the next eight days. Whilst he was hiking and camping in the Pyrenees, Charlie completed a major English Literature assignment for her. He began his eight-day 'adventure' by hitchhiking from Zaragoza to Jaca.

In Jaca, Charlie filled his half-empty backpack with canned food, several small baguette loaves, fresh fruit and fresh vegetables. Afterwards, he walked northwards along a steep and windy mountain road. Eventually, Charlie came upon a hiking trail. For the next seven nights, he either slept in 'hiker' huts or inside his pitched tent. In the evenings, Charlie created a campfire to either cook vegetables in a can partially-filled with water or used makeshift tongs (two small branches) to heat a can of food.

During the day, Charlie mostly wandered along the various walking trails. On the fifth day, he walked to the town of Aisa to replenish his food and beverage supply. As Charlie continued on one of the mountain trails in a westerly direction, he eventually came upon a snow-covered section – even though the summer season was only a few weeks away. On the sixth night, Charlie shared a hut with a young student (Miguel) from the Basque city of Bilbao. Miguel had been hiking through the Pyrenees for the past several weeks. He had commenced his trek south-east of the city of Donostia-San Sebastian (in the province of Gipuzkoa).

Miguel's level of spoken English was excellent and the pair was able to converse freely for several hours. Charlie was hoping to hike further westwards but Miguel informed him that there were still significant amounts of snow in certain sections of the Pyrenees Mountains. Charlie did not have adequate footwear for these particular conditions.

On the eighth day, Charlie hitchhiked back to Zaragoza by obtaining several lifts: one of which was with two young women aged in their mid-twenties. They were from Barcelona and heading towards Zaragoza. Using a mixture of English and Spanish, he learnt that both of them were journalists and they were travelling throughout Spain for the next several weeks. They had no particular travel itinerary and were just 'following their noses' or in other words, a loosely planned (but hopefully adventurous) road trip. Just over an hour later, Charlie arrived in Zaragoza.

Charlie stayed with Conchita for several more days before departing from Zaragoza on a Santander-bound intercity coach. As the coach entered the *Basque Country* (travelling along the AP-68), it was stopped at a roadblock manned by heavily-armed military personnel. The bus driver was immediately taken off the bus and questioned. Next, two of the military personnel boarded the bus. They checked items of identification but only from passengers who were sitting in the first few rows of seats. Charlie was seated in the rear section of the bus and, thus, was not required to produce any form of identification. Twenty minutes later, the intercity-coach resumed its journey.

Upon arriving in Santander, Charlie immediately made his way to the ferry port only to discover that the next ferry crossing to Plymouth (United Kingdom) was two days away. After a brief walk, Charlie came upon a campsite and pitched his tent. His next-door neighbours were a young couple from the African country of Namibia. They were also waiting for the next Plymouth-bound ferry.

Two days later, Charlie was amongst the horde of passengers waiting to board the large ferry. Passengers with *European* passports were automatically directed to board the vessel. People holding non-European passports (including Charlie and the couple from Namibia), however, were singled out and questioned by customs officials. Charlie's passport would be closely scrutinised as nearly every page was filled with numerous visas and entry/departure stamps. A stone-faced customs officer eventually located the *limitado* visa and stared at it for quite a while. Charlie had changed the three-day *limitado* visa to 28 days by using a thin black-coloured marker to cover over all the pen ink!

During these agonising moments, Charlie maintained a fairly calm demeanour. Judging by the expression on the customs officer's face, however, he felt that the sternly-looking gentleman probably realised that the handwritten entry on the visa had been tampered with – twenty-eight days was probably an excessive amount of time for a 'limited-stay' visa. As Charlie was departing from Spain, there was no attempt to extract a monetary fine from him. He boarded the ferry.

The ferry trip to Plymouth was just over twenty-two hours in duration. Charlie passed most of the time away by reading a large paperback (800+ pages) and drinking four litres of red wine (two two-litre casks). He tried to sleep several times but with minimal success. The ship eventually docked in the south-western English city of Plymouth.

As Charlie approached the English customs officials, he was still feeling the effects of the large amount of wine that he had consumed. Severely sleep-deprived, Charlie sensed that he may soon be embroiled in a 'verbal showdown' with a customs officer. During the lengthy voyage, however, Charlie had carefully devised a *watertight story* concerning his travel plans (and recent travels) and well-rehearsed responses had been prepared to any line of questioning by customs officials.

Passengers with 'European' passports, once again, were politely ushered through the customs area. The same group of non-European passport holders, however, were directed to a particular customs officer. The portly, fair-haired, female customs officer would subject each individual (or couple) to a rigorous interrogation process, typically lasting five to ten minutes. A now-irritable Charlie waited near the end of the queue. An hour later, it was his turn to be interrogated. The customs official greeted him coldly and then spent the next few minutes carefully scanning *every* page of his passport. With her face now a flustered-red colour, she commenced the intimidation process.

Charlie was soon bombarded with rapid-fire questions but in response, he pretended that his hearing and level of comprehension couldn't keep pace with the rapid questioning technique! Charlie irked the customs official by asking her to repeat *every* question: it was a ploy to allow him more thinking time. After interrogating and trying to intimidate Charlie for more twenty minutes, she eventually stopped trying to 'catch him out'. Despite being sleep-deprived and alcohol-affected, Charlie had remained quite calm throughout the rigorous ordeal. The female customs officer, on the other hand, was now well and truly flustered.

After a few seconds of silence, Charlie was then ordered to provide evidence of personal finances and he presented the following to her: traveller's cheques in both British Pounds and Australian Dollars; an American Express cheque; and, numerous cash currencies (Greek Drachmas, Italian Lira, Spanish Pesetas, Australian Dollars, German Deutschmarks and English Pounds). She *politely* asked him what the cheques and cash added up to in English pounds sterling. Although Charlie did know the equivalent amount, he casually retorted, 'I don't know... I'm not very good at Maths either!'

The customs officer somewhat reluctantly stamped Charlie's passport and allowed him to move on. He had only walked a few metres when two male customs officers decided to stand in front of him. They then asked Charlie several questions and he coolly responded to them with the same well-rehearsed answers. Five minutes later, Charlie left the

customs area and was soon enjoying a refreshing beer in one
of the local hotels.

$$\mathit{17}$$

Winter in the Vineyards

On a cool winter's day, Charlie boarded an Air New Zealand flight at Sydney Airport. Destination: Wellington (the capital city of New Zealand). After being in the air for three and a half hours, the aircraft landed on the tarmac of Wellington International Airport amidst atrocious weather conditions. The barely-tolerable blustery conditions were also intermixed with intermittent bursts of torrential rain. Due to the strong winds regularly passing through the Cook Strait, 'Windy' Wellington is regarded as one of the windiest cities in the world. The weather conditions were hardly welcoming!

In stark contrast to his previous visit to New Zealand, Charlie passed through the customs area fuss-free and within fifteen minutes. As the customs official stamped his passport, he even welcomed him with a friendly smile. Outside the Arrivals terminal, Charlie patiently waited in a partially-sheltered bus bay. Ten minutes later, he was boarding the *Airport Flyer*: a bus service that went directly to Wellington Railway Station. For the next twenty minutes, the bus swayed from side to side and the windows were pelted with heavy droplets of rain. The bus driver, however, was unperturbed by the treacherous conditions; he drove the vehicle as if it was just a clear, sunny and wind-free day!

Charlie stayed in a centrally-located hostel for the next three nights. He filled in his days with endless hours of sightseeing and the daily patronising of several hotels. Charlie was quite intrigued with the local dress sense – everyone wore at least one article of black clothing. He wondered if the 'conformist' dress sense was a result of the patriotic influence of the country's national rugby union team: the New Zealand All Blacks.

On the fourth day, Charlie boarded a Bluebridge Cook Strait ferry service (Wellington to Picton). The three and a half-hour ferry crossing passed through the Cook Strait, mostly in a westerly direction. For most of the trip, he gazed through the window at the unique and picturesque scenery; especially the numerous small islands the ferry passed by. The ship arrived at the seaside town of Picton (South Island) in the early afternoon. Charlie had intended to hitchhike to the town of Blenheim (28 kilometres south of Picton) but soon discovered that there was a bus service between the two towns. He would, however, have to wait two hours for the next departing bus. Whilst waiting at the port terminal, Charlie pre-arranged accommodation by telephoning one of the youth hostels (Jill's Backpackers) in Blenheim.

After the bus had arrived at the Blenheim i-SITE (Visitor Information Centre), Charlie walked for about fifteen minutes before stopping in front of Jill's Backpackers hostel. Charlie would stay there for the next four weeks. Inside the hostel, he was greeted at the reception desk by the female manager who introduced herself as Tulip Rose. After a brief chat, she directed him to a four-person room.

Inside the hostel, there was a mixture of young travellers from various countries. A plentiful supply of local vineyard employment (especially vine pruning) was available at the time. Obtaining employment, therefore, was a relatively easy task. A small number of the residents (mainly the New Zealanders and Australians) chose to adopt a somewhat care-free and sporadic approach to the employment opportunities provided, opting to just work 'now and then'. The rest of the hostel residents, however, were *on a mission*. They wanted to work hard, save hard and then continue with their travels.

Two French nationals (Francois and Algerian-born Muhammad) worked in the vineyards during the day and in the evenings, were employed at a local factory. They, literally, just *worked, ate and slept*. Besides the cost of weekly accommodation, the pair would only spend their weekly wages on rice and fresh vegetables. The rest of their earnings were frugally saved. After working two jobs for several months, Francois and Muhammad attained their financial goal. They left Jill's Backpackers to pursue extensive travel throughout New Zealand, Fiji, Tonga and Western Samoa. The pair regularly sent postcards to the hostel. Tulip Rose would then place them on the large noticeboard.

During his four-week stay at Jill's Backpackers, Charlie regularly conversed with Tulip Rose. Born in the latter half of the 1960s, she admitted she was conceived during the 'hazy, hippy-flippy' era. Her parents were living in a commune at the time. The pair would freely discuss a variety of topics: environmental issues, politics, religion, etc. Sporting topics, however, were never discussed – not even the fortunes (or rare misfortunes) of the All Blacks. Although Tulip Rose's political (and environmental views) were left-leaning and Charlie's views were right-leaning, the pair, however, actively sought *common ground.* As they respected each other's viewpoint, fruitful discussions continued to thrive.

From time to time, Tulip Rose would have to deal with several troublesome hostel residents: all were young 'Kiwi' (New Zealander) males. As she could not physically deal with these erratic youngsters, Charlie and another resident (a heavily-tattooed, middle-aged Kiwi gentleman named Alan) would assist her if required. The most troublesome of these young delinquents was seventeen-year-old Martin.

Solidly-built Martin, who had recently relocated from Auckland, was on parole at the time. For the previous three and a half years, he had been detained in several juvenile detention centres located in and around New Zealand's most populated city. His parole conditions primarily involved him being relocated to the Marlborough wine region. Employment in a local vineyard and accommodation for Martin had been pre-arranged.

Initially, it appeared that Martin was faring quite well with his parole conditions. By the end of the second week, however, his mood had drifted to a noticeably more sombre one. In vain, Tulip Rose and other residents tried to convince him that regular employment can be beneficial to one's self-esteem and overall mindset. Unfortunately, it soon emerged that Martin's basic mentality towards life hadn't changed. At one point, he cheekily declared, 'Why should I work for little money? I can easily steal thousands of dollars!'

Martin's childish and stubborn attitude would soon land him in a whole lot of trouble. Dressed in baggy black clothing, he decided to patronise the hotels in central Blenheim one Saturday afternoon. His choice of clothing would be in stark contrast to the conservatively-dressed locals!

Several hours later, Charlie was reading a book and sipping on a cup of black tea in the hostel's second kitchen, when suddenly a terrified Martin burst through the kitchen door. He was looking for somewhere to hide. An intrigued Charlie immediately quizzed him to what was going on. At first, Martin was reluctant to divulge any information but Charlie's persistence eventually persuaded him to reveal all. An hour earlier, he (Martin) had been involved in a volatile disagreement with a local youngster in one of the hotels. He then admitted that he produced a butter knife and a fork ('borrowed' from the hostel kitchen) and attempted to stab the young male in the stomach with both utensils!

Whilst Martin was nervously explaining the sequence of events, his mobile phone was ringing – constantly. Charlie suspected that the local police were trying to contact him. Martin further admitted that a group of young locals were probably looking for him as well and he wanted to lock the door (of this second kitchen). Charlie decided to relocate to the main kitchen.

As Charlie waited for the kettle to boil in the main kitchen, he peered through the kitchen window. An old and well-dented (and heavily rusted) car was parked in the driveway which ran along the side of the house. Seated inside the vehicle were two young males and a young female, casually passing a 'peace pipe' (a homemade bong) to each other after a brief usage of the implement. Although both passenger windows were rolled down several centimetres, there was still an easily noticeable smoky haze inside the vehicle! Suddenly, two police cars drove into the driveway. The police officers had arrived to arrest Michael but the activity taking place inside the vehicle immediately caught their attention. The three young occupants were questioned and searched. The vehicle was searched as well. A third police car soon arrived.

One of the police officers was still trying to contact Michael on his mobile phone. A loud ringtone from an unanswered mobile phone, coming from inside the second kitchen, soon prompted vigorous door-knocking from a senior police officer. Thirty seconds later, Martin unlocked the door and reluctantly walked outside. Handcuffs were placed on his wrists and he was taken away in the third police vehicle. Meanwhile, the other three youngsters were being informed of their upcoming court appearance!

After this incident, Charlie decided it was time to seek accommodation elsewhere. At the age of forty, he felt the *toleration of hostel adventures* was no longer for him. The next day, Charlie relocated to a 'motor camp' (a caravan and camping park): 1.5 km east of central Blenheim. The new style of accommodation for him was a small and quaint caravan: one that was probably constructed in a bygone era (e.g. the 1950s). The following morning, he purchased two blankets from an Opportunity Shop and a small bar heater from a Discount Warehouse. The nightly temperature in the caravan dropped significantly as the outside temperatures were regularly in the minuses. Charlie stayed in the motor camp for the next three months. The serene nature, along with quiet and peaceful neighbours, was in stark contrast to the hostel accommodation.

Charlie, by now, had been employed by a vineyard labour contractor for the past several weeks. The contractor had also loaned him a Toyota mini-van, mainly to transport co-workers to and from the vineyards. The meeting point and drop-off point, each working day, was at Blenheim's railway station car park.

Three of Charlie's co-workers, Don (an elderly New Zealander) and a South African couple (Kepler and Winnie) were also residents in the motor camp. He would drive them from the motor camp each morning and transport them back home in the late afternoon. Outside employment hours, Charlie was permitted to use the van but only within Blenheim and nearby surroundings. He had also been provided with a company-paid Caltex fuel card.

Charlie would rarely socialise with Don, Kepler or Winnie. He opted, instead, to walk or occasionally drive the van into central Blenheim several times a week on his own. One weekend in late-August, however, the four of them decided to travel together to Dunedin (the south island's second-largest city) to watch a Rugby Union international match between the *All Blacks* (New Zealand) and the *Springboks* (South Africa). They hired a car to travel south to Dunedin via State Highway 1 (SH1): a distance of 663 kilometres. Motel accommodation, for two nights and in the coastal town of Oamaru (120 kilometres north of Dunedin), had been pre-arranged by Winnie. Accommodation within Dunedin and surrounding areas had been fully booked out. Kepler drove the hired vehicle for the entire journey and received *two* speeding tickets. As he was leaving the country several weeks later, the speeding infringement notices would not be paid.

The international rugby match took place on a bitterly cold night in Carisbrook (stadium). The venue was colloquially known as *The House of Pain*: the All Blacks rarely lost a test match at this venue. As the Australian Wallabies was not one of the competing teams, Charlie didn't care who won. Nevertheless, he still enjoyed an entertaining match: a mixture of a try-fest and several on-field skirmishes. The lead changed several times during the match but the All Blacks emerged victoriously. The final result was 31-27. Don was quite thrilled with the result. Kepler and Winnie – devastated.

The next morning, they left Oamaru and arrived in Blenheim in the late-evening. During the return trip, the four stayed in the picturesque coastal town of Kaikoura for over two hours. After consuming a late-afternoon meal, they went sightseeing. One of the most spectacular views in this particular area is the Seaward Kaikoura Mountains (part of the Southern Alps) where the 'mountain meets the sea'.

Charlie worked in the Blenheim area for four months and only for one contractor (Rob). Rob employed a large number of vineyard workers throughout the Marlborough region. This large volume of employees was then divided into several groups. Each group had a foreman or forewoman. Len (a Blenheim resident) was the foreman of the group that Charlie was in. Aged in his late fifties, he was a typical 'no-nonsense' type of guy. Len, however, was a very effective communicator who clearly explained to the vineyard workers how to complete the various vineyard labouring tasks (especially vine pruning) effectively and efficiently. He had previously worked in vineyards for over twenty years.

The bulk of the vineyard employment was paid piece-rate where an individual is paid by the amount of work they complete. Len's *tips and tricks* enabled the vineyard labourers to complete the various tasks (especially anything related to vine pruning) to be completed efficiently and more importantly – quickly. As the season progressed, Charlie became more adept with the nature of vineyard labouring (largely due to Len's expertise) and his earnings steadily increased each week. Nevertheless, he realised that his income earnings would have been much higher in Australian vineyards for the undertaking of similar employment.

Throughout July and August, weather conditions on some days could be best described as *horrendous*. Life in the vineyard could be quite treacherous at times. On most days, Charlie wore full wet-weather gear: wellington boots; yellow rain-proof trousers; and, a yellow rain-proof coat with an attached head (or hood) covering. He had brought the protective clothing with him from Australia. Despite the less-than-ideal employment conditions, goodwill and humorous camaraderie still prevailed within the working group.

As the end of October neared, the vineyard pruning season came to an end one afternoon. The weather conditions during the second half of the season (throughout September and October) had been far more favourable: dominated by plenty of sunshine and a steady increase in daily temperatures. As a token of appreciation, Rob (the contractor) organised an end-of-season party in the beer garden of one of the local hotels. All food and beverages (except spirit drinks) were provided free for all employees.

Two days later, Charlie boarded a minibus (near Blenheim's railway station) and half an hour later, he was inside the port terminal in Picton. As the ferry sailed through Cook Strait in an easterly direction, Charlie watched an in-house movie and read a book. He stayed in Wellington for two nights before boarding an Air New Zealand flight, bound for Sydney Airport.

18

The Journeys In Between

After travelling for over two decades, Charlie reminisced over his past wanderlust adventures. Some of the more memorable and exhilarating components of his travel experiences were the *journeys in between*. By far, hitchhiking was Charlie's favourite means of transport: obtaining 1200-1500 rides from (mostly) kind-hearted motorists by the time he decided to stop travelling. Throughout his extensive period of travel, however, Charlie did move from place to place via more conventional methods: namely trains, buses, ferries and aircraft.

Elements of these 'in-between' journeys have been covered in previous chapters: the flight to London via the USA (chapter one); the flight from Athens to Chania (chapter five); ferry trips across the Celtic Sea between Swansea and Cork (chapter nine); and, the extensive night travelling by train throughout Poland (chapter thirteen).

For the seasoned world-wide traveller, air travel features prominently in their overall itinerary: both international and domestic flights. When Charlie decided to cease travelling internationally, he had been on 28 different airlines and had spent more than $40,000 (Australian Dollars) on air travel. The majority of flight journeys were largely uneventful and, at times, could largely be deemed as quite boring. Several flights, however, were quite memorable: commencing with Charlie's first experience with Aeroflot (or PJSC Aeroflot-Russian Airlines).

As Charlie boarded an early-evening Aeroflot flight at London's Heathrow Airport, a level of drama was about to unfold due to mass confusion over seating allocation on the aircraft. The seat numbers are usually located above the seating and just below the overhead luggage compartments – not on the back of the seats. A large number of passengers believed that their reserved seat was the one directly *behind* the actual seating number. The confusion led to the majority of them deciding to just occupy any seat! The (Russian) stewardesses, initially, tried to place all passengers in their allocated seats but defiant passengers, once they had sat down, refused to move. Eventually, the stewardesses gave up (several of them even throwing their arms haplessly up into the air) and made their way to their seats.

Charlie was one of the last passengers to obtain a vacant seat. He sat next to a retired couple from rural Queensland: Joe and Florence. Before the aircraft even commenced take-off proceedings, the three of them were conversing earnestly and the banter-filled conversation was largely dominated by the behaviour of the passengers and the stewardesses! The melodramatic events occurring before take-off had also irked the pilots. On several occasions, they calmly announced (in several languages) to the passengers that the aircraft would not be ready for take-off until *everyone* was seated and with seatbelts on. There was a considerable delay but, eventually, the Aeroflot flight would be airborne. Destination: Sheremetyevo International Airport (Moscow, Russia).

The flight to Moscow was mostly uneventful except for two things: more than three hours would elapse before passengers received their meals and requests for bottled water were slowly met. Requests for vodka, however, were swiftly met. Charlie felt that the onboard supply of vodka seemed to exceed the supply of bottled water! Before consuming his meal, he had already drunk four small glasses of straight vodka and one small bottle of mineral water.

After the aircraft had touched down at Sheremetyevo International Airport, the herd of passengers made their way through a series of corridors. Charlie, along with Joe and Florence, eventually found themselves in the large Customs room. As the trio made their way towards the lone customs check-in desk, the etiquette of queuing was practically non-existent. A *push and shove* approach dominated the overall slow progress. Customs officials and military personnel just stood there; they were probably enjoying the 'entertaining' mayhem! Joe, Florence and Charlie eventually made it to the lone customs desk where their passports were duly stamped. The three of them were then directed by a customs official to a nearby stairwell. The set of stairs took them to the transit lounge.

The transit lounge was spacious and, surprisingly, quite modern. As it was now after midnight, most of the shops/stalls were closed. A twenty-four-hour *Irish bar* (with a large Guinness sign above the doorway), though, was open. Joe and Florence decided to relax in one of the lounge areas. Charlie, on the other hand, walked into the bar. He would consume three pints of Guinness over the next several hours. Sitting on a stool at the bar counter, he occasionally conversed with the two bar attendants (both Irish nationals).

Later that day, just after 3.00 pm, Charlie was aboard another Aeroflot aircraft. According to his flight itinerary, the next stopover was supposed to be New Delhi (the capital city of India). Several hours later, however, the chief pilot announced that there would be an unscheduled stopover in Tashkent (Uzbekistan). Once again, the food and beverage service during the flight was sub-standard – except for requests of small glasses of vodka. The stewardesses were regularly asked to when food and drinks (especially water) would be served and they consistently responded in either English or Russian what appeared to be a well-rehearsed statement, 'Please be patient… meals and drinks are on the way!'

As the passengers were consuming their late-evening meal, the aircraft began its descent to Tashkent: the capital of Uzbekistan. The aircraft landed on what appeared to be an *abandoned* airfield. The significant rebuilding of Islam Karimov Tashkent International Airport was still many years away!

From the warmth of the inside of the aircraft, the passengers made their way down a portable staircase to the tarmac and were unpleasantly greeted with blizzard-like weather conditions. The passengers were then escorted to a nearby building, after passing through two rows of military personnel (each holding a sub-machine gun) who were well rugged-up and wearing *ushankas* (a Russian fur cap/hat with ear flaps).

Inside the building, passengers were directed to walk up a flight of stairs and then into a large room. Inside this room, several long wooden (and antiquated) bench tables had been set up. On each table, there were numerous small bottles of mineral water. In a minor frenzy, thirsty passengers quickly grabbed a bottle – or several. Charlie pushed his way through the horde of passengers and hastily grabbed three bottles: one for himself, two for Joe and Florence. The overall mood of the passengers, by now, was largely one of fatigue and grumpiness. Most of them were quite content to just 'chill-out' (rest and relax) on one of the numerous wooden bench chairs or cold plastic chairs, sipping contentedly on their cherished bottle of mineral water.

At the far end of the large room, there was a raised platform. A group of musicians were standing on it. They all had beards and hairstyles, reminiscent of the bygone hippie-era – and wore ageless paisley shirts. There was also an array of musical instruments on the stage. Suddenly, one of them bellowed into the microphone, 'Good evening everyone and welcome to Tashkent… are we all feeling groovy tonight?'

For the next hour and a half, the passengers were 'entertained' with covers of songs that were predominantly released before 1970 – especially songs by Elvis Presley and The Beatles. Somewhat surprisingly, passenger spirits did seem to lift a notch or two, although it was quite apparent that many of them still regarded the band's *enthusiastic* performance with a mixture of disdain and hilarity. The situation was probably best summed up when a Sikh gentleman loudly blurted out in a 'cockney' (East Londoner) accent, 'What the fuck is this?'

Several hours later and just as dawn was breaking, the aircraft was above the Himalayan Mountain Range at a relatively low altitude. Having a window seat, Charlie was able to gaze at the picturesque mountains for over an hour. Whilst he enjoyed the spectacular scenery at close range, Charlie was hoping that the aircraft maintain a reasonable distance from any mountainside! After passing over the mountain range, the plane commenced its descent to Indira Gandhi International Airport (New Delhi, India).

Throughout the steady descent, the chief pilot reminded passengers (several times) that they needed to be seated and with seatbelts on. He further added that everyone needed to remain seated until the aircraft came to a *complete* halt. A sizeable number of excitable passengers, however, blatantly ignored the safety instruction and were retrieving their luggage from the overhead storage compartments – even before the aircraft had touched the tarmac.

The stewardesses, initially, tried to persuade these excitable passengers to get back into their seats and to put the seatbelts back on. Their efforts, however, were in vain. After a lot of arm-waving and frantic nodding to each other, the bewildered stewardesses moved away from the disobedient passengers and promptly decided to go to their seats. Even as the aircraft gently 'bounced' up and down on the tarmac, a large number of passengers were standing in the aisles. Charlie, cheekily, quipped to Joe and Florence, 'I wonder what will happen if the brakes were suddenly slammed on!'

As the aircraft travelled along the tarmac, Charlie noticed that the airfield was largely in a dilapidated state. There was a considerable amount of rubbish lined along the grassy area that bordered the runway and he also noticed a few cows in nearby and poorly managed fields. In some sections, there was only collapsed fencing separating them (the cows) from the runway. Charlie wondered if any of them had ever wandered onto the tarmac; he could picture frantic runway attendants shooing the cows off the tarmac as the aircraft approached the runway!

By the time the aircraft had come to an abrupt halt, a large number of over-eager passengers were already lined up at the main exit door! The cabin crew, however, were in no rush to open the sealed doors. Instead, they made the standing passengers move *backwards* and thus, allowed plenty of space for some of the airline crew to exit first. More than twenty minutes would elapse before the cabin crew were satisfied that the passengers had moved back a sufficient distance. The release mechanisms on the doors were then activated.

Passengers travelling onwards were directed to the transit lounge and many of them would wait there for a connecting flight to Singapore's Changi Airport. Later, they would be reboarding the same aircraft. The stopover in New Delhi was only meant to be for about three hours. The transit passengers, however, were soon informed that a considerable amount of ice had built-up on the wings (whilst flying above the Himalayas region) of the ongoing aircraft. The stopover, therefore, would be longer than initially planned.

As the hours ticked by, the mood of the transit passengers gradually transforming into one of 'aggravated restlessness'. The occasional announcement of a *further delay* only exacerbated the situation even further. Just after 2.00 pm, the passengers were informed that they would be provided with a meal at 3.00 pm; they had been already waiting in the transit lounge since 7.30 am. After conversing with several other passengers, Charlie felt that they will be boarding the aircraft before 3.00 pm. At 2.45 pm, there was an announcement to reboard the aircraft!

The six-hour flight from New Delhi to Singapore was much more comfortable for Charlie. He had a row of seats to himself and, thus, slept through most of the journey. The Aeroflot flight touched down at Singapore's Changi Airport in the early morning hours. Inside the transit lounge, Charlie relaxed in a comfortable lounge chair for the next few hours. Later that morning, he left the airport and boarded a bus which took him into central Singapore. Charlie soon located a *crash pad* (a cheap, but illegal-operating hostel) and stayed there for the next three nights. On the fourth day, he boarded a bus, bound for the Malaysian capital of Kuala Lumpur. The bus trip took just under eight hours.

The bus arrived in central Kuala Lumpur just as the night darkness began to creep in. A short time later, Charlie was negotiating with a taxi driver over the cost of a 'reasonable' fare to the coastal city of Klang: 33 kilometres from Kuala Lumpur. The pair eventually agreed on a fare of $28 Malaysian (equivalent to about $14 Australian at that time) and Charlie was on his way to catch up with an old friend: Chan. He had previously worked and travelled on the itinerant fruit-picking circuit with him in Australia: two tomato-picking seasons in Bowen (North Queensland) and during the fruit season (cherries, pears, soft fruits and apples) in Orange (New South Wales).

After arriving in Klang, the taxi driver soon located Chan who amongst family and friends, was known as *Frankie*. His family was well known throughout the district of Klang as his long-deceased father had been involved in politics for over twenty years and had also been a senior government minister in a previous Malaysian government. The upmarket family residence owned by his mother (Frankie also resided there) was located close to the palace owned by the Sultan of Selangor.

As Charlie enjoyed a thirst-quenching beer in a red-themed plush bar, Frankie introduced him to his friends and acquaintances. They were all of Hokkien (or Hoklo) Chinese descent and spoke fluent English. Over the next seven days, Charlie regularly conversed with them and soon learnt that they were all *businessmen*: they owned numerous bars, restaurants, pool/ snooker halls, massage parlours and 'gentlemen' clubs. The red-themed bar belonged to George (an old school friend of Frankie) and his family was also well known throughout the district of Klang. A multi-millionaire, he was widely known amongst the local community as the 'mayor'.

George owned numerous businesses throughout the district of Klang and in the city of Kuala Lumpur, often employing a large number of young males who were former 'gangsters' (mainly from street-crime gangs). He felt that gangster-related crime was a major problem throughout the region and he was quite keen to *clean it up*. Charlie deemed George, basically, a 'nice guy' but also realised that he wielded a lot of power within the local area and beyond.

Charlie stayed in Klang for a week and was chauffeured several times to regions outside the city of Klang. This included: an extensive tour of Kuala Lumpur; a day trip throughout the state of Malacca (including several hours in Malacca City); and, two trips to the seaside town of Port Klang where Frankie took Charlie to a fishing village on a motorised longboat. The small fishing village was entirely built on stilts. On both visits, Frankie also purchased a sizeable amount of fresh fish from several fishmongers who he had known for many years.

On the last day of his stay, Charlie was dropped off at the central bus station in Kuala Lumpur – in a shiny black Mercedes. A short time later, he boarded a Singapore-bound bus and arrived in the city in the early evening. From central Singapore, Charlie boarded another bus, taking him to the international airport. His flight to Sydney was departing the next morning, so he decided to stay at the airport overnight.

As Charlie relaxed in one of the lounge areas, he was hoping to gain some sleep throughout the night. Inside this lounge area, however, was a large group of talkative Cambodian-born Americans and Charlie soon found himself in an earnest conversation with several of them. The group had also decided to stay at the airport overnight as they would be boarding an early morning flight to the Cambodian capital of Phnom Penh.

They, firstly, explained to Charlie how their families had managed to escape the atrocities of the Cambodian Civil War (1968-1975). Next, several of the group discussed the process which allowed them to be relocated to the USA as political refugees. The majority of the group had been children at the time. This monumental occasion would be the first time the group had returned to their country of birth – an absence of more than fifteen years.

A severely sleep-deprived Charlie boarded a Sydney-bound flight just after midday the following day. He had slept for several hours before the aircraft commenced its descent to Sydney (Kingsford Smith) Airport. Charlie was hoping to pass through the customs area with a minimum of fuss but, alas, this was not going to occur. Firstly, there was a lengthy delay for passengers waiting to reclaim their major luggage items – an empty carousel went round and round for nearly an hour. Eventually, Charlie was able to retrieve his luggage but along with other Aeroflot flight passengers, was directed to a luggage inspection area. The entire contents of each item of luggage (or baggage) were emptied onto a large table for closer inspection. An hour later, he walked out of the arrival terminal and, fifteen minutes later, boarded a bus which took him directly to Sydney's Central Railway Station.

Three years later, Charlie was once more aboard an Aeroflot flight which had departed from London's Heathrow Airport. This time, however, there were no Aeroflot flights between any south-east Asian airports and Australian airports. From Ninoy Aquino International Airport (Manila, Philippines) to Sydney Airport (Australia), he was aboard a Philippines Airlines flight.

In stark contrast to Charlie's previous experience with Aeroflot, the cabin crew were far more pleasant, helpful and better organised. During the flight from London to Moscow, he sat next to a very attractive red-haired Russian woman: Tatiana. As the pair conversed, Charlie learnt that she was employed as a Russian-English translator: mostly working for Russian government officials. Tatiana stated that she regularly travelled between Russia and the United Kingdom (or the occasional trip to the USA and Canada).

As they chatted amicably throughout the flight, Tatiana asked him if he was going to stay in Russia for a while. Charlie responded that he would only be in transit (at the airport) and further explained to her the complicated and expensive process for Australian passport holders (at the time) in their quest to be granted a tourist visa before entering Russia. Tatiana said to Charlie that if he did have a tourist visa, she could offer him accommodation in her apartment, along with being his tour guide in and around Moscow. Charlie thought to himself, 'Wish I did have a tourist visa… what a lost opportunity!'

Inside Moscow's airport, Charlie bid farewell to Tatiana and then walked up a stairwell, taking him to the transit lounge. Very little had changed in three years – and, the Irish Bar was still there. Whilst waiting for his next flight, he sipped on a Guinness beer and conversed with one of the Irish Bar staff members, along with several transit passengers.

Just before midnight, Charlie waited patiently in a lengthy queue; he was waiting to board the New Delhi-bound aircraft. A large number of the waiting passengers were Australian-Macedonians and earlier in the day, had been aboard a flight that had arrived from the Macedonian capital of Skopje. When these passengers were making their way through the customs area, they were reminded by customs officials: 'one litre of alcohol, per person, allowed on this flight only'. A large number of them were carrying an amount of alcohol – well above the allowable one-litre limit. They were singled out and subjected to an extensive luggage search.

Instead of being allowed to take a maximum of one litre of alcohol (per person) onboard, the surly customs officials (aided by the presence of military personnel) decided to confiscate *all* the bottles/containers (most were unlabelled). Charlie suspected that most of the alcohol was home-made. He also wondered whether the seized alcohol would even be disposed of or not. The possibility of excessive alcohol-fuelled gatherings, amongst airport staff and military personnel, had also entered his mind!

After departing from Moscow Airport, there were a lot of *unhappy* Australian-Macedonian passengers on board the aircraft and two of them, a middle-aged couple, sat on the same row of seats as Charlie. He conversed with them throughout the flight to New Delhi.

As the Aeroflot aircraft steadily zoomed along the tarmac at New Delhi's Indira Gandhi International Airport, Charlie noticed that the landscape had changed significantly in comparison to what he had viewed three years earlier: the grasslands bordering the tarmac was well maintained; barely any rubbish or litter could be seen; and, and there was sturdy high-wire fencing – and not a cow in sight. After waiting in the transit lounge for just under three hours, Charlie reboarded a half-emptied aircraft. Next stop: Manila (capital of The Philippines). At Manila's Ninoy Aquino International Airport, Charlie boarded a Philippines Airlines flight: the final leg of the long journey to Sydney (Australia).

Inside Sydney Airport, Charlie made his way to the customs area. All passengers on the Philippines Airlines flight, unfortunately, would be subjected to a luggage search.

Before this luggage search, however, a severely-fatigued Charlie had to deal with an irksome female customs official. Checking his passport, she *slowly* perused each page. Most of the pages of Charlie's passport were covered with an array of visas, work permits and numerous entry/departure stamps!

Deciding to be unnecessarily intrusive, she sarcastically quipped, 'How do you afford to do all this travelling?' 'Regular incoming family revenue,' was Charlie's snappy reply.

The customs official, quite surprisingly, didn't ask Charlie to elaborate on his statement or even respond with a follow-up question. Instead, she promptly handed back his passport and ushered him to the luggage inspection area. During the over-the-top luggage search, every item of clothing was removed and scanned thoroughly. At the bottom of Charlie's backpack, a plastic bag containing a pair of runners/sneakers was taken out and put aside. He had intended to dispose of the well-worn (and partially-soiled) footwear in the United Kingdom but, alas, Charlie had completely forgotten about them! The male customs officer then asked him if he had been working on any farms or orchards during his lengthy stay in Europe.

A composed and quick-thinking Charlie replied that he was an avid hiker/walker and had walked many kilometres within various European countries. The customs official then arranged for the 'offending' footwear to be taken to a room for closer inspection. Twenty minutes later, the well-worn runners/sneakers were returned to Charlie – in a waterlogged plastic bag. Shortly afterwards, he sought a rubbish bin. Charlie soon found one and, subsequently, disposed of the washed footwear.

Although some flights could be deemed as memorable, most were generally quite boring – especially long-haul flights. One particular long-haul flight was a direct flight from Seoul (South Korea) to Paris (France) via the sparse Siberian plains of Russia. Charlie boarded a Korean Air flight at Sydney Airport and nearly eleven hours later, arrived at Seoul's Gimpo International Airport in the early evening. His connecting flight to Paris wasn't until the late-morning of the following day. Charlie had planned to stay at the airport overnight but just before 10.00 pm, he (along with several others) was informed by patrolling military personnel that the airport was about to be closed for the night.

Charlie walked outside the airport terminal and half-expected that he might be 'sleeping under the stars' that night. Outside the airport, however, there were several hotels nearby. After a certain degree of haggling at one of the hotels, Charlie agreed to a 'competitively-priced' accommodation arrangement ($60AUD). The next morning, Charlie casually ambled towards the airport's departure terminal. After paying a departure tax, he boarded the aircraft. The direct Korean Air flight to Paris would take nearly sixteen hours.

The tedious long-haul flight was exacerbated by several large on-board screens where each of them displayed a world map and a curved line, showing the intended flight path to Paris. The pop-art image of an aeroplane would *creep furtively* along this curved line for the next sixteen hours but, even worse, a digital clock above the world map displayed the remaining flight time – to the exact second.

Charlie, fortunately, had a window seat. As the aircraft passed over the north-eastern Russian landmass, he was quite content to just stare for hours at the endless white and lifeless terrain of the Siberian region. On several occasions, Charlie lapsed into a state of partial-sleep and contemplated on how the 'Eastern Front' would not have been a desirable destination for *disobedient* soldiers (especially during World War II) or political dissidents within the Soviet Union. Eventually, the aircraft landed at Charles De Gaulle Airport in Paris. A relieved Charlie was happy that the long monotonous journey had come to an end.

Besides memorable flight adventures, Charlie also had fond memories of several land-based episodes of travel, perhaps best described as a *character-building* time in his life. One particular land journey was a treacherous two-day coach trip from Poznań (Poland) to Rome (Italy).

After staying with Ivana (chapter 13) in Poznań for eight days, Charlie departed the city aboard a minibus (near the main railway station) amidst persistent falls of snow. The

280km journey to the city of Opole would take nearly five hours, largely due to the treacherous and slushy road conditions. After arriving at the main bus station in Opole, he immediately boarded a coach. The large Rome-bound bus would travel through the countries of the Czech Republic and Austria, before arriving on Italian soil.

According to Charlie's travel itinerary, the journey from Poznań to Rome was meant to take about 23 hours. The coach, however, drove into the bus station (near the Roma Termini Railway Station) 48 hours after departing from Opole. For the first part of the trip, the weather conditions after departing from Opole were largely quite favourable. Despite the temperatures being in the minuses, the roads were relatively slush-free. The coach passed through the Czech Republic and Austria incident-free. However, at the Austrian-Italian border checkpoint (ten kilometres north of the Italian town of Tarvisio) the *real adventure* was about to begin.

The Italian military personnel guarding the checkpoint were not satisfied with the coach company's paperwork: a 'letter of permission' from the Polish Department of Transport. Secondly, several of the passengers (who were non-Polish passport holders) did not have a visa to enter Italy. Charlie, as a holder of an Australian passport, did not need a visa to enter the country. After an hour, several Polish passengers (holders of Italian or German passports) decided to walk to a nearby railway station, on the Italian side of the border. The standoff between the coach driver and border patrol, meanwhile, would last for several hours. At one point, Charlie considered the possibility of even hitchhiking to Rome but icy temperatures and consistent snowfall quickly quelled that thought!

The coach driver, eventually, directed all of the passengers to reboard the bus; he now intended to enter Italy via Slovenia. At the Slovenian–Austrian border, patrolling border guards boarded the bus to check passports. Fortunately for Charlie, passengers were only required to show the covers of their passports. The dark blue cover of his passport was the same colour as the cover of the Polish passports (at the time). Two border guards entered the bus but stopped halfway down the aisle. Charlie was seated near the rear of the bus and the border guards only saw his passport cover from a distance! Australian passport holders, at the time, required a visa to enter Slovenia. Passengers with different-coloured passports were taken off the bus and made to pay for a transit visa.

The coach passed through Slovenia by travelling uphill (mostly) through the Southern Limestone Alps: the driver was attempting to enter Italy at a Slovenian–Italian border checkpoint (near the Slovenian town of Rateče). Once again, the Italian border patrol was not satisfied with the paperwork and the driver was forced to turn the coach around, driving back along the same road to the Slovenian–Austrian border.

The return trip, therefore, was mainly downhill. Freshly-fallen (and heavy) amounts of snow were now covering the road, making the downhill journey a potentially hazardous one!

For the next twenty minutes or so, there was an eerie silence amongst the passengers. It soon emerged, though, that the coach driver appeared to have had a fair amount of hazardous-driving experience on previous journeys. He calmly and slowly drove the vehicle down the steep decline in quite treacherous conditions. As there was a substantial amount of ice on the road, the coach's braking system was largely ineffective. The driver, therefore, would only touch the brakes gently and had already chosen a low gear for the descent. The coach 'roared' loudly as it slowly made its way down the steep decline. Charlie, who had a window seat, occasionally gazed at the steep embankment below – there was no protective railing. When the vehicle finally made it to level ground, there was a loud collective sigh of relief from the passengers! After passing through Austria for a distance of 15 kilometres, the coach was once again back at the Austrian-Italian border checkpoint near the town of Tarvisio.

After a lengthy discussion with the Italian border patrol, the coach driver rang the coach company's office in Rome. As the border officials were adamant that the Polish-registered coach would not be allowed entry into Italy, the company decided to send an Italian-registered coach to the border checkpoint from Rome. The passengers, therefore, were stranded at the border for several more hours and the snow continued to fall.

The Italian-registered coach arrived at the border checkpoint, late in the evening. The passengers boarded the newly-arrived coach and the Polish coach-driver drove back to Opole with an empty bus. The journey throughout the night, along several snow-free autostradas (motorways), was quite a peaceful one. The majority of the passengers (including Charlie) slept through most of the trip. The coach arrived in Rome just after 8.00 am, amidst blue sky and emerging sunshine.

After alighting from the coach, Charlie immediately made his way to the nearby Roma Termini Railway Station and purchased a train fare to the port city of Brindisi (477 km southeast of Rome by rail). His intended final destination was the Peloponnese region of Greece. Several hours later, he was aboard a Brindisi-bound train. The train journey took just over five hours. Inside the carriage compartment, Charlie shared a large bench seat with two young Italian females. Two males sat on the opposite bench and spoke to each other in English – in a distinctive accent. Charlie soon interrupted their conversation. Dave and Jim (from Brisbane, Australia) were also on their way to Greece.

Throughout the rail journey, the trio exchanged 'travel adventure' tales: both recent and past ones. The train arrived at the Stazione di Brindisi just as dusk was merging with the darkness of the night. Dave, Jim and Charlie then walked to the ferry port: a twenty-minute journey. The ferry service to the city of Patras (Greece), fortunately, was due to depart in two hours.

The ferry crossing would take over sixteen hours, along the calm waters of the Adriatic Sea and the Ionian Sea, thus, ensuring a relatively comfortable and relaxing voyage. The only stopover (before reaching Patras) was at the Greek island of Corfu. After disembarking from the ferry, the trio immediately sought accommodation and soon located a youth hostel. The next day, Dave and Jim boarded an Athens-bound bus. Charlie boarded a bus that would take him to the ancient city of Corinth. In Corinth, he boarded another bus which was going to the Peloponnese seaport town of Nafplio. Charlie would live in the village of Tolo (12 km from Nafplio) for the next two and a half months.

The Wanderlust Withers

On a typically cold June day, Charlie boarded a Qantas flight at Sydney (Kingsford Smith) Airport. The aircraft soon ascended into the greyish-white clouds, intertwined with a mixture of gusty winds and persistent rainfall. Six and a half hours later, the aircraft came to a smooth halt on the runway of Ngurah Rai International Airport, Denpasar (Bali, Indonesia). As passengers disembarked, they were greeted with a clear blue sky and outdoor sauna-like conditions.

Whilst Charlie was still inside the airport arrivals terminal, he organised (by telephone) accommodation for the first two nights. After venturing outside the terminal, Charlie headed straight for the taxi rank. Moments later, he was inside a cab which would take him to an address in *Jalan Legian* (Legian Road), located in the tourist area of Kuta. Charlie stayed in a plush villa for the next two weeks. In the centre of the villa complex, stood a large swimming pool; it was surrounded by poolside sunbeds/banana lounges. A bar serving both alcoholic and non-alcoholic beverages was close by.

For the next several days, Charlie filled in his days by wandering throughout the district of Kuta. Enjoying a mixture of sightseeing and exploring many of the local bars/eateries (but avoiding well-known American restaurants), he quickly took a dislike to the persistent and tiresome practicing of *haggling*. Charlie soon learnt that the worst offenders were Javanese, *not* the Balinese people.

Charlie's favourite eatery (a combination of a café and a bar) was situated next-door to the villa. Every morning, he casually wandered into the café to consume a large 'continental' breakfast. In the evening, Charlie returned to this venue as it was now operating as a fully-licensed bar. By the third evening, he was well on his way in creating a friendship with one of the female bar staff: Indah.

Aged in her mid-twenties, Javanese-born Indah stated to Charlie that she had relocated to the island of Bali, solely to earn and save as much money as possible. Indah had been employed by the café/bar for over a year and stayed in a room, located at the rear of the premises. Indah further added that she was hoping to return soon to her home village (in the Javanese province of West Java), primarily to assist her mother's quest to expand the family 'business venture'.

Indah's level of spoken-English was relatively advanced. Although she learnt English at school for several years, Indah admitted her employment at this café/bar had significantly assisted her to achieve a higher level of spoken-English. She further admitted that she had also learnt quite a few German, French and Dutch words, courtesy of past interactions with European tourists. Indah finished her shift at 10.00 pm each working night but would continue to chat amicably with Charlie until the bar's closing time at midnight.

Every evening, Charlie purchased food for Indah during her meal-break. As a 'token of friendship', he also bought several non-alcoholic drinks for Indah throughout the evening. During the day (or outside her hours of employment), she was Charlie's tour guide. Hiring a motor scooter, Indah would steer the bike whilst Charlie sat behind her. He had, previously, never ridden on a motor scooter or motorcycle.

Whilst Charlie enjoyed walking, Indah didn't – she refused to walk a distance of more than fifty metres. A motorised scooter was her favourite mode of transport. On the fifth night, Indah invited Charlie back to her room and he stayed the entire night. Nine days later, the pair was aboard a Garuda Indonesia flight, flying to the Indonesian capital of Jakarta (on the island of Java). Outside the arrivals terminal of Soekarno–Hatta International Airport, Indah immediately approached eagerly-waiting taxi drivers and for the next few minutes, she haggled *ferociously* over the cost of a taxi fare to her home village of Cikampek (Karawang district). A price was finally agreed upon. Charlie paid the fare and they were soon on the way to Indah's home village, 104 kilometres away.

After a journey of just over two hours, the taxi cab stopped on a dirt thoroughfare, near a small convenience store. In front of the building, an enthusiastic crowd of more than twenty had gathered. They had been eagerly awaiting Indah's arrival! In front of the crowd stood Indah's mother and she immediately hugged her daughter – for quite a long time. Charlie was then introduced by Indah to her mother and two of her sisters (a third sister resided in the city of Bandung).

Charlie stayed in the family home for the next four weeks. It was located about two kilometres from the store. The store served as a confectionary shop (inside) and as an outdoor café. Indah and her two younger sisters resided in the family residence. Her mother, however, mostly stayed in a small room, at the rear of the shop. The family residence had been owned by the sisters' father, who had passed away several years previously. Their parents had already been separated for a few years before his death.

During these four weeks, Indah used a large portion of her savings, primarily as a means to help expand the small family business, mostly controlled by her mother. She wished to provide a wider range of confectionary (and non-confectionery) items to sell. Several days before Charlie's departure from the area, he decided to give Indah's mother a wad of cash in a further attempt to boost the 'business venture'. She had already developed a deep liking of Charlie and via several translators (although Indah was the main one), attempted to converse with him on numerous occasions. He quickly deemed her as a kind-hearted woman. Aged in her late forties, Indah's mother regularly tended to others – especially the small children and teenagers in her neighbourhood. She regularly provided them with free snacks/meals and confectionery treats as well!

There was a high level of unemployment within the area and varying levels of poverty were quite evident. Many individuals, however, were quite *resourceful* and were able to eke a living via various means. A common one was to use their tricycle or motorcycle/motor scooter as a taxi service. Another idea saw many individuals go door-to-door and attempted to sell 'home-styled' rice-based or noodle-based meals. Charlie and Indah purchased at least one of these meals each day.

A small percentage of the local male population had obtained employment within a nearby industrial area. All the company factories that operated within this area were European-owned (predominantly German, Dutch or British) and employees were paid substantially higher than the average wage. Charlie soon learnt that some of the 'out-of-work' males had previously worked inside these factories. After being employed for several years, many had saved enough money to launch some kind of family-run business: a grocery store or mini-supermarket; a fruit and vegetable shop (greengrocery); a café/bar, etc.

Charlie enjoyed his four-week stay in Cikampek: each day was filled with a variety of activity. Indah, once again, was Charlie's tourist guide. Riding a motor scooter, she regularly showed him various landmarks within the Karawang Regency (including the village of Cikampek). There were also several trips to the city of Bandung (80 kilometres south of Cikampek) where Indah would use this opportunity to visit her older sister.

Indah wanted to teach Charlie how to ride a motor scooter but he was quite hesitant of the idea. Riding amongst the ever-present chaotic and often gridlocked traffic, along with the almost-daily bump from four-wheeled motor vehicles, was hardly appealing! Additionally, a large number of unsealed roads and trails/paths were quite treacherous to travel along – littered with numerous potholes of varying shapes and sizes.

On two separate occasions, Charlie and Indah were *escorted* to coastal fishing villages. Her mother wanted her to purchase a substantial quantity of fresh seafood. As a security measure, the pair was accompanied by several local males, riding motor scooters or motorcycles. Indah informed Charlie that crime rates in some of the fishing villages were quite high. Lone 'westerners' would be an easy target. Two of the accompanying males also informed him (Charlie) that prostitution in these areas was absurdly cheap!

Each day, Charlie spent a certain amount of time just 'chilling out' with local individuals, sitting on one of the tables situated in front of the store and would converse with them with the assistance of several interpreters. He attempted, however, to add some school-learnt *Bahasa Indonesian* words to the conversation but with minimal success. The local population mostly conversed with each other in *Basa Sunda* (Sundanese language) and, generally, only spoke *Bahasa Indonesian* with non-Sundanese speaking Indonesians or foreign speakers of the official Indonesian language.

Sixty metres from the café/store stood a bar. It was regularly frequented by many of Indah's male friends. Two or three times a week, Indah would take Charlie to the bar – on a motor scooter. A popular pastime at the bar centred on the frequent pool games (subjected to local rules) where participants played each game for a 'money pool'. Each participant would place a small amount of money on a plate before each game. The local males soon discovered that Charlie was an excellent pool player!

Charlie, however, never kept any of his winnings. Instead, he purchased cups of coffee/tea or soft drinks for his fellow pool players: a move that was happily accepted by all. Charlie would occasionally purchase alcohol (mainly wine) if requested. Excessive consumption of alcohol, however, was widely discouraged within the local community.

The main highlight of Charlie's four-week stay in Cikampek involved a day trip with Indah's family (two of her sisters, her mum and an aunt) and three of her male friends.

A minibus was hired (which Charlie paid for) to transport the group around throughout the day. The day trip comprised of several activities: visiting a fishing village built entirely on stilts; visiting a large crocodile breeding farm (containing several hundred scaly reptiles of varying sizes); and, a two-hour trip in the relatively shallow Java Sea on a motorised longboat.

The minibus was stopped several times at military-controlled checkpoints. The military personnel inspected the vehicle and then requested identification from the driver (and even from several passengers at two of the checkpoints). At the time, the Indonesian government had implemented a policy which amounted to a severe crackdown on any potential *terrorist activity*, along with attempts to quell localised ethnic conflicts.

On the day of Charlie's departure, Indah and her mother accompanied him on the journey to

Soekarno–Hatta International Airport (Jakarta) in a four-wheel-drive vehicle, driven by a family friend. He paid the driver a return 'taxi fare' – negotiated by Indah. After bidding farewell to a slightly tearful Indah (and her mother as well), Charlie was aboard a Garuda Indonesia flight, bound for The Netherlands capital city of Amsterdam.

Throughout the direct fourteen-hour flight, Charlie had two seats all to himself as the aircraft was barely half-full. Two hours into the flight, he was conversing with a young female student from the Javanese city of Bandung. Grace (sitting directly across from Charlie) was going to Amsterdam to stay with her Dutch boyfriend for several weeks. She had met him whilst they were both studying in an English-speaking university in Bandung. Charlie discussed his recent four-week stay in the village of Cikampek. Grace knew the Cikampek area quite well, citing that she had relatives who resided in the village and nearby Karawang Timur as well. The pair conversed throughout the long haul flight.

After arriving at Schiphol Airport in Amsterdam, Charlie decided not to leave the airport. Instead, he purchased a one-way ticket to London Luton Airport (United Kingdom) and two hours later, Charlie boarded a Ryanair (an Irish low-budget air carrier) flight. There was no seat allocation on the aircraft, so the passengers were practically *herded* onto the aircraft. The 'no-fuss' flight took just over an hour. Food and beverages (except for water) were not provided.

Inside the customs area of London Luton Airport, passengers carrying 'European' passports were quickly waved through to the Arrivals lounge. The rest of the passengers (including Charlie) were required to wait in an orderly queue, before being tended to at a customs desk. After waiting in the line for nearly half an hour, he was called to the customs desk. The middle-aged female customs officer was soon 'harassing' Charlie with a bombardment of questions: similar to ones he had become quite accustomed to on previous visits to the United Kingdom!

This time, however, Charlie had a relatively new passport: one which mainly contained blank pages. Unlike previous visits to the United Kingdom, he now possessed two credit cards (Visa and MasterCard). Charlie was also carrying £200 sterling on him. The customs officer quizzed him extensively in regards to his employment situation in Australia. Charlie casually responded with a *watertight* story about his 'family-owned' business – one which didn't exist. Fifteen minutes later, he gleefully strolled through the terminal exit and made his way to the nearest railway station.

In central London, Charlie alighted from the train at London St Pancras (now known as St Pancras International) railway station. Half an hour later, he boarded a Maidstone-bound train, one that took him to Maidstone West railway station (one of three railway stations that served the large town of Maidstone, Kent). After alighting from the train, Charlie walked to a nearby *Bed and Breakfast* establishment where he would stay there for the next two nights.

The next morning, Charlie boarded a train to the nearby market town of West Malling. Eleven years had elapsed since the last time he had been in this town. After walking along the main street and several adjoining streets, Charlie noticed there were now fewer hotels but more restaurants/take away shops. One of his favourite *drinking-holes*, however, was still in existence and he entered the premises.

Charlie instantly recognised two of the patrons who were sitting on stools near the bar. He had previously worked with them at Broadacre Wood Farms. Quite surprisingly, they instantly recognised Charlie and one of them greeted him with the line, 'The prodigal son has returned!' The trio conversed earnestly for the next several hours. John and Bob informed Charlie that the orchard had now been under new management for the past two years. Colin (the former manager) had been at Broadacre Wood Farms for over twenty years.

At one point during the conversation, Charlie was told of the upcoming cherry-picking season and was interested in obtaining fruit picking employment. John further added that the orchard was currently looking for cherry-pickers. Several minutes later, he telephoned Ben (the orchard manager) and informed Charlie that he could commence cherry-picking in three days.

Charlie was hoping he could pitch his tent on the main orchard of Broadacre Wood Farms. Ben, however, had replaced the camping area with several demountable multi-room cabins. After Colin's departure, the new manager immediately prevented the New Age Travellers from staying and working on the orchard. The demountable buildings were reserved solely for Eastern European students: predominantly from Romania, Bulgaria, Ukraine and Belarus.

On the day before Charlie commenced employment, he relocated to the Gate Hut Forest Tourist Park (three miles west of West Malling). The facilities for tent-dwellers were excellent – especially the camp kitchen area. The camping and caravanning park would be his home for the next three weeks. During the cherry-picking season, a major hassle for Charlie was *transport*.

Each working day, he would firstly walk to a bus stop: 200 metres from the tourist park. After alighting from the bus in the main street of West Malling, Charlie then walked two kilometres to the orchard. The total travelling time to Broadacre Wood Farms took nearly an hour. On Saturdays, however, bus services between the camping park and West Malling were severely limited (only between 9.00 am and 3.00 pm). Charlie's only option: walking to *and* from the orchard (a two-way distance of 9 miles/14.4 kilometres). The total travelling time for the day was around three hours!

The short cherry-picking season came to a halt in the last week of July. The apple-picking season, unfortunately, was still at least six weeks away and there was no other orchard employment available for Charlie during this time. Hourly-paid employment on Broadacre Wood Farms, during these six weeks, was only available for the foreign students. He decided instead to relocate to the West Midlands region, endeavouring to seek further employment.

After leaving West Malling, a week would pass before Charlie arrived in the West Midlands area. For the first two days, he stayed in a coastal village in the county of Essex. On the third day, departing from the Kent town of Dartford, Charlie hitchhiked along several motorways and A-roads (M25, M3, A303 and the A37) towards the southern seaside town of Weymouth (county of Dorset).

For a large part of the journey to Weymouth, Charlie obtained a lift from a lorry/truck driver. The burly driver chatted with him somewhat incessantly throughout the trip. At one point, as the heavy vehicle travelled along the A303, it passed near the prehistoric Stonehenge monument, located on the Salisbury Plain. From the cabin of the lorry, they could see the tourist buses and a sizeable number of *sheep-like* tourists. Much to the pair's amusement, scores of tourists were walking around the group of rocks in a circular formation, sheepishly following the 'leader of the pack'. An hour later, the driver dropped Charlie off in Dorchester (a county town in Dorset). After several more lifts, Charlie arrived in the town of Weymouth. It was now mid-afternoon.

Charlie walked for nearly four kilometres from central Weymouth, until he reached the Ocean Breeze holiday park. Before pitching his tent, the holiday park manager decided to only charge him the unpowered *puppy tent* rate which cost less than half the normal rate! The tiny tent was surrounded by medium to large-sized caravans and 'family-sized' tents (consisting of several rooms). Charlie stayed in the holiday park for four nights.

For the first two days, Charlie wandered throughout Weymouth and the surrounding area. On the third day, he boarded an early-morning ferry at Weymouth Ferry Port. Several hours later, Charlie arrived at Saint Peter Port: the capital of Guernsey (one of the British Channel Islands). He was met at the port ferry terminal by Sabina. The Belgian national had previously worked with him on an orchard in the Shepparton area (Victoria, Australia).

Sabina had been residing in Saint Peter Port for the past nine months. For the remainder of the day, she took Charlie on a bus tour of the island; he would only be on the island for eight hours. In the evening, Charlie boarded the ferry returning to Weymouth Ferry Port. It arrived there just after midnight. Several months later, he returned to the island of Guernsey, via a return flight from London's Gatwick Airport.

After departing from Weymouth, Charlie hitchhiked along the A37, A38, M5 and the A417 to Ledbury (Herefordshire). His final lift dropped him off on the outskirts of the town in the early evening. He slept in a 'comfortable' paddock that night. The next morning, Charlie casually ambled towards the Visitor Information Centre in central Ledbury to seek accommodation options. Half an hour later, Charlie walked to the village of Holyhedge (3 miles/4.8 kilometres from Ledbury) along a woodlands walking trail. Due to a recent heavy downpour of rain, sections of the trail were quite muddy and slippery at times. Eventually, he arrived at a family-friendly accommodation facility (in Holyhedge) – wearing a muddy pair of footwear.

Charlie, initially, had intended to seek orchard labouring employment in this particular area, using the relatively cheap hostel-style accommodation as a living-base. Another employment opportunity, however, would present itself – less than fifty metres away.

The hostel-styled accommodation was a series of former horse stables converted into living quarters. There were eight rooms of varying sizes: from a single-person room to a six-person-sized room. Charlie's single-person room was *quaintly* comfortable. The accommodation also contained a communal kitchen, a communal common room and a shared amenities block. There was also a small camping area behind the building. The entire accommodation facility was owned by the Connor family.

After paying a week's rent, Charlie informed the Connors of his intention to seek orchard-based employment. Jim Connor, however, suggested to him to visit their next-door neighbours (Percy and Molly) who were seeking someone for a variety of outdoor tasks: gardening, landscaping, wood chopping, etc over the next few weeks. Percy and Molly, a semi-retired couple aged in their mid-fifties, owned what could simply be described as a large estate. Besides the five-bedroom house that they occupied, there were two cottages on the spacious property. These two small dwellings were rented out. The estate also contained several gardens, rockeries and sizeable 'neglected' yards.

Charlie resided in Holyhedge for the next five weeks and during this time, mostly worked for Percy and Molly: six days a week, eight hours a day (8.00 am-4.00 pm). He was paid (in cash) at a fixed rate of five pounds sterling per hour. Every weekend, Charlie would move to the camping ground and pitch his small tent. All the rooms in the converted horse stables were full of longtime pre-bookings.

Outside the work environment, Charlie enjoyed a thriving social life in which Percy and Molly played a major role. The trio shared an interest for watching live music (two or three nights per week) and midweek trivia nights at several different hotel venues: located in Ledbury and the city of Hereford.

After four weeks of 'outdoor tasks', Charlie's period of employment for Percy and Molly came to an end. They were quite grateful for his many hours of *hard yakka* (An Australian term for hard or vigorous toil). The couple, a few months later, was planning to be in their holiday home, located in the south of France. They invited Charlie to travel with them, offering him free accommodation and paid employment:

mainly gardening and landscaping. Their holiday home was near the village of Ceret (located next to the Pyrenees Mountains). Several years earlier, he had stayed in this particular village and, unsuccessfully, had sought cherry-picking employment. Charlie declined their offer as he would have returned to Australia by then.

During his final week in Holyhedge, Charlie undertook five days of landscaping employment for the Connor family. Jim Connor wanted to convert a patch of land into a small tar-sealed carpark. Charlie's task was to level this patch of land with 'landfill' (namely rocks, stones and large clumps of dirt) and then cover everything with large amounts of loose dirt. As payment, he received a week's worth of free accommodation, free grocery items and two bottles of red wine!

On the last day of his stay, Percy drove Charlie to the southern outskirts of Ledbury and dropped him near the A417. Fifteen minutes later, he obtained a lift and was driven along the A417 towards the city of Swindon. During the journey, the motorist turned off the A417 and went along a narrow road, passing by the hill that held the annual *Cooper's Hill Cheese-Rolling* event. Charlie was eventually dropped off at the junction of the A419 and the M4. After waiting for over an hour, he finally received his next lift – in a shiny, black Ferrari. The driver, Ahmed (a Turkish-born Londoner) was a fashion designer. Judging by his vehicle, along with expensive-looking jewellery and clothing, Charlie assumed that he was quite a successful one!

Ahmed, however, was a friendly and down-to-earth character and Charlie enjoyed conversing with him. At one point during the conversation, Ahmed stated that he had been to Australia on five separate occasions. As the vehicle approached London along the motorway (M4), Ahmed asked Charlie if he wanted to view the mansion of a well-known Australian entertainer who was now-retired and had been living in the United Kingdom for the past several decades.

Charlie wasn't overly enthusiastic about the idea but Ahmed added that the picturesque neighbourhood (near the River Thames) was *overwhelmingly spectacular*. The Ferrari left the M4 and zoomed through a nearby village. Casually driving along a quiet street, parallel to the Thames River, the Ferrari came to a halt in front of a mansion. Ahmed excitedly declared, 'There it is!'

Charlie was dropped off near the junction of the M4 and the M25. With a protruding left thumb and a cardboard sign ('Tonbridge') in his right hand, he waited for over an hour for his next lift. After obtaining several lifts, Charlie arrived in the market town of Tonbridge (county of Kent) in the early afternoon. He boarded a bus in central Tonbridge, taking him to the village of Five Oak Green. After consuming two pints of ale in one of the local hotels, Charlie walked to Crispies

Apple Orchard which was located less than a mile from the village.

Crispies Apple Orchard was home for Charlie for the next six weeks. The pear-picking season only lasted for three days but for the rest of the fruit-picking season, it was solely apple picking. During these six weeks, he worked every day (9-11 hours per day) and in any type of weather. The wet-weather gear was provided by the company. The accommodation was a large caravan which Charlie shared with two other people. The caravan was one of ten large caravans. There were also six demountable homes which housed up to four people. By the end of the fruit-picking season, he had saved just over £3000 sterling.

After leaving the orchard one morning, Charlie was in London several hours later. During his three-day stay in the city, he purchased a return airfare from London's Gatwick Airport to Guernsey Airport (4.1 miles southwest of St. Peter Port, Guernsey's capital). Eager to see Sabina again, Charlie boarded the flight just after midday. At Guernsey airport, he boarded a bus, taking him to the Saint Peter Port bus terminus. Sabina was waiting there for him and Charlie stayed with her for the next seven days.

Throughout the week, Sabina showed Charlie the numerous landmarks on the island, far more than on his previous visit. On two separate days, the pair also ventured to the nearby islands of Herm and Sark via the local ferry service. On *car-free* Sark, Sabina and Charlie spent a large portion of the day cycling on the island. On Herm, however, the only way to explore and view the historical features of the island was by walking. Cars *and* bicycles were banned.

Walking in and around Herm involved a mixture of sandy beaches, walking paths and stony cliff paths. Sabina and Charlie walked around the perimeter using several paths of the island: a distance of 3.9 miles (6.3km). They accomplished this feat within two hours. On one of the paths, the pair eyed what they thought was a 'snake'. However, later in the Mermaid Hotel, bar staff informed them that they probably saw a slow-worm (Anguis fragilis). The creature is neither a worm nor a snake, but a legless lizard. Charlie's glorious week with Sabina soon came to an end and he boarded a return flight to Gatwick Airport.

After staying in a youth hostel in London for two nights, Charlie boarded a Malaysian Airlines flight at Heathrow Airport (UK) in the early afternoon: bound for Jakarta (Indonesia). The return leg of the flight to Sydney was supposed to be with Garuda Indonesia airlines, flying from Schiphol Airport in Amsterdam (The Netherlands). However, due to the mysterious death of a well-known Indonesian political activist on a flight two months previous, all subsequent Garuda Indonesia services between Indonesia and The Netherlands had been suspended.

Charlie arrived at Soekarno–Hatta International Airport in Jakarta and was greeted by Indah (and several family members) inside the Arrivals terminal. Several hours later, he was in Cikampek once again. In front of the café/store, the *welcoming committee* (Indah's neighbourhood friends and other family members) greeted him enthusiastically.

Whilst Charlie had been residing in the United Kingdom for the past four months, the café/store had undergone extensive renovations. The premises had been refurbished inside and outside. It was now more like a minimart. Even the outside café had a more 'up-marketed' appearance: a raised (and shiny) wooden platform had been installed and was covered with several rubber mats, under the new tables and chairs.

Charlie stayed in Cikampek for the next four weeks. The last two weeks of his stay coincided with the Islamic holy month of Ramadan. For the first few days, Indah fasted from dawn to sunset. Her family and the majority of her neighbours, however, did not. Once the sun had fully disappeared into the night sky, she would then gorge on a large meal. But on the fifth day, Indah succumbed to severe hunger pangs just after 4.00 pm – and hungrily 'devoured' a whole roast chicken.

As alcohol consumption was practically banned during the time of Ramadan, Charlie was a teetotaller for two whole weeks! He, however, suspected several of his fellow pool/

billiard players were *discreetly* consuming a small level of alcohol consumption from time to time. In the last week of his stay, Charlie decided to financially assist Indah who had endeavoured to open her own bar/café. During this week, she also raised the possibility of *marriage* with him. Charlie then asked Indah would she be prepared to live in Australia. She, however, wished to remain in Cikampek. Over the past several months, he had already thought about relocating to the city of Melbourne to commence a *new life*. Charlie was happy to stay in Cikampek for several weeks or months during any calendar year, but he didn't want to live permanently in the village.

Charlie stayed with friends in Sydney for several days before driving his vehicle nearly 700 kilometres to a small town in northern Victoria: his home base at the time. He would never see Indah again but they kept in contact (mainly by email) for the next several years. She responded with a follow-up email, along with numerous photo attachments – especially ones of her new bar/café. Indah, eventually, married a former school friend and all correspondence between Charlie and her ceased.

During his four-month stay in the United Kingdom, Charlie planned to make major changes to his life once he returned to Australia. After being involved in the *wanderlust spirit* for over twenty years, Charlie relocated to Melbourne. After five years of study, he graduated with a Bachelor's

Degree in Information Technology (IT). Charlie adopted two new passions: novel writing and trivia (both online and hotel trivia nights). The *wanderlust journey* was sadly over for Charlie but he would soon embrace and relish his new lifestyle!

About the Author

P.J. Kropp was born in rural New South Wales (Australia) in 1965.

After completing a Diploma in Education (high school teaching) in Sydney 1987, P.J. Kropp decided not to enter the teaching profession the following year. Instead, he returned to his home city (Orange) in December 1987 and commenced employment (fruit picking) in one of the local orchards.

In May 1990, P.J. Kropp boarded a one-way flight to London and, thus, began his overseas wanderlust journey.

In mid-2008, P.J. Kropp decided to farewell the itinerant lifestyle and the overseas wanderlust journey. He relocated to the Victorian state capital: Melbourne. At the age of 43, and after an absence of 21 years, P.J. Kropp was a full-time student once more!

P.J. Kropp completed a Bachelor's Degree in IT (Business Information Systems) in 2014 and the following year, commenced two literary projects: *The Itinerant Way* and *Travelling below the Surface.*